# Sugar
## A NOVEL

Zoe Shae

This book is a work of fiction. While some places or people are real – Seattle, WA being an example – most names, characters, places, and incidents either are products of the author's imagination or used fictitiously.

SUGAR

ZOE SHAE

https://linktr.ee/AuthorZoeShae



Cover Design: Luisa Sipia, @luy_co

Cover Text by: Torie Jean

Editing: Writers Untapped

Formatting: Starla DeKruyf

For information of subsidiary rights, please contact the author at authorzoeshae@gmail.com

Hardcover edition ISBN: 979-8-9871328-1-4

Print edition ISBN: 979-8-9871328-0-7

Digital edition ASIN: B0BMPV4LMT

*To all the people out there who identify with this story – I see you, and I'm sorry. Hopefully you feel seen as you read this and know that it was not your fault. It's never your fault.*

*To my beta readers, alpha readers, those who gave me glowing praise and constructive criticism, I wouldn't be the writer I am today without you. I wouldn't have this book without you and I can't thank you enough, truly.*

*To my Dad, I miss you every single day. Thank you for being my rock and my safe space. I'll see you again someday.*

*To my daughter, don't read this book. It has too much sex and I don't want you anywhere near it until you're at least fifty. Know that this book really wouldn't exist without you, my girl. Becoming your mother changed my heart in the most profound way and your refusal to sleep anywhere but on me forced me to sit down and write. You're an angel and I love you forever.*

*And to you, reader, thank you for taking the time out of your life to read this book. I appreciate you more than I can express.*

---

## Author's Note and
## Content/Trigger Warnings

---

Thank you for picking up Sugar. If you don't want any spoilers and are okay with the possibility of being triggered, please skip this page. If, however, you would like to avoid certain triggering topics, here is a list of the ones that appear in this book. Please protect your own mental health.

- Parental Abuse; includes physical, emotional, and mental abuse
- Negative self-talk
- Explicit sexual content
- Therapy
- Explicit language/cursing
- Two instances of referenced homophobia

# Chocolate Chip Frappuccino
# with Extra Whipped Cream

"*J*esus, Darby, how do you look so fucking perfect this fucking early in the morning?" Casey's words bounce off the walls of the Starbucks, despite the long line of people. Her words go unnoticed by the zombies awaiting their daily addiction.

"I'm going to ignore that remark, seeing as you haven't had your morning coffee yet," I reply, redoing the black bun on top of my head.

"Well, I would've already had it if this line would move fucking faster!" She pointedly stares down the poor, flustered barista behind the counter.

"You were the one who refused my generous offer of freshly brewed coffee at home. You know how grouchy you get, and yet you still insisted on coming to the overcrowded Starbucks." I grin guiltily at the barista. Casey Fairbanks may be my best friend, but that doesn't mean she gets a free pass for her behavior. The place just opened right underneath our apartment—still has that new coffee smell and everything.

"You're annoying. And I wanted a pumpkin spice latte, which we don't have."

"You're such a basic fall bitch." I pause. "Wait. It's spring. You can't get a pumpkin spice latte."

"You can get anything you want if you know how to order it." She winks. "And you love my basic ass."

For some reason, I do. I love that basic fall bitch more than pretty much anyone on this Earth. As Casey finally steps up to the counter to order, my eyes sweep around the coffee shop. It's cute for a chain, what with the soft chairs and inviting little nooks. One corner has the plushiest blue couch and the optimum amount of sunshine. It would be the perfect place to sit down with a hot drink and a good book—well, once it's not so crowded.

"You want a drink?" Casey asks, pulling away my wandering eyes.

"Nah. I had coffee at home. But if you're buying, you could get me a cinnamon bun," I reply with a smile. I'm not one to refuse an opportunity for free baked goods. Or baked goods in general.

"I'm only doing this because I'll regret my general grouchiness eventually. This way I don't have to apologize." She turns with a whip of her chin-length strawberry blonde hair to pick out my pastry. "When do you have to be at the office?"

"Not for another hour."

Casey pays and we make our way to a secluded spot in the corner to people watch as we wait. I pull apart the warm pastry and am immediately assaulted by the scent of cinnamon and sugar. Two of my favorite things. My mouth waters as I almost inhale it. The flaky, buttery confection melts in my mouth. God, that's good.

"Why haven't you quit that awful place yet? You're such a kick-ass finance lady and they treat you like crap." Casey stares longingly at the cinnamon bun until I rip her off a piece. The little giddy noise she makes at the gesture sounds more like a mouse than a grumpy coffee addict, but I know better than to mention it.

"I need a job, Case. You pay enough of the rent as it is. On that note, have I mentioned lately that you're amazing and I love you?"

"Speaking of love . . ."

"Casey?" a barista calls from the counter. She prances up to get her coffee, eye fucking it already. Without missing a beat, she takes a long gulp of it before sitting back down across from me. The freak. Who just downs scalding hot coffee like that?

"Right, where was I?" Casey snuggles in, kicking her shoes off and tucking them underneath her. "Speaking of love, didn't you have a date last night? Your first date in ages?"

"Yes, and I was reminded how thoroughly disappointed I am in the male population. All he did was stare at my breasts and nod. Hence why I was home and in my pajamas by nine."

Cherry lips blow a strand of hair off her face. "Men. That's why I don't fuck with men or fuck them in general. But, and I have to ask, did you give him a chance?"

"I told him I was toying with the idea of getting my MBA and he asked my breasts what that stood for." I raise an eyebrow at her.

She stares at me for a full two seconds before breaking down in giggles. "Okay, okay, *fine*. Not a winner. They can't all suck, though. I bet the next guy who asks you out will be better."

"If you say so." My heart throbs. According to my mother, I'm a waste of space who doesn't deserve a good man. At this point, I'm certain she's right. Twenty-five years old and I'm single, in a dead-end job, and watching so much of *The Great*

*British Baking Show* that I've turned into a pastry. Eat your heart out, boys.

"By the way, you are looking so annoyingly hot in your fancy little work outfit. Are you sure you don't want to model?" Casey winks at me.

"Shut up, you horny bastard, and drink your coffee." I roll my eyes and sink my teeth back into this delicious morsel. Mmm. Eat all the sugar or be a model? Sugar, please.

"Hannah has been visiting her parents in Wisconsin for two weeks now. She may be coming back tomorrow, but I'm going insane!" Casey whines pitifully, slouching down in her plushy chair.

"I don't know how Hannah puts up with you. If I were her, I'd take a two-month vacation instead of two weeks." I nudge her arm with a smile.

"See, I know you're lying because you've been my best friend since we were five. And you've lived with me since we were eighteen. So shut up."

I love my grouchy best friend. I wouldn't trade her for the world.

I hate my grouchy best friend. Because of her, I'm late for work, which somehow makes me late for my first meeting, which snowballs into me running around like a chicken with its head cut off. I get she misses Hannah, I do, but I had to literally *run* my ass three blocks. I'm lucky I work so close to where I live, sure, but a bitch is wearing heels. No thank you. Stupid date last night. Stupid Casey. Just *ugh*.

"Clarke!" my boss, Mindy, calls from her office once I finally have my shit together. Which means it's noon. I emerge from the bland white cubicle I spend far too much of my life in and cross the bland white room. Everything at Xerx & Hoff Law Firm is bland, from the antiquated cubicle setup, the lack of any plants or paintings, to the scent of old man that permeates every inch of the building.

"Yes, Mindy?" I ask, standing in her doorway. To call this an office would be kind. It's more of a shoebox with a desk and computer.

"I need coffee. Get me some," she demands, not lifting her eyes from her screen.

My teeth grind together in an attempt to mitigate the headache I've had since this morning. I'm not an assistant; my job title is literally financial analyst. I remember a time when I used to love numbers, love Excel sheets. This place has beaten it out of me without so much as a 'sorry'. But I need this job.

"Sure."

"Not too much sugar this time," she calls after my retreating form. In my defense, last time she said the coffee was too milky and didn't have enough sugar. If she's so particular about her coffee, she should just make it herself. Or hire an actual assistant.

The kitchenette in the office smells of coffee, chicken salad, and some of the stuffy cologne Jason in HR wears. *Delicious.* I may gag. If I didn't need the paycheck, I'd be gone. As it stands now, I need the experience and the money. Damn Seattle cost of living. I pop just a teaspoon of sugar into Mindy's coffee and head back.

"Thanks," she grumbles as I place the mug on her desk. *Yeah, you're fucking welcome.*

"I'm taking my lunch," I warn her while she's distracted. She's much less likely to deny me when she's not focused on me. Without sitting down, I grab my phone on my desk and oh . . . oh great. Just what I needed today.

Mother.

THE MOM-STER

Miss you. You'll never have a chance at meaningful relationships if you continue ignoring me. Don't live your entire life alone.

Remember the fifth commandment. Honor thy father and thy mother. God loves you and so do I.

Fucking hell. You spent most of my life calling me a worthless piece of crap, Mom. I don't think a meaningful relationship is in the cards. Even if that means I'll be alone forever. You'd think after years of me ignoring her, she'd get the hint by now. I should block her number. I tell myself every time this happens that I'll do it. And yet, somehow, I never do. Maybe I like picking at my childhood scabs and festering in my own self-pity.

With a shake of my head, I delete her texts and focus on getting out of here for lunch. I won't do anything about that particular issue until I'm good and fucking ready.

"'Sup, Clarke?" Jason from HR nods at me as he strolls past my desk with his typical group of friends. Let's see how long it takes him to stare at my ass and then giggle about it with his bros.

Three . . .

Two . . .

One . . .

"Hey, Chase. Do you know why I love that Darby is the one handling the company's finances?"

"Why's that Jason?"

"Because she has the best ass-ets I've ever seen."

I hate this place.

*I*'m far too cranky when I return home, so after changing into sweatpants and a T-shirt, I find myself wandering back into the Starbucks. Maybe I'll get a chocolate chip croissant and some ridiculously sugary frappa-something. I deserve a treat after today. What's a few extra thousand calories? It would make my mother sick to watch me stuff my face. Which is what seals the deal.

"Hi . . ." The barista recognizes me from this morning. Her judgmental eyes going from the tips of my toes to the top of my head are pretty damn hard to miss. I witnessed it daily growing up, after all. "What can I get you?"

"A venti double chocolate chip Frappuccino with extra whipped cream, a chocolate chip muffin, a piece of coffee cake, and"—the muffin is pushed into my hand with *vigor*—"a chocolate croissant. Please." And a little less attitude.

"Wow, that's a lot of chocolate." A male voice envelops me.

Oh goodie, someone else who has an opinion about me.

"Listen, dude." I turn to defend myself and my right to eat as much damn chocolate as I please when . . . *oof*. I land nose first into a crisp white button-down shirt covering the firmest chest I've ever encountered. Apparently spinning too fast plus man leaning over your shoulder in close proximity equals boom.

"All right?" His warm, low voice asks as big, calloused hands grasp my arms to steady me. I lift my face and meet a broad-shouldered Greek statue standing somewhere over six feet in an impeccably tailored black suit. Short brown hair with —oh Lord—little specks of gray at his temples morphs into a stubble-covered, razor-sharp jawline. I could cut my finger on that jaw and part of me really wants to try. I catch his sky blue eyes and my entire body goes up in flames. Am I . . . Yeah, I'm wearing sweatpants and a T-shirt. Fuck. And, yes, my muffin is also smeared all over his shirt.

Double chocolate chip fuck.

"Chocolate is a food group in my world!" I reply, backing out of his embrace. A food group? Good comeback, Darby.

"Huh." His eyes twinkle. Fucking *twinkle*! "You misunderstand. I was impressed. I thought I was the only one with that intense of a sweet tooth."

Great first impression, Darby. You fall on him, get chocolate all over him, and then can't even get your foot out of your mouth long enough to apologize? Can I blame this on triggered mommy issues?

"I'm sorry about your shirt." My cheeks burn hotter with every second.

"That'll be twenty dollars." The barista huffs. Someone else obviously has had a long day too.

I turn toward the counter, cheeks aflame. "Do you have any napkins or something?"

"It's my own fault for making you think I was insulting you. Plus, it's just a shirt," the man behind me interrupts, taking a few napkins off the counter. Where they are placed, but I didn't see them. Because I'm apparently stupid now.

"Twenty dollars," the barista repeats.

"I'll have what she's having, except make my coffee black." He hands over a black credit card.

"What's the name?"

"Benjamin James. And. . .?" Benjamin smiles at me expectantly.

"Darby. Darby Clarke. And you don't have to," I protest. I'd really rather go home and drown myself, thank you.

"I insist." And apparently that's that, as he steps up to the counter to retrieve his card. I stand off to the side, my palms a little sweaty. Can I discreetly wipe them on my pants or am I just stuck like this?

"Do you have a few moments to sit down?" the man asks once his order has been placed. The amused smile on his face is reassuring, but how have I not scared him off? He's covered in chocolate. And not in a fun way.

*Oof,* there's an image.

"Oh! Um, sure. Yeah," I very eloquently reply. I'm being hit on by the embodiment of a sexy older man. A sexy older man with a sweet tooth! I must've fallen asleep at my desk because this can't be real life. I'm wearing sweatpants for God's sake! Still convinced this is a dream, I follow him to the most secluded corner of the shop, which has the exact blue couch I noticed earlier. He smiles and gestures for me to sit first, and if this continues like my other dreams, Paul Hollywood is going to pop out of the kitchen any second.

"It's nice to meet you, Darby," he says once we're sitting down and comfortable. Well, as comfortable as I can be with sweaty fucking palms.

"Nice to meet you. I . . . thank you for paying for my things. You didn't have to, especially after I ruined your shirt," I reply.

"I know, but I wanted to. Take it as an apology for the misunderstanding." Despite sitting down, a certain rigidity remains in his shoulders. As if he doesn't know how to relax. "So while we wait for our drinks, tell me about you."

"Oh." He actually wants to know about me? Most of the time I can't get guys to pry their eyes away from my chest for longer than five seconds. It's always about sex, sex, and more sex. But, to his credit, he's kept eye contact this entire time.

Maybe, just maybe, he's different. "I never know what to say. I'm in finance. I work over at Xerx & Hoff."

"Really? That's interesting." His eyebrows raise.

I cock my head to the side. "What does that mean?"

His grin turns sheepish. "I used to do some work with them about ten years ago. Let's just say I wouldn't expect anyone under the age of fifty to be working there."

"Darby. Benjamin!" Our names are called from the front.

"Allow me, Darby." He smiles and stands before I can. As he walks to the counter, I wipe my palms on my pants. Despite my mommy issues, and my date from hell last night, I can't bring myself to run away to my apartment.

"Thank you," I respond when he returns, taking my drink and desserts. "Turnabout is fair play. Tell me about yourself."

"Ahh." He chuckles, taking a sip of a very normal looking cup of coffee. "I'm the CEO of Streemz."

"Holy shit," I reply before I can stop myself. Streemz? He's the *fucking CEO of Streemz?* Of course he is. Of *course* he is. It's not like Streemz is the biggest video streaming service in the country or anything. No wonder the man can't relax. I'm going to need Paul Hollywood to come running in from the kitchen because there's no way this is real.

"I figured I'd get that out of the way." His fingers drum against the side of his coffee in a restless beat.

"Wow. That's very impressive. We used your company as a case study in one of my college classes."

"That's a little flattering." He scratches at his stubble. "Hopefully we weren't an example of how not to be."

I smile. "Don't worry, you were one of the good ones."

"Good, I'd never live it down otherwise." His phone rings from his pocket. "Shit. Give me a second?"

"Of course." I reply. He stands and walks off, speaking into the phone. A man like that is probably busy . . . and very easily

Google-able. No! No, Darby. He deserves to be treated like a normal human, not a super-rich business god.

*Oof.*

"Darby, that was the office. Seems I'm needed. So as much as I'd like to watch you try and eat all of that chocolate . . ."

"Yeah, I bet you like watching." I narrowly succeed in keeping my head from thunking onto the table in front of me. I spend way too much time with Casey.

A surprised snicker draws my gaze up to him. His eyes are doing that twinkling thing again, and his shoulders seem to have dropped to that of a normal human.

"May I call you?" he asks, with a grin so large little dimples have formed. "I don't think I've smiled this much in months, and I'd really like to see you again."

"Oh!" How have I not fucked this up? Casey said the next guy who would ask me out would be decent. CEO of Streemz seems pretty fucking decent. The fact that he's actually been addressing me and not my chest this entire time is certainly a bonus. "Yeah, I'll give you my number."

"Here." He hands me his phone as if it's nothing. Does he not understand that most men guard their phones with their lives? What if I saw his texts with another girl he's talking to? I punch in my number and hand it back without snooping.

"I'll talk to you soon, Darby." He lifts my hand and kisses the back of it. His stubble gently rasps against my skin, and I have to stop myself from melting into the couch.

"Yeah," I dazedly reply. With a smile, and a wink of that perfect blue eye, he exits the shop.

*B*ack in the apartment, Casey's sitting on the worn, hand-me-down fabric couch her parents gave us, and staring at me.

"What?" I finally ask, throwing my bag on the table by the door.

"Why is your entire face pink?" she asks, crossing her arms. Ah, shit. I walk into our kitchen, which is unfortunately completely visible from the living room, trying to avoid her.

"I'm not pink. And if I am, it's just because of the chill in the air," I deflect, running my hand along the basic cream countertop. It's not a super fancy place, but it's homey and warm.

"The chill in the air? I thought we established already that you're too pretty to lie." She rolls her eyes and flops back on the couch. Ugh.

"Shut up." I glare at her back and fish around inside the refrigerator for dinner. The literal pile of desserts I just destroyed doesn't count. I settle on making up a stir fry, thanks to the extras Casey brought home from the restaurant. She may be an assistant chef for now, but I know she'll be getting promoted to sous chef soon. The downside is she rarely cooks at home. Something about being too sick of making food all day to make food for my lazy ass.

"I know I mentioned it earlier, but Hannah comes back tomorrow. So I'll be out at her place until she gets sick of me and makes me come home," she yells over the now un-paused TV show.

"So I'll see you about two minutes after you leave?" I snicker under my breath.

"I heard that!"

Yeah, I meant for you to hear it, dingus.

I smile as the veggies sizzle in the pan. My spatula scrapes against the bottom, dragging butter and soy sauce over the meal. Benjamin James. *Benjamin. James.* Even his name is sexy. My cheeks heat at just the thought of him. Images of his fingers drumming against his coffee cup flood my mind. I want to know exactly what those fingers can do.

"Ah!" I yelp as a drop of butter splashes up on my arm.

"You dead?" Casey calls.

"Shut up!"

That was new. Men don't usually distract me this much. Not that I believe he'll stick around for any real length of time. According to my own mother I'll never have any meaningful relationships. Fuck, I almost forgot she texted today.

"Hey, Case?" I slowly say after I'm done eating.

"Mm?" she replies, not taking her eyes away from the TV.

"My . . . my mom texted me today." I sigh.

Casey scrambles up from her lounged position immediately. "Fuck. Why didn't you tell me sooner? Are you okay?"

"I guess, yeah. I just . . . I don't even know why I'm telling you, to be honest."

"Come here," she snaps, holding out her hand to me. I take it and let her pull me down with her on the couch. "Look at me. You are a beautiful, intelligent, funny woman, and you do not need her. Just because she gave birth to you doesn't mean she can treat you like dirt and get away with it. You are not obligated to humor her bad behavior. Someday you'll realize that you are so much more than she ever made you think you were. Someday you'll see the woman I see."

"Thanks, Case. But she's my mom. I don't really know what to do with that."

"You'll figure out that you are a genuinely good person who deserves more than this. And once you do, you will feel so much lighter. Trust me."

"That's what Dad tells me all the time. It's just easier to give advice when it isn't you."

She nods and smiles. We've had this discussion so often that she knows there's no good in continuing. With a flick of her wrist, she's pulled the soft zebra print—Casey's choice—blanket on top of both of us and switched over to *The Great British Baking Show*. No matter how much we bicker like an old married couple, no matter how different we are, Casey will always be there for me. And I will always be there for her.

# Flourless Chocolate
# Cake Bomb

*P*ure, untouched winter snow crunches underneath my brand-new pink boots. I've never seen it this deep, this luscious, in my eight years of life. According to Dad, Seattle never gets snow, and I have no idea how to function in the face of this. My head tilts toward the cloud-covered sky as my tongue peeks out. People catch snow in their mouths in the movies, so why can't I?

"Darby, what in the world are you doing?" Mom asks from the relative warmth of the porch screen door. She's in her fluffiest bathrobe and thick Ugg slippers.

"Look!" I exclaim, twirling in a circle. "Snow!"

"Yes, we can all see it's snow," she snaps. "You look ridiculous like that. What in the world will the neighbors think? Come back inside!"

I reluctantly trudge back to the porch but stop in front of her. "May I please play outside?"

She slowly trails her gaze from the tip of my pink boots to the top of my floppy blue hat. "If you must. Just don't expect me to listen to you complain about being cold for the rest of the day."

*"Yes, Mom," I whisper. The sound of laughter pulls my attention to the lawn next to ours. Chris and Willow Turner, who are four years younger than me, are having a snowball fight with their parents. Not for the first time, my heart pangs in my chest. By the time I turn my head again, Mom has already closed the door and retreated into the warm house. I guess I'll teach myself how to build a snowman, and maybe he'll come alive and love me just like Frosty. Just like Frosty.*

***

My phone vibrates in my pocket the next day, during our weekly departmental meeting where I have been replaying last night's nightmare on repeat. I don't recognize the number and immediately the hopeful part of me wonders if it's Benjamin. I can't very well leave in the middle, no matter how mundane this is, so I keep checking until I see the little voicemail notification pop up. People don't leave voicemails anymore. It has to be him.

My foot nervously taps against the long glass conference table, hoping against hope that time will speed up so I can check the voicemail that is waiting for me. Mr. Carmelon stands hunched over a dinosaur-era laptop at the front of the room, trying repeatedly to get the presentation to work. I'd offer my help, but last time I did I was told to *mind my place.* According to my mother, my place is at home with any man who can stand me. Spoiler alert: no man can so far.

Once the meeting is over, I almost sprint out of the room and outside to find a little corner of privacy and soon I'm in my favorite little cove. Two small, wooden benches on a rare patch of grass sandwiched between two tall buildings. The sounds of the city are muted by the tall pine trees.

"Hi, Darby. This is Benjamin James calling, from yesterday. I'm hoping you're free tomorrow evening to join me for dinner. Please let me know!" I can't help the giddy grin that lights up my face. He called! And the next day too! Maybe it's the warm blue eyes, or the attention to my actual interests, but I haven't felt this excited for a date in a while. And I barely know anything about him other than the fact he can potentially eat as much sugar as I can. I have continued to show restraint and haven't Googled him. Yet. I'm not sure how much longer I can hold out, but I want to give him the benefit of getting to know him. He deserves that much. My fingers are moving before I realize it and then the phone is ringing.

"Darby?" Benjamin's voice floods through the phone. God, I like how he says my name.

"Hi Benjamin. I'm just returning your call. I'm sorry I missed you, I was in a meeting," I reply, somehow feeling like a teenager all over again. Why didn't I practice speaking in the mirror beforehand?

"Please, call me Ben. And I figured that was the case. I don't know your schedule, so I just took a chance. How are you?"

"Ben." I test the name on my tongue. Yeah, I like how that sounds. "I'm well. My workday is almost over. How are you?"

"I'm well. Just working on a major project." He sighs. "You're lucky to be going home soon. So would you like to join me for dinner tomorrow night? I would love to spend some time with you."

He would love to spend some time with me. I don't think a man has ever said that to me in that way before. It almost sounds like courting.

"That would be wonderful. What time?"

"How about seven? I'll pick you up. You can text me your address."

"Oh, I live above the Starbucks actually. . ." I break off with a nervous chuckle.

"Perfect. Listen, someone just walked into my office, but I'll see you tomorrow night at seven. I'm looking forward to it, Darby."

"Me too, Ben. I'll see you soon!" I hang up and twirl in place. My God, who am I? I'm acting like an honest to God teenager right now. It's just a guy, Darby, just a gorgeous, older, super successful guy with a sweet tooth. Fuck.

With one more fist pump, which I will never mention to another living soul, I run back up to my desk. Hopefully no one noticed I was gone.

"Clarke!" Mindy calls, tone cold as ice. Shit. So much for hoping no one noticed. I stand from my cubicle, smooth my skirt, and walk into her office.

"Yes, Mo—" Jesus Christ, I was about to call her mom. I'm stabbing myself in the face with a pen the minute I get back to my cubicle. "Mindy. Yes, Mindy?"

"Sit for a second." She gestures to the chair in front of her wood desk. She brushes her chin-length brown hair behind her ears as I lower myself into the most uncomfortable chair I've ever sat in. It's a wooden frame with no cushion to speak of. I think my dolls had better chairs as a kid.

"Listen. We've been asked to put together a presentation for the partners. They want to see projected budgets, opportunities for charity, and an overall snapshot of our growth over the last five years. I want you on this."

Me? *Me?* The woman who I'm convinced doesn't know my first name wants *me* on this? "Definitely. How can I contribute?"

"I want you to put together the entire presentation. The annual meeting is in three months, and the partners will be meeting with each department. I trust you to wow them and prove that we're doing a good job."

She . . . she trusts me. This. This is exactly what I've been looking for. An opportunity to prove that I have the intelligence to be useful to this company. I can do this!

"I won't let you down, Mindy."

"You don't have a choice, Clarke. Now get to work. I want to see a rough outline in a week." She pointedly stares at her door.

I scramble out of the chair like it's on fire. "Yes, ma'am!"

I'll make you proud. You'll see.

Despite how often Casey tells me I need to get out there, I don't date much. And every first date I've had has sucked. I've had one boyfriend in all my years, and it only lasted six months. No man has ever cared to get to know me. For some reason, guys take one look at me and think "piece of ass." But Ben? Ben seems different. Maybe it's because he's successful and intelligent in his own right, but I feel like he sees me. Not just my ass.

So when it comes to picking out an outfit for my date Friday night, I'm totally lost. It doesn't help that a man like Ben definitely won't be taking me to the Waffle House. I'm certain we'll be going somewhere nice, and I don't know how to dress for nice. I may have to do the one thing I don't want to do—ask Casey. And I really, *really* don't want to ask Casey.

I have no choice.

"Case?" I call from my closet. It has just barely enough

room for me to stand in it and stare hopelessly. Casey gave me the bigger bedroom when we got the place, insisting that she'd spend so much time with Hannah that it would go to waste. She was right. It's a nice size room, almost as big as the living room, with a bathroom en suite. I've spent days in the bathtub at this point.

"Yeah?" she calls back from deep in the apartment somewhere. She's grabbing some things and then heading back to Hannah's.

"Could you . . ." I cringe. "Could you help me?"

A herd of elephants come trampling into my room.

"What am I helping you with, dear?"

I regret this, I so regret this.

"Be nice, Case," Hannah calls from the doorway, hip cocked against the wall. Naturally a quiet person, Hannah makes up for that in her taste in fashion. Every outfit glows against her dark skin as if to say "I know exactly who I am and I embrace it." At some point I really should learn how she does it.

"I'm always nice. Now tell me what's up," Casey says, practically pushing me against the wall of my closet.

"I'm going out tonight . . . somewhere potentially fancy. And I need help figuring out what to wear."

"Are you going on a date?" She bounces up and down like a puppy.

"Casey, just help me," I whine. It's already six thirty, and at this rate I'll be going in my pajamas.

"Okay, okay. Do you want to look good, or do you want to look appropriate?"

". . . Good."

"So it *is* a date!! I'll be expecting all the details later. Now, get out so I can take a look."

"Bossy." I back up and let her take control of my closet.

She's going to pick out something crazy, and because I'm running late, I'm going to have to wear it. My future with Ben will be ruined by this single decision.

Look at me, pretending my unworthy ass has a future with a man like him.

"Since this is a first date, I'm assuming you don't want to go too hard. Don't want to give the poor guy a heart attack with all that sexy you got goin' on. But you want him to be impressed. I suggest the classic little black dress. This one specifically," Casey announces, exiting my closet with said dress in hand. It's simple but short enough that it shows off my legs—despite the fact that they're my least favorite feature. Not a lot of cleavage, but tight enough that my breasts are slightly emphasized. It's a good choice.

"Huh. Thank you," I reply, taking it from her.

"We'll want to see the final look before you leave," Hannah adds as Casey walks toward her.

"Yeah, yeah, get out," I grumble as they close the door behind them.

It's annoyingly perfect. The dress comes down to just above my knees and has short little sleeves. I pop on a pair of low black heels and take one last look in the mirror. Will he still like the girl he met a few days ago? The girl with sweatpants and a messy bun is still here under all of this. The girl with a brain. The girl worth loving for more than her boobs. Theoretically, anyway.

"Hot damn, it's been a minute since you dressed up. Like, shit . . ." Casey circles me as soon as I exit the bedroom. "You look hot."

"You do. You look beautiful, Darby," Hannah seconds with a smile.

"Thank you, Hannah," I reply, laughing at the "hey!" that Casey whines. "I'll see you guys later."

"Just, one thing first." Casey stops me with a hand on my wrist. "I know you probably said yes to him because I was all up in your business about it. But try to give him the benefit of the doubt and give him a chance, okay?"

I nod and give her a quick hug. I'm certainly not going to admit that he gives me butterflies and I wasn't thinking about her advice when I accepted his invitation. Nope.

*I* step onto the sidewalk at precisely seven, because I'm always annoyingly on time, and get to see him before he sees me. Ben is leaning on a smooth, black Audi in a gray suit and white button-down. The hands in his pockets emphasize how perfectly the pants fit over his strong thighs. Fuck, my mouth is watering.

"Darby." His low, warm honey voice melts over my name with something like reverence. "You look beautiful."

My eyes glance up from his thighs to meet his. "Oh, thank you. You look very handsome."

A soft grunt that sounds suspiciously like a laugh is my response as he works his hand along his chin. "Shall we?"

I nod and he opens the passenger door for me like a true gentleman. Ben has this calming effect on me. He's incredibly confident and something about that makes it hard not to feel safe. With a click of his own door, we are alone. The car itself smells like Ben, a dry cedar, sandalwood blend with just a hint of sharp citrus. I could easily get addicted to a smell like that.

"You do look beautiful tonight," he murmurs after a few moments. "I'm looking forward to dinner."

"Me too. Thank you for the invitation." I glance down to my fidgeting hands.

"How was your day?" He is the picture of confidence as he lets one hand settle on the arm rest beside him and one on the wheel.

"Oh, um, fine, I guess. Fridays are usually pretty slow in the office as most of the execs are out wooing clients. How was your day?" He wouldn't want to hear about my project. No one ever enjoys hearing about my work. I just say the word "finance" and most people's eyes glaze over.

"Busy, as always. My assistant, Xavier, insists it's because I'm too much of a control freak to delegate. He says I need to get out more," he admits with a chuckle.

"Well, do you?" I tease in a sudden burst of confidence.

Ben shrugs and glances at me. "Probably. But look at me now: I'm out and about."

"Xavier would be so proud."

"To be honest, he's right. I need to relax a bit. And if in the process I get to spend time with a beautiful, intelligent woman, then I'm certainly not going to complain." He shoots me a crooked smile before fixing his eyes back on the road.

"Smooth," I reply, winding my fingers together on my lap.

The restaurant itself is nestled in the heart of downtown Seattle, and I thank God he didn't bring me to the space needle. I hate heights. Vanlis is a gorgeous place, and I am once again ecstatic that Casey picked out a suitable dress. The views are mesmerizing from the floor-to-ceiling windows in the mid-century modern home turned restaurant. The city itself is the other direction, but in front of us sits a small harbor on the Puget Sound and a lush hill covered in homes and evergreen trees. The stone fireplace in the center of the entrance is blazing, creating a warm, romantic glow.

"Do you have a reservation?" the host asks as Ben leads me toward him with a hand on the small of my back.

"No, but I'm friends with the owners. Benjamin James," Ben replies with a confident smile. I've never been in this restaurant, but I've heard stories from Casey that you need to get reservations at least a month in advance.

"Oh! Of course, sir. Let me prepare a table for you. One moment, please." The host dips his head before scurrying off.

Ben winks in my direction, oozing confidence out of every pore.

This isn't something I've ever experienced. The ability to get used to name-dropping, to people tripping over themselves to accommodate you, is beyond my comprehension.

"Right this way, please." The host returns, picking up two menus on his way. We follow him up the wooden stairs to a roped-off area. "A little privacy."

"Thank you, it's very much appreciated," Ben replies. When they shake hands, Ben covertly passes the man a tip. I've only ever seen that maneuver in old movies. Ben pulls my chair out for me, and I sit down, trying not to trip all over myself.

"The view is gorgeous," I gush, my gaze following the lights of the harbor.

"I'm glad you're enjoying it. I'll admit, I wanted to impress you." He sits across from me, leaning back in the chair.

"Consider me impressed. I may have to bring back some leftovers for my roommate. She's a chef, and I think she may kill me if I tell her I was here without proof."

"That can be arranged. I wouldn't want to be the reason you're murdered, after all."

With a smile, I look down at the menu. I had a feeling this would be out of my price range, but they don't even list the price of a basic salad. What's the cardinal rule? If you have to ask how much something costs, you can't afford it. Casey may just murder me after all.

"How do you feel about red wine?" Ben asks, pulling my eyes away from the extravagant menu.

"I'm not much of an aficionado, but I like reds usually. Just nothing too dry," I reply with a weak chuckle. I don't want to know how much a bottle of wine costs here.

"There's no delicate way to say this, but please order whatever you like. This evening is on me." The blush that lightly stains his cheeks is endearing in all the best ways.

"That's very kind of you, Ben. Considering all goes well, I'd be happy to get the next one."

"Deal." His face lights up with a grin so large those dimples resurface on his cheeks.

"Are you two ready to order a drink?" our waiter asks a few moments later.

"Do you mind if I order that bottle of red?" Ben asks.

"Please go ahead." I close the wine menu and place it on the white tablecloth.

"We'll have a bottle of the Giuseppe Rinaldi Barolo, please." Ben gestures to his own wine menu.

"Absolutely, sir. I will return with that shortly. If you have any questions about our menu, please don't hesitate to let me know. My name is Bernard." The waiter dips his head and exits our table.

"So." Ben relaxes back in his chair. By the way his menu lies abandoned in front of him, it seems he's in no hurry. "I know you work in finance at a law firm. Tell me more about that, and you."

I lift an eyebrow. I mean . . . really? You don't have to pretend you care about *finance*.

"Well, this is my first job after graduating so I can't complain too much. . ."

"I'm not interviewing you." He chuckles. "Go ahead and be honest."

Honest? This won't last anyway, may as well stop trying to impress him.

"I'm . . . underestimated by upper management. They treat me like a glorified assistant. I get coffee more often than anything else and it's frustrating. They put me on a new project, but even so I've been playing with the idea of getting my MBA. I'm just not sure if it's worth it."

"I'm sorry they can't see what an intelligent woman they have on their team. I got my MBA when I was in my twenties, and it helped a great deal with my image professionally. Although, even with that, my friends and family thought I was insane for starting Streemz. There's something to be said for knowing your own worth."

"Huh." I grin. "Maybe I'll take a more serious look at that after all."

"And what about when you're not working? What do you do to unwind?" Did I imagine the low tone his voice took on when he asked that? Because . . . wow. He can talk in that voice all day long.

"I run. I did a 5k for breast cancer research not too long ago. I also enjoy painting and watching movies. . ." I trail off.

"Ahhh, running. I miss running. It's a little too high impact on the old knees for me now." He winks.

"Old? You can't be that old, Ben."

"I'll be forty in two years," he deadpans.

"Yeah, like I said, not old," I sass back.

"You're kind, whippersnapper."

"Thank you, Grandpa. What about you? How do you enjoy your free time?"

He gives me a look. "What free time?"

"You're telling me you work every single minute of every

single day?" I cross my legs at the ankle like a lady—just as Mother taught me—and sit back. "Because I don't believe you."

"Well, you should." His eyes twinkle. They *twinkle*. And my belly is definitely not filled with butterflies because of it. "When I can, I try to get to the gym in the office. I can be a bit of a homebody when I do have free time. I don't have an artistic bone in my body, so I try to steer clear."

"Everyone has a little bit of creativity in them," I argue. "I can't believe a man who built one of the biggest streaming services in the country doesn't have some creativity."

"I'll prove it." He whips out a pen from inside his jacket pocket and presses down on the paper square underneath his water glass. His lips thin in concentration as he scratches along.

"There!"

I look down. "What in the world is that?"

It is as if a dog somehow morphed with a horse, a man, a monkey, and a. . . worm?

He quickly crumples the napkin in his hand with a smile. "Told you."

"The wine, sir," Bernard says, having materialized by our sides. It is only with the greatest self-control that I don't jump ten feet in the air.

"Excellent, thank you," Ben replies as Bernard opens the bottle, showing off the cork, displaying the label in a very old-school movie way, and pouring a sampling into Ben's glass. I'm transfixed by the way Ben delicately lifts the glass and swirls it. With an elegant sniff, Ben lifts the glass and takes the smallest sip.

"Delicious," Ben says with a nod. Bernard smiles and fills up my glass before topping off Ben's.

"Have you two had a chance to look at our menu? I'm happy to answer any questions." Bernard places the wine bottle on the large table.

"No, we haven't had a chance," I pipe up.

"Of course, madam. I'll return in a few moments." With that, Bernard disappears again.

After a few minutes of careful consideration of the menu in silence, I feel confident enough to order. For a second I was tempted to text Casey and ask her what to get. She'll be eating the leftovers, after all. As I wait for Ben to finish perusing his own menu, I pluck up the courage to taste the wine. Being twenty-five, I've had a few occurrences with wine, but it's usually cheap. I haven't gotten much of a taste for it yet. However, I don't want to be rude and ignore it when Ben specifically picked it out. With a prayer to God that I don't hate it, I lift my glass to my lips.

*Ohhhh.* A small moan leaves my lips involuntarily. I didn't realize wine could taste that good. My eyes flicker up to see Ben watching my mouth with an almost hungry gaze.

"Sorry." I self-consciously clear my throat. "That's delicious."

"Yes, delicious." He smirks, eyes never leaving my lips. "I fell in love with wine while traveling through Italy in my mid-twenties. I feel, admittedly, a bit pretentious about my hobby, but we can't all be perfect."

A bit? Dude, you walked into a restaurant and expected them to give you a table based on your name. It's more than a *bit.*

"I'd love to travel to Italy. What prompted the trip?" I ask. His face shifts from light and relaxed to scrunched up. The hand that had been holding the menu goes up to rub at his chin.

"Right . . . well. I was there on my honeymoon."

Ah, fuck me.

"I'm divorced," he continues. "Have been for seven years now."

"Oh." Thank God he's not married. He's gorgeous but I'm

no homewrecker. "I'm sorry." That's what you say right? That you're sorry?

"I'm not. We weren't right for each other, and in the end it was better that we split. She ran off with some wellness guru, and now he's the one who has to deal with her." His shoulders relax. Maybe he was just worried about my reaction.

"Hmm . . ."

"I realize it's a lot." He grins guiltily. "But I'm not one to hide things like that. I'm an open book."

"I appreciate that. Honesty is important to me, and I'm glad it's important to you too." I raise my hand and squeeze his forearm. *Fuck, it's hard as a rock.*

"Speaking of honesty, I should probably find out just how young you are," he jokes, taking my hand from his forearm and placing it in his.

"I'm twenty-five. Does that bother you?" Not that I've even given our age difference more than a passing thought, myself.

"No, it doesn't bother me at all. Age is just a number." He shrugs, running his thumb in little circles on my knuckles. Goosebumps prickle against my skin. "Does it bother you? I'd understand if it does."

My eyes fall to our hands gently clasped together and I smile to myself.

"No, I don't mind at all."

***

The food is delectable. The steak is perfectly pink and practically melts in my mouth, and the asparagus is crisp and fresh. While the wine is a perfect pairing, I'm doing my best to pace myself. It's a first date, after all, and I don't have much of a tolerance. No one wants a drunken Darby stumbling around like an idiot.

"How is it?" Ben asks after a long silence. We are both far too engrossed in our food to make much conversation.

"Delicious! Without a doubt, the best steak I've ever had," I assure him.

He smiles, taking a slow sip of wine. "Good. I'm having a really nice time getting to know you, Darby."

"Oh." My cheeks flame. "I am too." Wait. "Having a nice time getting to know *you*, I mean."

"How is your meal this evening? May I get you anything?" Bernard saves me from my floundering. *Thank you, Bernard.*

"It's wonderful," I say, turning my attention back to my food.

"Yes, it is," Ben says with a nod. "Darby, would you like to see a dessert menu when you've finished? They have excellent chocolate dishes."

*Considering how delicious you look covered in chocolate with clothes on, I bet you look delectable covered in it without them.*

"Chocolate, huh?" My smile grows.

Ben's eyebrows raise, looking me up and down with a slow bite of his lip. *Mmm.*

"Take your time, and I will return with our dessert menu," Bernard interrupts, snapping my eyes away from Ben's. With a nod, he elegantly strides away.

"If you want to finish your dinner, I'd be happy to order Casey something and have it boxed up. Whatever you like," he insists, his gaze fixed on my unfinished main course. His blue eyes are earnest and kind in a way I've never experienced.

"No, that's alright. It's a lot of food," I reply, putting my hand back in his. His fingers, slightly calloused, clasp around mine in a gentle hold.

***

"I can't eat another bite! I couldn't possibly!" I exclaim, flopping back in my chair. The chocolate *monstrosity* we ordered is just one bite away from being gone, and my belly has never loved me more. It was rich, thick, and delicious . . . just like Ben. How much wine did I drink?

"Are you sure? There's only one bite left, my dear," he croons, waving the full fork over the plate.

"Stop!" I whine. "Please eat it and get it away from me!"

"If you insist." He lifts the fork up and wraps his full lips around the bite. *Holy moly*. It'd be entirely inappropriate for me to climb into his lap and suck on his bottom lip. But that may not matter.

Who am I? I've never felt this way about someone before. It's the physical reaction, sure. Woof. But he listens to me. He cares about the things I say, and that's something I've never experienced before. Even the actual boyfriend I had never cared about anything that came out of my mouth. But it's the first date, and I can't let myself get too excited.

"I'll have Bernard bring us the bill and Casey's box," Ben says with a wicked smile. There's no way he knows what I'm thinking. No way.

"Alright," I reply, suddenly bashful.

Once everything is settled, Ben stands and offers me his arm. I wind my hand through the crook of his elbow and allow him to lead me back through the restaurant to the entrance. The valet grabs the car and Ben insists on opening my door and helping me inside. As I sink slowly into the comfortable leather seat, Ben takes off his jacket and places it on the backseat with the bag of food.

"I had a wonderful time tonight, Darby," he says as he rolls his shirt sleeves up to his elbows and puts the car in drive.

"Yeah, me too," I reply, my eyes cataloging every vein and muscle in his exposed forearms. This is a man with strength, a man that I could spend hours talking to—I just had, after all.

"Darby?" At the concerned tone of voice, I reluctantly rip my eyes from the flexing muscles.

"Mm?" I smile.

"Are you okay?"

"Yes. Ben, I had a lovely evening. Thank you for inviting me," I reply. He probably thinks I'm nuts. With a sideways grin, he lays his hand, palm up, on the armrest between us. I link our fingers together and don't hold back the sigh of contentment. I could get used to this.

Too bad it won't last. A man like this is far too good for me, and it won't be long until he realizes it.

The drive back is too quick, in my humble opinion. However, I can't complain. Going over the bridge in the moonlight with Ben is something I'd love to do over and over again.

"May I walk you up to your door?" he asks as we approach my apartment.

"Sure. Here, let me show you where to park." I point toward a hidden lane. I direct him toward some guest parking spots for the high rise and wait for him to bring the car to a stop. He lifts his hand at me, signaling me to wait, before grabbing his jacket and coming over to open the door for me. *What a gentleman.*

"Thank you." A slight shiver travels down my spine in the cool night air. Without prompting, Ben drapes his suit jacket over my shoulders and wraps an arm around my waist.

"Lead the way," he rasps. *Fuck.* With a grace I have somehow summoned against all odds, I lead us to the entrance to my building. The building itself is mostly glass and modern. The reception area where we wait is white and gray, with black and white artwork on the walls. The elevator itself is completely reflective, and I watch as four pairs of us enter and press the button for my floor.

"May I see you again?" Ben whispers in my ear, pulling me closer. His grip is light, easy to escape if I wanted to. I don't want to.

"Yeah," I whisper back, turning to face him. His eyes act as magnets, drawing me closer until our noses practically touch, until . . . the bell for my floor dings, and the doors open. With great reluctance, I pull back and walk toward my door.

"This is me." I shrug, turning to face him in front of door number 3116. His hand slowly, so slowly, comes up and brushes a lock of hair behind my ear.

"May I?" His thumb caresses the apple of my cheek. I nod, not trusting my voice at this point. My throat feels dryer than the Sahara. The other hand comes up to my neck, tipping my head back just a fraction as his head dips down. Our noses touch, a gentle rub that sends bolts of electricity down to my toes. The first press is soft, so impossibly soft. With a dazed blink, I wrap my hands around his back and pull him in. *Hungry.* That's the only way I can describe the desperate slip of kisses. Before I know it, my back is against the door and his hand is in my hair. The slight tug on my roots is a sensual prickle of pain, and I moan into his mouth. I can sense every inch of him pressed against me, all clean lines and muscle.

"Soon. I want to see you again *soon,*" he implores, breaking our kiss. It's now that I remember I have neighbors. Neighbors that don't deserve a show.

"Soon," I agree, slipping his jacket off my shoulders. "Goodnight, Ben."

"Fuck." He grins, giving me one last fleeting kiss. "Goodnight, Darby."

# A Bag of Cookies

I do *not* skip into the apartment. I don't. Except for I do, and then twirl around in circles once I've closed the door. My lips still tingle in the most delicious way.

"Welcome back, Darby-kins."

I snap my head to that stupid hand-me-down couch where Casey is waiting with Hannah. Hannah, at least, has the courtesy to look moderately guilty.

"Why are you guys still here?" I ask, already knowing the answer. The downright evil face Casey makes is confirmation enough that I'm right.

"We just want to hear all about your date," she replies. "*All* the details."

"Or instead of interrogating me, you could snack all over these leftovers from Vanlis that I brought for you." I swing the bag in front of her.

Her eyes grow as big as saucers. "Vanlis? He took you to *Vanlis*? Marry him and give me that bag!"

"Here, you ridiculous creature. I'm changing into my pajamas." I laugh, placing the bag on the coffee table in front of her.

In record time, I'm in my comfy pajamas and a messy bun. Thank goodness for slippers—my feet hurt like crazy.

"How much did you two eat? Because if this is just left-overs, I may have to have a talk with you," Casey says. She's opened the bag in my absence and has four takeout boxes open in front of her.

"I—" How did he . . . *when* did he?

"I think he surprised her," Hannah remarks, nudging Casey with her shoulder.

"Hmmm . . . he's trying hard, huh? What did you *do* to the poor man?" Casey chuckles, looking over her spoils. "Oh, I think I'll start with these noodles."

"We didn't even have noodles," I murmur, still staring at the feast. When did he do this? I whip my phone out lightning fast and type away.

ME

Thank you for the extras you snuck for Casey. I can't believe you did that! You really didn't have to—but thank you.

"You do realize there's at least three hundred dollars' worth of food sitting in front of me, right? Is this guy Jeff Bezos?" Casey says after swallowing a big forkful.

"No, but you're not far off." I flop onto the mismatched armchair that rests next to the couch. None of our furniture goes together, due to budgets, but I kind of like it. It adds a certain artistic chaos to our apartment that matches Casey and me perfectly.

"Wait, what?" Casey puts down the fork to stare at me. "Elaborate."

"You promised not to interrogate her in exchange for the food," Hannah reminds her.

"She won't take it from you, you eat some." Casey pushes

the box and the fork into Hannah's hands and rounds back on me. When I don't respond, she lifts a single eyebrow and crosses her arms across her chest. So she's not going to let this go.

"Fine. His name is Ben, and he's the CEO of Streemz," I mumble.

"*What?*" Hannah and Casey exclaim at the exact same time.

"You're dating my boss's boss's boss's boss?" Hannah continues. "Benjamin James?"

I pick at the hem of my shirt. "Yep."

"Shit, he could probably afford to buy the restaurant." Casey relaxes back on the couch. "How'd you meet him?"

"I met him in the Starbucks downstairs. I didn't know who he was at first," I admit. I contort my body to rest my head on the armrest and my legs over the side. "I forgot you work there, Hannah."

"Well, it's not like I've ever met him for more than three seconds or anything. He's far too up the chain for that. But he seems decent enough. He gives good vacation time and bene- fits." She shrugs with a smile.

"You're dating a God with an unlimited income . . . Good for you! And you're welcome. If I hadn't mentioned something earlier, you may have passed him up." Casey cheers, stealing back the fork from Hannah.

"Right." I'll let Casey have the win, even though I know she has nothing to do with how I feel about Benjamin James.

"Wow, could he be any more pretentious?" Casey says, stuffing her face with one hand and staring at her phone in the other.

"Wait a minute! What are you doing?" I scramble over to the couch.

"I'm scrolling through his Instagram like a normal person.

Duh." She rolls her eyes. "Have you not looked at his socials yet?"

I shake my head and crane my neck to see over her fork. Her thumb is flicking by quickly, but even I notice that all his photos are of him, in his office, in a multi-thousand-dollar suit.

"Xavier must take these," Hannah remarks. "Ben's assistant."

"Yeah, he's mentioned Xavier."

"Are these all fucking sponsored?" Casey snorts, clicking on one to see the caption.

I make a grab for her phone, which she evades. "Stop!"

"Absolutely not. What do you two even talk about? I mean, sure, objectively he's attractive, but this is a little sad."

Hannah smacks Casey's arm. "Be nice!"

Maybe it's just his persona? Or Xavier insisting that Ben needs to be seen a certain way since he's in the public eye. But the man who just kissed me isn't this guy.

Casey's gaze burns a hole into my side until I meet it.

"Alright, I'll shut it down," she says, throwing her phone on the floor. "This food is more important anyway."

I've never been more grateful for her ability to read my mind. With an exasperated sigh I retreat to my bedroom, confident that she'll stay off his social media. At least for the rest of the night.

Thankfully, my bedroom has a TV that my dad graciously purchased for me. Or guiltily purchased for me because of Mom stuff. Sometimes, no matter how much I love her, I need a break from Casey and the world in general. My room is my oasis. It's the only room in the house where the furniture matches and there's an actual color scheme. Shades of blue decorate every inch of the space. Light blue bedspread, ocean-colored curtains, a navy rug . . . and all it does is remind me of Ben's blue eyes. With an exaggerated flop, I land face first on my soft bed. I believe in an abundance of pillows. My phone buzzes and I fish it out of my pocket. *Oh!* Ben! My heart flutters as I read his message.

BEN

I wanted to do something nice for you. I hope she enjoys it, and I hope she shares. There's another dessert hidden in there, after all.

At this rate, my ass will be as wide as a truck. Images of my mother having a heart attack at my size flit across my mind. Maybe I should go steal that dessert.

ME

It's long lost to me. She's been devouring all of it since I returned. I'm glad you made it home safe.

At least, I assume he made it home safe. I hope he's not the type to text and drive. Despite being the type to pose like a model on Instagram. I scroll through Streemz, not paying attention to what I'm looking at.

BEN

Safe and sound. When do I get to see you again?

ME

When would you like to see me again?

I hope that my message comes off teasing and flirtatious, not like a brush off. Oh God, I'm going to be that girl that analyzes every single word in our conversation.

BEN

I didn't want to leave you tonight. What are
you doing tomorrow?

I squeal at his response, cheeks heating involuntarily, and roll onto my stomach to reply back.

ME

Nothing planned . . . yet.

BEN

What if I wanted to surprise you? Would you
come with me?

ME

I think that could be arranged. My only
requests are that you tell me what time and
what to wear.

I'm not letting him leave me to Casey's outfit decisions again.

BEN

I'll let you know the answer to both of those
questions in the morning. Give me a little time
to plan ;)

ME

I'll hold you to that.

BEN

So . . .

How are you?

Hours later, I look up to see that stupid message from Streemz. Are you still watching? No, no I am not. I'm texting Ben. And I plan to until I fall asleep.

*I'm eight again, running around outside in the summer sun. Daddy is at work and Mom is inside, and I am free as a bird. The entire world is in each leaf on each tree, in the blades of grass beneath my bare feet. I tumble, cart-wheel, run . . . I'm free.*

*"Darby, what are you doing? Your room is a mess!" my mom calls from the back porch. A single drop of fear runs down the length of my spine as I turn to her.*

*"I'll go clean it," I say, walking toward the house.*

*"Don't bother," she snaps. Her eyes are as cold as ice. "You're useless when it comes to cleaning, and I'll just have to redo it anyway. I swear, I don't know what I did to deserve you."*

*"I can try harder," I murmur, my gaze on my bare feet. Just don't be mad anymore.*

*"The only thing you'll ever have is your face. That's all you're good for. One day, I hope you have a daughter that's exactly like you. Then you'll understand." She scoffs and slams the door behind her.*

***

Tears slowly trickle down my cheeks as I wake. With a heaving sob, I scrub at my face. This must stop. I can't keep having these dreams. Rolling over, I look at the clock with a groan. Four a.m. Fucking balls. My entire body is tensed up, my nerves frayed. I'm not going to be able to sleep like this. Sighing, I pull myself out of bed. This situation calls for a bubble bath, a bag of cookies, and a good book. And then a nap.

The bath water is scalding once I slip in. All the better to burn away those awful dreams. The scent of cassis fills my nose as I snuggle deeper into the pink, bubbly water with one of my treasured romance novels. There's nothing an expertly crafted man in flannel can't solve. Or a real-life man in expensive suits with blue eyes, dimples, and a little bit of gray in his hair.

Everything will be okay.

# Chocolate Chip Pancakes and Vanilla Cake Coffee Creamer

*M*y eyes blink open again at ten, having dragged my sleepy self back to bed after my bath. Checking my phone, I see a new text from Ben.

BEN

Wear something casual, something you'll be comfortable walking around in. I'll be there to get you at 1:00.

I reply in the affirmative and kickstart my day. That hiccup earlier was nothing, and I refuse to let it impact my date with Ben. This broken-ass woman can attempt to be worthy of his love and attention, but not if I keep wallowing. Push it down and focus on Ben.

*Ben, mmm.*

Since I have an actual idea of what to wear, I feel confident starting in the kitchen rather than the closet. Girl's gotta eat. And what this girl wants to eat is chocolate chip pancakes and a hulking cup of coffee. Do we still have that vanilla cake creamer . . . Oh, thank goodness. Casey didn't use it all. Within a couple of movements, I have music playing and pancake batter stirring. This can still be a great day. This *will* be a great day. Especially once I scarf down these pancakes. Fuck you, Mom.

A ridiculous amount of coffee and pancakes later, and I'm ready to go. I've pulled on a semi-low-cut, black, long sleeve shirt, my favorite blue jeans, and a cute pair of leopard print sneakers. Casey gave them to me, and as much as I hate to admit it, I love them. They're obnoxious and cute all rolled into one. A confident knock jostles me out of my thoughts and I practically bound toward the door, flinging it open.

"Darby." Ben grins, dimples and all. Has it been just a few hours since I've last seen him? It feels like an eternity. Without a thought, I bounce into his embrace and wrap my arms around his neck. Digging my face into the soft skin there, I finally relax my muscles. This. This is what I needed. His arms wrap around my middle, pulling me closer into the best hug I've ever experienced. I inhale his scent—cedar, sandalwood, citrus—and smile. Yes, I needed this.

"Hi." My voice is muffled by how deeply I'm burrowed into him.

"Hello." He chuckles, the rumbles making my body shiver.

"Hi," I repeat, pulling back a hair to see his face.

"You ready to get going?" he asks, pressing a kiss to my forehead. I'm going to melt into the floor. I am puddle, hear me roar.

I'm nodding before he finishes the question. "Mm-hmm. Let's go."

"I just don't understand why people go into shark cages. Do they not realize sharks are terrifying? Has no one seen *Jaws*? *Jaws 2*? *Jaws 3*?" I ramble, walking hand in hand with Ben. He surprised me with a trip to the aquarium, which I love. It's not my fault that I'm terrified of sharks, however.

"You couldn't pay me to get into one of those." Ben nods with a smile, squeezing my hand. "I'll stay in the boat." The light blue glow from the tanks falls on Ben's navy blue polo shirt and jeans. I'm certainly not opposed to how delicious the shirt looks straining against his broad chest. Flannel who?

"Oh! Belugas!" I tug him forward like a child to see the adorable whales. The three of them look so content as they play together in the calm water. "This was a wonderful idea, Ben, thank you."

Another gentle squeeze of my hand. "I'm glad you're enjoying it. I'm a bit out of practice at dating."

I scoff and let my gaze lift from the whales in front of me to him. I expect to find a haughty smile or a smug look, but he just grins at me like I'm the source of the sunshine.

"What?" he asks.

"What do you mean what? I'm just finding it hard to believe you're out of practice. I mean, not to be blunt, but you're attractive, wealthy, and incredibly sweet. I'm sure there'd be a line out the door of women happy to date you." I mean, seriously. Does he not realize how out of my league he is? I'm not sure we're even playing the same sport.

His nose scrunches up. "Sweet?"

"Sweet."

"If you insist. I haven't dated in about a year. I have no time with work being as busy as it is."

"Right, I remember you saying your assistant was telling you to get a life."

"Anyway." He gives me a mock glare. "I'm sure you have more practice than I do."

The indelicate snort of laughter in response is downright embarrassing. "No way."

"What?" he asks again as we move toward the stingray pool.

"I don't date much either."

"I'm surprised to hear that. You have to know what a woman you are, Darby. I'm lucky to be out with you."

My cheeks heat up from his compliment and I duck my head. No one has ever said that to me before. No one. It's like I'm a middle schooler finding out that a boy *likes* me. At least for now.

"Yes, well, we're both lucky," I brush off, pulling him along. If my behavior seems strange to him, he doesn't mention it. Just follows me with a kind smile on his handsome face.

That is, until he sees the gift shop. He turns to me with a dimply smile and kicked-puppy eyes.

"Wait here. I'm going to get you something!" He runs off without a second glance.

"Ben? You really don't—" I call after him.

He turns, running backward through the glass double doors. "You better not look. Don't make me blindfold you!"

That's an image. I don't remember how to breathe. What is breathing? How? Help.

***

"You didn't have to," I implore, snuggling into the arm wrapped around my shoulder. The parking garage is cold, okay? At least that's my excuse.

"You'll remember this date whenever you see it," Ben fights back, grinning at the beluga stuffed animal in my arms.

"I'm a grown woman. I don't need a little beluga." I pout, pulling it tighter into my chest.

"Uh-huh." The permanent shit-eating, cocky smile on his face is unnerving. It's like he doesn't believe me! Rude. Oh well, it's my beluga now.

"Are you hungry? I was thinking we could stop for an early dinner, then maybe see a movie?" he asks as we approach his car. He brought some fancy BMW today, and I have a strange feeling he's got a fleet of vehicles at his home.

"On one condition."

"What's that?" He opens the car door for me.

"You let me pick the restaurant and pay for dinner."

He walks around the car and sits with a sigh. "Okay. But I'm getting the movie."

"Sounds good to me." I nod, clicking my seat belt.

***

Benjamin James just may be the most perfect man I've ever met. Even if he is thirteen years older than me.

He raises a brow at me, smiling broadly when I cast my eyes back to my hands. And now he caught me staring. Ugh.

The fact that a man this rich, this powerful, can be this kind. It's mind-blowing. He bought me a fucking beluga! It's like he doesn't even realize who he is or what he could do. Yes, he's a bit pretentious, but there's a sweet, down-to-earth guy underneath it all. Even if he does throw down a grand at one dinner.

"Enjoying it?" I ask, nibbling on cheap pizza. I just said I wanted to pay for dinner, not that I could afford anything worth eating.

"I'm enjoying you." He winks. "And pizza is always good."

"Smooth talker," I say, slurping some more Coke out of my pink paper straw. We're in a little booth in the back of the nearly empty fluorescent-lit pizza joint. It's old, cheap, and Ben has never seemed more out of place. It's almost comical to see his rich, pampered ass on a sticky cushion. "How long has it been since you've been in a place like this anyway?"

"A place like this?" he repeats.

"A hole in the wall," I explain. My foot is just forcing itself further down my throat with each word. "You just don't seem the type to go somewhere like this, especially after looking through your Instagram."

"Shit, you saw that?" He groans.

I cock my head. "Yeah."

His hand scrubs through his stubble. "That's Xav's pet project. The *public facing* Instagram. I just let him do whatever he wants. I'll get you my private one."

It's reassuring knowing that the fake, sponsored-post guy in expensive suits isn't the man sitting in front of me. That my instincts were correct about him.

"So our choices for a movie are super cheesy romance, over-the-top action, or kids movie. What do you think?" he continues, scrolling through the options on his phone.

"Depends on if you want to make out in the back of the theater or not." I shrug, eyeing him playfully when his gaze snaps away from his phone.

"Which movie gets me that option? Because I want that option."

"Ahh, you must figure that out for yourself."

"Challenge accepted," he replies, looking back down to his phone. "Movie starts in an hour." Truthfully, it doesn't matter which one he picks. I plan on jumping his bones no matter what.

Okay . . . maybe not if he picks the kids movie.

***

Ben picks the action movie. Because, apparently, no matter how much of a sweet, beluga-buying softie he is, he is still a *guy*. This is one of those fancy movie theaters, with the private loveseats just made for snuggling. And the tickets that cost twenty-five dollars a pop. Yikes. Ben, however, doesn't look phased and picks up two boxes of candy for each of us. He knows the way to my heart. Not that I've made the bottomless pit I call a stomach any sort of secret. We enter theater four, and I pick the loveseat in the back with the darkest of shadows.

"Here." He smiles, handing me my boxes. My hero. After draping his coat behind us, he wraps his arm around me and snuggles into the plush couch. He probably doesn't expect I was serious about kissing him silly during this movie. I just barely restrain myself from giggling. The previews blare and I rest my head on his shoulder. Despite my evil plans, I'm rather enjoying just being here with him. Ben came into my world like a wave, crashing in like he belongs here. With me. I didn't even kiss my first boyfriend until our third date, and here I am planning semi-public make-out sessions on date two. It's as if my entire world has shifted on its axis, like the hemispheres have flipped. And I'm enjoying it. Maybe I'm not as broken as I thought.

Ha! Good one, Darby.

This movie is shit. Thankfully, my expectations weren't that high to begin with so I'm not disappointed. Crash, crash, boom, boom is the general synopsis, so I know I'm not missing much by focusing on Ben instead. He's a bit more amused than I am, but not seriously engrossed.

"Hey Ben?" I whisper about halfway through the film.

"Mm?" he whispers back, turning his gaze to me.

"I like you."

The explosion on screen lights up his face at the exact moment he breaks into a large grin. Oof, those dimples kill me every time.

"I like you." He leans in and kisses my cheek. His stubble rasps against my skin and my heartbeat picks up. He must be able to hear it over the main character's swearing; my heart is practically beating out of my chest. Before he can sit straight once again, I reach my hand out and settle it on his cheek. I playfully rub my nose against his just to see those dimples again. With a gentleness no man has ever shown me, he closes the distance and kisses me. It isn't the full-blown make-out that I had planned . . . It's better. Softly, slowly, his plush lips guide me through a slipping and sliding that has my eyes closing immediately. Those large, calloused hands are rubbing my sides, my thighs, wherever they can reach in the limited space of the movie theater seat. My fingers trail up from his cheek to settle in his hair, scratching his scalp when he gives a pleasured groan.

"Darby," he murmurs, his mouth trailing down to the sensitive places on my neck. "Darby, Darby, Darby."

"Mm?" I moan, head tipping back to give him access. Whatever access he wants. Wherever he wants.

"You taste *delicious*," he growls in my ear, causing my entire body to shiver. Fuck me, he's good. So good. All the good.

"Come back," I whine. Using the hands I have buried in his short locks, I pull his mouth back to mine. *This* is what I had planned. I suck harshly on his bottom lip as his hands tighten around my waist, pulling me as close as our little seat will allow. A tongue dances along my lips until I allow it entrance with a groan. My brain short circuits at the playful dance. God, I will never get enough of this.

With a pitiful whine, which I will deny ever happened, we break apart at the end of the movie. I'm half convinced we would've never even noticed if that teenager hadn't started screaming how awesome the movie was as the credits rolled. My lips ache in the best way, in a way that'll be impossible to hide. Everyone will know exactly what we were doing. I'm kiss-swollen and dazed, and my jaw will hurt for the rest of the night.

Worth it.

Ben looks slightly more put together, however his hair is an absolute mess from my wandering fingers.

"We should see movies regularly," he whispers, smiling when I snort-laugh.

"I've already spoiled you. There'll be no living with you now." I sigh dramatically, pulling myself together.

"It's your own fault." He stands and extends his hand out to help me up.

"Maybe so," I allow. I take back my hand for just a moment to attempt to straighten his hair. At least one of us should look presentable, and it sure as hell isn't going to be me.

"Alright, alright." He pulls my hands away and wraps his arm around my shoulders. "Let's get out of here already." We're the last people in the theater, and I didn't even notice. I sling my arm around his waist and walk with him out of the room.

"One more box of candy for the road?" he asks as we pass the counter. Well, fuck me, he's trying to make me fall in love with him.

"I've never said no to candy." I smile, dragging him over.

*I* don't want to say goodnight. I *really, really* don't want to say goodnight. The only way tonight could be better is if tonight didn't end. The little voice inside my head keeps repeating *invite him in*, but I shove it down. As much as I want it to be, I know this isn't forever. I'm not willing to give myself to him just to have him leave.

"Drive safe," I murmur into Ben's neck. His arms feel so good around me; I don't ever want him to go.

"Always do. What are you up to tomorrow?" he asks, not releasing me yet. *Good.*

"What, miss me already?"

"Obviously." He chuckles. "I have some work I need to get done that I blew off on Friday. But I'm hoping that I could text you a bit if you're not too busy."

"Sundays are my Dad days. I pretty much spend the whole day hanging out with my dad. But I'll have my phone." I smile, nuzzling further.

"Awwww," he coos.

I lightly slap his chest and *oof,* hi muscles. "Shut up!"

"No, it's sweet."

I glare up at him. Judging from the continued laughing, I must not look that menacing.

"I'm not judging!" he insists. "Really, it's sweet."

"Yeah, yeah," I grumble, returning to his neck. Mmm, sandalwood, cedar, citrus—my happy place. A gentle finger comes and lifts my chin out of his neck. He pecks my lips, kissing away the pout.

"I'll see you soon, sweetheart."

"Good."

We disentangle and I open the apartment door. "Good-night, Ben."

"Goodnight, Darby."

My neck cranes to watch his ass as he leaves. Those jeans look *good*.

# French Toast and Maple Syrup

$\mathcal{C}$asey isn't home, thank God. I can't imagine the torture I would be put through if she had witnessed that. Not to mention what she would've done to Ben himself. I throw the empty candy carton in the trash, only slightly regretting eating it all in the car. I worked up an appetite, and I'm still famished. Opening the stainless-steel fridge, I take a peek to see if Casey left anything easy. Like, a few minutes in the microwave easy. There, nestled on the middle shelf, is the untouched dessert that I brought home last night. A little post-it note sits on top saying, *Go ahead, Darby. You deserve it. Love, C.* I am so spoiled. With a squeal, I pull out the—oh, cheesecake!—dessert and unwrap it. Prepare to be devoured, friend.

A belly full of cheesecake later, I settle in for a marathon of *The Great British Baking Show* on Streemz in bed when my phone buzzes. *Ben!* My heart flutters with a million little butterflies that all die a painful death the moment I see the name.

No, not Ben.

Mom.

THE MOM-STER

> I remember the day you were born perfectly.
> You were such a pretty baby. Call me.

Well, there goes my good mood. I swallow down the cheesecake that threatens to make a reappearance. No. I will not let this get to me. I had a good day, damnit, and I . . . my hands are shaking. She may remember the day I was born, but I remember all the other days. The days I was told I'd never be worth anything, the days she spent critiquing every minute detail, the calorie counting, the degradation. The moments when I knew this woman would never love me. The moments when I knew I wasn't worth her love.

Why did I have to send Ben away? Then again, I don't want him to see me like this. I don't want him to know these dark and twisty places that live inside me. As if all the warmth in the apartment has been sucked out the window, I shiver. Alone. By myself. The shadows are longer and darker, seemingly coming to swallow me whole. I burrow deeper under the blankets, holding my beluga tight against my chest, as the tears start to fall.

Fuck.

"*K*iddo!" My dad pulls me into a bear hug as soon as I enter his home in the morning. Every feeling of self-doubt melts away in that hug. I'm no longer the girl who hates her job, who has nightmares most nights, whose own mother couldn't find a way to care for her, who is convinced no man will ever love her. Now, I'm Darby. Just a girl loved unconditionally by her dad.

Dad stands at around five foot nine and has mostly gray, short hair. At sixty, he looks damn good for his age.

"Hey, Dad." I wrap my arms around him just as tightly. He's been my one source of safety for so long that I don't know what I'd do without him. It's purely because of his influence that I'm able to function on a daily basis. Hawke, the family black Labrador, circles us during our embrace.

"You ready to start our day?" he asks when he pulls back, his eyes sweeping me. Ever since I was a kid he almost unconsciously checks me after every hug. I don't know what he's looking for. None of my damage was ever visible by the naked eye.

"Yep! Let's get going." While Dad grabs Hawke's leash—we would never leave without him—I take a few steps through his house. It's the quintessential Seattle mid-century modern split level. I lived in the house for a couple years after my parents divorced, so it doesn't feel like mine, no matter how often my dad tells me it is. He means well, wants it to feel like home. I'm just glad it feels like home to him; he deserves it, after all.

"I was here a week ago! When did you get a new couch?" I call, appraising the living room. It's full of furniture my dad has "collected" over the years. He loves adding *authentic* pieces to the house. The dork.

"Wednesday?" he answers, walking into the room with Hawke at his feet. "You know me."

"I do. I also know that you have an addiction. Doesn't he, baby?" I coo when Hawke comes over for pets. He's almost immediately on his back, woofing at me.

"I have a healthy appreciation for a certain type of furniture. I see nothing wrong with it," he says with a decisive nod of his head. Despite his attitude, he's more than used to my teasing by now.

"So what's new in your life? How was this week?" Dad asks over our brunch. We're sitting on the outdoor patio of 7720 Bar & Grill in downtown Bellevue next to the tall hedge, Hawke happily lapping at a bowl of water at our feet.

I drizzle maple syrup over my fluffy French toast and scrambled eggs as the waiter drops off extra whipped cream without prompting. They know me too well. This place has that quintessential homey feel that's needed for a perfect brunch. It's in the older part of Bellevue, the part that's a little quieter than the city center. The storefronts have that small-town feel to them—flowers in front, bowls for thirsty pups.

"Good," I reply, my cheeks heating up. The space heater standing next to me doesn't help the situation. I've never been good about lying, but I'm not sure how my dad will react to my dating someone so much older. Unfortunately, I'll have to tell him sooner or later.

Dad quirks an eyebrow. "Spill it, kid."

Apparently sooner. "I went on a date."

"A date, huh? What's so embarrassing about that? Is he ugly?"

"Dad!" I cry, laughing into my food.

"Well, if that isn't it, then spill."

"He's . . . he's wonderful. We've gone on two dates already and I just met him this week." I smile at the thought of Ben.

"Wonderful, huh? Don't think I've ever seen you make that face before. Must be someone special."

"I think he is. He's funny, sweet, kind, and might love sugar as much as I do."

"Sounds like a winner. I'm glad you're happy, kiddo. If it all works out, I'll be looking forward to meeting him. What's he do?" Dad cuts his egg so that the yoke trickles all over the plate.

Avoidance tactics engage. I didn't hear him ask about Ben's occupation. "What about you? How've you been this week?"

"Oh, you know, same old same old. Work, taking care of Hawke . . . went out with Lisa on Tuesday. The usual."

I relax back in my iron-wrought chair with a smile, breathing in the fresh air. Avoidance tactic successful.

"How is Lisa doing?" I ask, patting Hawke on the head.

"Good. She was asking about you, wanted me to send her good wishes along."

Lisa is a much better partner to my dad than my mom ever was, despite her general boring-ness. Problem is, I don't think he'll ever want to get married again. Not that I blame him. As much as I suffered at the hands of the mom-ster, Dad suffered too. How do you see marriage as a positive thing after an experience like that?

"Back to the guy. Want to tell me about him? Or is that not a conversation you want to have with dear old Dad?" He leans over to scratch Hawke behind the ears.

I scrunch up my nose. So much for that. "I guess I can give you the highlights if you really want me to."

He bats his eyelashes exaggeratedly, causing me to giggle snort.

"His name is Ben, and he . . ." Here comes the boom. "He's the CEO of Streemz."

"Seriously?" His jaw drops a little. Funny, I've never seen that happen in real life. "You're dating a big-time CEO?"

"I've been on two dates with a big-time CEO," I correct, shrinking down in my chair.

"How old is this guy?"

One boom down, another to go. "Thirty-eight."

I'm given a hard stare. "Okay . . ."

"I know it's a big age difference—"

He interrupts, "That's an understatement."

"But he's a good guy, Dad. You know me, you raised me to have a good head on my shoulders. I wouldn't fall for some creep."

He scrubs his face with his hands, actually raising his brows at Hawke. As if the dog would help him. "I'm not pleased with the idea of you dating someone so much older. But you're an adult. I can't very well lock you in your room and ground you. Just be careful. That's all I'll say."

"I know, Dad." I'm not going to try to convince him that Ben is special. I'm hoping that Ben will be around long enough to convince him himself. That's if me and my damage don't send him running for the hills.

"Okay, okay, backing off." He holds his hands up in surrender. "You ready?"

We stand, Dad throwing the exact amount of cash on the table, and walk to the farmer's market down the road. Traditionally, we always hit up the local farmer's market after brunch on Sundays. It's not a big one, not like the one in Issaquah; there's only fifteen wooden stands clustered together in the park.

"These blueberries look good," Dad praises, perusing one of the local farm stands.

"It's two dollars a pound," the older woman wearing a humongous straw hat replies with a toothy grin. With a nod in agreement, he pulls a few bundles together. Despite my being an "adult"—whatever that means—he always buys everything at the farmer's market. I tried to contribute to a carton of straw-berries once . . . it did not go well.

"You think Casey will want some zucchini? I know you hate it, but these are gorgeous. . ." Dad trails off, muttering to himself. As much as my dad adores me, Casey is his number two. She's been a permanent fixture in our house since we were kids and even calls him dad. Probably because he's been a better father to her than her own.

"You know Casey never says no to good produce," I reply with a chuckle. "Plus, whatever she doesn't eat, Hannah will steal."

"Those two ever going to tie the knot? It feels like they've been dating for years now."

"That's because they have been dating for years." I groan. "I keep telling Casey to propose. Hannah is too good for her. She's finally starting to talk about shopping for a ring."

Dad hands the woman some money and takes a large bag of fresh fruits and veggies in return. "No one is too good for my girls."

"*Dad.*" I roll my eyes.

"*What?*" he mocks.

"You know what? Nothing. You just keep doing your shopping."

"That's what I thought. How about some flowers for your coffee table?"

And he's off.

My phone buzzes, and I hope to God it's not my mom. I can't deal with that right now, especially with Dad. He had to deal with her enough.

BEN

Missing you. Hope you're having fun with your dad.

My heart does a full swoop up into my throat and my cheeks are on fire. He misses me. Me. How in the heck have I bamboozled this man into thinking I'm worth missing?

ME

> I miss you too. I'm having a good time. How are you? Still working?

I hope that doesn't scream how much I wish he were here. I can almost imagine him walking along with my dad, patting Hawke on the head. I like to think they'd all get along.

"Hurry up, kiddo!" Dad calls. He's gotten a few stalls down now and will probably need help holding his horde soon. Wait. I could use this stuff to make a homemade meal for Ben. I'm nowhere near Casey's level, but I can whip up a dish. Better than anything I could afford to pay for in a restaurant, anyway.

BEN

> Still working. Thought it would only be an hour or two, but a couple lawyers requested some paperwork. I'll be stuck here for days. I'm glad you're having fun.

"Hey!" I run to catch up. "Have you been to the butcher yet? I'm thinking of picking a few things up there."

"Nope, but it's next on my list. Let's go!"

ME

> How about I make you dinner some night this week? Something to look forward to!

Dad and I peruse the butcher as I nervously wait for a response. I can't imagine Ben wouldn't like someone making him a home-cooked meal. Ooh they have some nice pork chops today.

I bark out a laugh and quickly school my face when Dad whips around.

"Are you texting during our father-daughter day?" he teases, pulling out his credit card.

"Maybe." I duck my head. Hawke woofs at another dog and draws my dad's attention away. Thank you, pupper.



We drop our purchases off at Dad's house before walking over to the park. Hawke always gets special play time after behaving so well during brunch and the market. He's a silly pup that we got two years before my parents divorced. I'm not sure how my dad, or I, would've held up without him.

"You keep glancing at your phone and blushing like a schoolgirl," he comments once we sit on our usual bench. Hawke is off-leash and seems to be making friends with an enthusiastic border collie.

"Thanks for pointing it out." I roll my eyes, stuffing my phone back into my purse.

"Just sayin." His gaze travels over the dog park and then returns to me. "It's nice to see you happy. I'm not fond of his age, but I can't deny that you look good."

"I barely know him still. I've only been on two dates."

"Maybe, but you've got the look. And the look doesn't lie."

"You just stay over there." I smile. "With your looks and such."

"Alright, alright." He lifts his hands in mock surrender. With a shared smile, we both return our eyes to Hawke. The ridiculous animal is now fending off two border collies that have obviously not been fixed. Poor Hawke doesn't have the *equipment* to handle them. I cackle into the back of my hand.

God, I am so immature.

"*W*here's Dad?" Casey asks the moment I step into our apartment. Sometimes he'll come over for dinner on Sundays to finish off the day together.

"He was worn out, and so was Hawke. No dinner today," I reply, taking my farmer's market haul into the kitchen to put away.

Casey, unable to help herself, meanders in behind me to appraise the goods. "Fuck, that's a sexy zucchini." She lifts it and slowly runs her hand up and down, waggling her eyebrows.

"You know, I'm not going to encourage you. I'm just not." I snort, opening the fridge.

"I'm disappointed in you!" She flops up onto the counter, still stroking the zucchini. The little freak. "Good day? How's Dad?"

"He's good. Working too hard, as usual, but it makes him happy, so what can I do?" I reply. I push off my ingredients for Ben's dinner to the side and leave them packaged.

"What's that pile?" Casey asks, swinging her legs.

"I'm going to be making dinner one night and those are my supplies. So"—I turn to her—"*do not touch.*"

"Fine." She huffs. "Are you making this dinner for me?"

"Nope."

"Rude. And after all I do for you."

"How about I make you some ravioli now instead? I got some of the handmade stuff from the market," I sing-song. She's right; she does a lot for me, and she deserves some pampering.

"I've been appeased," she announces, jumping down to the floor. "I will pick out a disgustingly cute movie for us to enjoy as we eat."

"Sounds fabulous, darling." I smack her bottom as she leaves. What a dork. While the water boils, I bounce with energy. Ben and I decided I would go over on Wednesday as a midweek pick-me-up. The thought of seeing him again has me physically unable to keep still. I've had a stupid smile plastered on my face all day, and there are butterflies in my belly. All of this because of a guy. A sweet guy, a beluga-buying guy. A fucking sexy guy. I pour the four-cheese raviolis in the boiling water and grin. This will be a good week.

# Double Chocolate Fudge Chip Muffins

y bitten-down nails clack against the keyboard rhythmically for the entirety of Monday morning. I have an opportunity to show everyone here that I wasn't hired for my ass. Or to get coffee. I'm pulling data from the last five years to prove we've been spending less money overall. I've also already found three places we can trim the fat, without layoffs, to increase our charitable givings. Fuck an outline, Mindy is going to get a fully formed first draft this week if it kills me. She will be proud of me—and proud of her decision to ask me to step up, despite the certainty that I'm giving myself carpal tunnel. Ouch.

Foot rapping against my cubicle, I clutch my stomach as it rumbles. I'll burn out if I don't get something to eat—and fast. I save my work and close my computer, stretching out my back as I stand. What I wouldn't give for a better chair. My mind wanders as I walk the bland, uncovered hallways to the kitchenette. I walk completely unnoticed by most of the employees, except for the few who watch my ass as I turn the corner. It's almost disgusting how used to it I am. How used to feeling like

I was only hired because I'm hot. I need to get the fuck out of this office, either that or earn some damn respect.

"'Sup, Clarke?" Jason from HR calls. I pretend I don't hear him.

I've barely been able to talk to Ben since yesterday afternoon because his company is going through some acquisition that's dominating all of his time. I can't imagine how much pressure he's under, and I just want to help him.

Lightbulb! I'm a genius! I should bring him some lunch during my break. I can bet he's not taking care of himself. Maybe if it's me who brings something to him, he'll take a breather for five minutes. Casey is working the lunch shift today at the restaurant, and she always gives me her employee discount, which means I can give him something that won't suck like that pizza. This will be perfect.

*A*fter a thoroughly abusive line of questioning from Casey, I have a double-decker gourmet grilled cheese, a half cup of tomato soup, and a ginormous chocolate chip cookie. No one, not a single person, could say no to this feast. Especially not when it smells so good. *Mmm.* Feed Ben first, then me. I drive over to the Streemz headquarters and park in the guest parking space out front. Considering Ben doesn't know I'm coming, will I even be allowed in? Shit. I should have thought this through beforehand. With a deep breath, I walk up to the glass building. It's not a tall building, but it's huge in width. It sprawls over a manicured green lawn riddled with benches and trees. Most people would love to work here.

I'm buzzed in by the calm woman at the front desk. "May I help you?"

"Uh, yes. I'm here to see Benjamin James." I didn't think this through. I can't imagine how many people try to see Ben without an appointment.

"Okay. . ." She raises her eyebrows. "Is he expecting you?"

"No. I, well, I brought him some lunch as a surprise. I was hoping to get him to take a break." I sheepishly smile.

"Uh huh . . . Let me call his assistant." She trails her eyes from the tips of my toes to the top of my head.

"Could you please ask him not to mention me? I want it to be a surprise. My name is Darby."

She scoffs quietly and dials the phone. "Xav, there's some woman here for Mr. James." A pause. "She says her name is . . . Darby? She wanted to bring him lunch or something." Her voice is steadily dropping in volume until I'm sure she assumes I can't hear her. "Seriously? Well, fine, but it's on you if she's some psycho."

I breathe a sigh of relief. Ben must have mentioned me, which means, Ben *mentioned* me. Must suppress the need to squeal.

"His assistant will be by to pick you up. Please wait a moment," the woman says, hanging up the phone. She gestures to the gray armchairs in the sitting area in front of her.

"Thank you." I smile and drag my feet over. The inside of the building matches the modern feel of the outside. Sharp lines, lots of whites and grays. It seems very Ben. I'm drawn to a small marble fountain in the corner. It makes the softest noise possible, with little gray and blue rocks submerged under water.

"Darby?"

I turn to find a short man, about my height, with dark brown "I just had sex" curls smiling at me.

"You must be Xavier," I reply, walking toward him. "It's nice to meet you."

He makes a point of appraising me, a big grin on his face. "It's nice to meet you too. So you're the one who ruined his brand-new Armani suit with that chocolate monstrosity." The words would seem almost aggressive from anyone else, but for some reason he isn't threatening.

"Brand new?" I wince. Shit.

"Armani," he says with a wink. "Don't worry, it's one of countless others. I think he'll be very happy to see you."

"He needs a break. I just didn't think about how I'd get to him," I admit, my cheeks heating.

"You're lucky he tells me pretty much everything. The minute Maxine mentioned your name, I knew who you were. It's kind of you to come." He leads me back through the building. Offices line the walls, but the middle is open. No walls, no partitions . . . just open space for people to talk and collaborate. The desks are small and they roll, allowing for easy maneuverability.

"Here we are!" he announces. Ben's office is at the back of the building and is the only one without windows into the main area. I assume it's for privacy.

"Thank you, Xavier. I appreciate you keeping my secret. Is he free?"

"As free as he'll ever be this week. Which means, get in there before someone else does." He winks and sits at his desk. Right. Deep breath.

I knock twice on the office door.

"Come in!" Ben calls from inside. Opening the door, I find Ben at his large, glass desk typing away on his computer, not looking up at all. "What's up, Xav?"

"I thought you may be hungry." I smile when his eyes snap up.

"Darby." His grin lights up his entire face. His dimples deepen with each passing second. "I can't believe you're here."

"I hope it's okay." I step in and close the door behind me. "You've been working so hard, and I know I always forget to take care of myself when I'm in the middle of a big assignment. So I wanted to bring you some lunch."

He's up and across the room in moments, placing his hands on my cheeks. "You're welcome here whenever you want. Thank you, sweetheart."

My entire insides turn to goo and my legs wobble at the thoroughly adoring gaze. He looks like I've hung the stars and the moon just for him.

"I'm glad you're happy," I dazedly reply, a dopey smile on my face. He leans in and meets me in a gentle press of his lips.

"I couldn't be happier," he promises, still so close that his mouth tickles mine with each breath.

"Eat," I insist, pulling away just a hair. "Then kisses."

"Fine." He pouts, taking the bag from my grasp and drawing me deeper into his office with a hand on the small of my back. The office is large, but not overly so. There's a bookshelf along one wall, and the other three walls have windows. It's light, simplistic in its decoration. A few plants are the only real color in the room, and I expect they are kept alive by Xavier's determination.

He leads me to the plush chairs in front of his desk and places the lunch bag down.

"I still can't get over this." He dives into the bag. "You're spoiling me left and right."

"I don't trust you to have eaten anything in the last twelve hours," I say, brushing off his adoration.

"You would be incorrect. I ate eight hours ago." He smiles triumphantly. "Fuck, this looks delicious. Have you eaten? We could split this."

"I have something waiting in the car for me since I didn't know if you'd have time to hang out."

"I really don't." He sighs. "But fuck it, I can take five minutes to eat."

"As you should," I insist. "Wait . . . eight hours ago . . . you haven't eaten since six a.m.? How long have you been awake?"

He takes a huge bite of the grilled cheese. "I don't want to answer that."

"Ben."

"Don't look at me like that," he whines. "This acquisition is huge. I have to be on top of it or this whole thing could go sideways."

"You also have to take care of yourself, or *you* could go sideways. And then down. On the ground. Because you passed out."

"I'll be fine."

"Uh huh." I roll my eyes. Typical workaholic. I snuggle down deeper into the deceptively comfortable chair with a sigh. He'll do as he pleases.

"I promise things will lighten up in about a week or two. I'll sleep for as long as you want me to then, okay?"

"Mm-hmm."

"How are you doing? Lunch break?"

"Yep! And I'm fine." I smirk at how he's annihilated his sandwich. Despite anything he's said, the man was hungry. Real hungry if the way he's ripping into his soup is any indication.

Xavier's voice comes through on Ben's phone. "Mr. James, that obnoxious lawyer Carver Something-or-other is on the line. He's demanding to speak to you about some clause in the contract."

"This guy is a fucking nuisance. One second, sweetheart."

He clicks a button on his phone. "Xav, did you tell him to call my lawyer? I mean, seriously."

"I did, and he's on the line as well," Xavier responds.

"Jesus," Ben mutters.

"I'll let you handle that." I stand. "Finish your soup and your cookie, and I'll see you tomorrow for dinner."

Ben snaps the cookie in half and waves it in front of me. "One kiss for the road?"

"Ahhh, bribery will get you everywhere." I chuckle, walking around his desk. He places his hands on my hips and stands, blocking out the sunlight from behind him.

"And I know *exactly* where I want to go," he purrs, leaning in. My brain short circuits as he presses against me, the harsh edge of the desk digging into the backs of my thighs. My fingers wind into his hair of their own accord, getting tangled in the gray-streaked tresses. *So soft.* He continues pressing into me, dominating me with harsh kisses that have me forgetting everything but more. I want more. One hand slides up my front and squeezes my breast, and I let out a far too loud moan at the feeling.

"Mr. James!" Xavier snaps again through the phone.

"*Fuck,*" Ben growls, pulling away.

"My sentiments exactly," I breathe, trying to regulate my stuttering heartbeat.

"We'll pick this up Wednesday?"

"Yes. Yeah."

I walk out of Ben's office with an entirely stupid grin plastered on my face.

Fuck.

If I don't say hi to Hannah, Casey will give me shit for days. I can already hear her voice: *you drove all the way out there and didn't even say hello?*

"Hey, Xavier? Do you know where Hannah from HR is?"

We walk through the bullpen until we come across her little wheelie desk and she lets out a small squeal when she sees me.

"Darby! What're you doing here?" She jumps up and gives me a big hug. Casey better fucking marry this girl or I will be pissed.

"I was just visiting Ben for a moment, making him eat lunch. So I thought I'd say hi before I head back to work," I admit.

"Ben, huh?" She winks. "I'm so glad you're happy. It's nice to see you smile like this! You know, I haven't taken my lunch yet. You want to sit outside and eat with me? Do you still have time?"

I check my phone. "I've got about twenty minutes. I'll grab my food from the car."

Despite my rush to get back to work, I want to use this opportunity to get to know her better. I've known her for a few years now, but she's the shy type. Surprising, considering who she's dating, but opposites attract and all that.

"I can't believe you're dating the CEO." Hannah smiles conspiratorially, leaning into my shoulder. "He's always so private. And busy."

"It all seems a bit unreal still, to be honest. I keep thinking I'll wake up and have dreamt all this, but considering Paul Hollywood hasn't attacked me with sugary kisses, I think it's reality," I admit, nibbling on a roll. Rare spring sunshine beats down on our little bench as we munch together.

"You're definitely not dreaming. Or, at least, I don't think you are."

"Thanks, Hannah," I say. "Anyway, tell me something about you I don't know. Casey does most of the talking when you guys are around."

Hannah's permanent smile turns dreamy, her eyes glossing

over just a smidge. "I love how outgoing she is. She's so good at pushing me out of my shell."

"I knew that! Tell me something I don't know."

"Hmm . . ." She twirls her fork in the remnants of her reheated spaghetti. "I have an older brother named Marcus. He's in the coast guard and currently stationed in Boston."

"That has to be tough. Him living across the country and being hard to contact most of the time."

"It's harder on my parents. They always connected with Marcus a little bit more than me." She pauses, lifting her eyes from her plate. "Don't get me wrong! They loved us both equally, and still do, but he's more like them than I am."

"Huh. I'm an only child, so I can't relate. But I'm glad you have a good relationship with your family. That's so important." My gaze lingers on my sandwich. How different would my life be if my family was whole like Hannah's?

"It's hard to be so far from them, but Casey is my family now anyway."

"*We* are your family now," I promise.

Hannah giggles, her eyes a little misty. "If this is any indication of the sweet things you'll say if Casey and I get married, I know I'm going to ruin my makeup. Do you think you'll ever get married? Have babies?"

My heart sinks into my belly. How do you tell someone as pure and sweet as Hannah that you doubt yourself too much? That you want that future more than anything but can't imagine someone choosing you for a lifetime? Who would want you when your own mother doesn't want you?

"Maybe someday," I reply instead, a fake smile plastered on my face.

## Chocolate Cheesecake

*I*'ve been jittery all day. My legs bounce, my hands twitch, and I can't stop biting my lip. It's Wednesday. It's *Ben* day. *Ben day!* Despite my need to perfect my outline for Mindy, I can't do anything but fixate. She's on my calendar for Friday, which means I can worry about this then. I have everything ready to go in my fridge for his romantic dinner: apple and honey glazed pork chops, green beans, mashed potatoes, and a chocolate cheesecake—courtesy of Casey—for dessert. Granted, I have to cook everything but the cheesecake, but I got this. I've never burned anything in my life, and I'm not about to break that streak tonight.

"Hey! Hello? Woman in towel?" Casey calls, waving a hand in front of my face. "As much as I'm enjoying the show, why are you standing naked in the living room?"

I look down at the single pink towel covering myself and smile. "I was checking the marinade on the pork chops, and I guess I got distracted."

"Right. Well, like I said, you're naked in the living room. So maybe remedy that?" She smirks, closing the front door behind her and placing her keys in the bowl. Right. I should focus on getting ready and not on how excited I am to have Ben in my arms again.

For the first time in my life, I want to feel sexy. My looks have always felt like they belong to other people. I've never taken control, but tonight I want to. I want to walk into Ben's house and intuitively know that all he wants is to strip me down and take me. I want to watch his eyes burn with restrained passion. I want to be wanted for all that I am. Truly, deeply, wanted. I curl my long black hair into playful, loose waves that rest against my chest. My eyes are rimmed with a dark purple-y, brown smokey liner that brings out the golden undertones in my brown eyes, and I'm almost poured into a flowing dark blue dress. It's not too fancy of a dress, which is perfect since I don't want to show up to his house looking like I'm ready for a gala.

"Well?" I ask as I exit my room, twirling in front of Casey where she sits on the kitchen counter.

She wolf whistles, a shit-eating grin on her face. "God-damn, woman."

"That's exactly the reaction I was going for." I nod, pleased.

"How old is he? Because you could give him a heart attack." She hops off the counter as the oven beeps.

"He isn't *that* old." I roll my eyes, grabbing my things out of the fridge. "I won't be back until later."

"You sure you're coming back at all? You're dressed for a slumber party, honey, not a visit." She plates up some ridicu-lous vegetable-looking dish that she pulled out of the oven. It smells like zucchini. Ick.

"I'm coming back," I insist. My items are tucked away into a reusable, insulated grocery bag for the trip.

"Uh huh. See you in the morning." She winks. With a wave of her hand, her and her plate are off to the living room.

The drive is easy, up until I get to the gate. He lives in an actual gated community. I have no idea how to proceed here. Does the guard know I'm coming? Do I just tell him who I'm seeing? Should I call Ben? Before I'm able to fully commit to the rabbit hole I'm jumping down, my car is up to the gate house and the guard is smiling at me. I roll my window down.

"Hey." He smiles, giving me a once over. Yuck, he reminds me of Jason from HR.

"Hi," I slowly reply, wishing I had put on a coat or something.

"Who're you here to see?" He leans against the doorframe. *Not you.*

"Benjamin James."

The guard's body language instantly changes. His back straightens, shoulders square, and he leans back a considerable distance. "Yes, of course, miss. He told me to expect you. Please go ahead once the gate opens."

"Thank you?" I can't keep the question out of my tone. I don't even want to know what kind of interactions he's had with Ben to produce that reaction. Well, whatever happened apparently people don't fuck with Benjamin James.

The house is breathtaking. I almost unconsciously slow my car as I approach. It sits at the top of a small hill, where it over-looks the water and the mountains. I can't imagine the view from the inside. The house itself is like something out of the year 2050. It's a futuristic mixture of glass, white walls, wood, and concrete. It reminds me of his office building in that they both share the large windows and sharp lines. This is something I never imagined I'd ever get to see in person, let alone step inside. It's a dream, it must be. But no, because there—stepping out of this testament to architecture—is Ben. And not Paul Hollywood.

"Darby," he mouths as I pull up the drive and park.

"Ben." I get out of the car as fluidly as I can. "This house is incredible."

"Not nearly as incredible as you are," he replies, pulling me into his arms. Sandalwood, cedar, citrus. Mmm. I wrap myself around his middle, twirling my fingers into the back of his shirt.

"Does that line usually work?" I tease.

With a big squeeze, he releases me and laughs. "Fair enough. I was just trying to be sweet. Plus, you do look incredible."

"Thank you." I turn to the car and open the backseat to grab the food.

"Nope," he interrupts. "Let me." He grabs the bag and closes the door, offering his free hand for me to hold. I lace our fingers together and let him lead me toward his home.

As we enter, my mouth drops. It's even more stunning inside than outside, which should be impossible. My gaze is drawn to the back of the house and the wall of windows. Although . . . no, they're not windows. They're open. The doors are folded into the wall so that the entire back of the house is open to the yard and the view.

"Go explore a little, I'll put this in the fridge. Then, I'll take you on a tour." Ben kisses my fingers before releasing me. I nod, unable to speak, and let my feet take me exactly where they want to go. The view. My feet carry me to the edge of the house, and then I step onto the stone patio. It's not yet sunset, but the springtime sky is beginning to turn a gorgeous shade of orange. The mountains are lit up on the side and the calm waters of Lake Washington lay out before me like blue glass. The backyard itself is simple and tasteful, with a large infinity pool right on the edge of the hill. I never want to leave.

"That's why I bought the land," Ben says, coming up behind me. "That view is worth all the money in the world."

"The land?" I can't tear my eyes away to watch his approach. "Does that mean you built the house?"

"It was my gift to myself after my divorce. While it was the right decision, divorcing Jennifer was draining. I needed to do something for me. So I found an architect and we worked together to create my dream home," he explains, handing me a tall glass of wine. When my parents divorced my dad bought himself a fancy bicycle as his gift to himself.

"It's beautiful, Ben. I can't wait to see the rest of it." I take a sip of wine and almost melt into the ground. It's a fresh, crisp white that somehow tastes like pear and sunshine. Apparently, I've just been trying the cheap shit, and wine is delicious.

Good to know.

"Then let's not wait another moment. If you'll follow me . . ." He walks inside and I spare the view one last glance. It's like a storybook.

"I went a little overboard with the house, I'm the first to admit it." Ben grins over his shoulder at me. "But I'm never moving again. This is it for me."

"No, I get it. If I had the opportunity to create my dream home, I'd jump on it." I never will though because I will never have this much money.

"This is the kitchen."

Holy *fuck*. Can a room be sexy? Because I'm pretty sure I'm drooling. The stainless-steel appliances, the black cabinets, the truly sexual marble countertops . . . This is a chef's dream. Casey would self-combust if she ever stepped foot in here.

"Question," I pipe up. "If you don't cook, why did you create the most beautiful chef's kitchen in existence?"

"I said I don't cook, not that I can't. I always want to take the time to cook a meal for myself, but cooking for one is depressing."

"I mean, fair. So does that mean you're going to help me with dinner?"

"Of course I am. I even got us matching aprons!"

A startled laugh escapes my lips. "No you didn't!"

"So what if I did?" He pouts, pointing to two aprons draped over one of the modern barstools.

"You're something else, Benjamin James. Truly something else." I smile, wrapping my free arm around his waist. Ben mirrors my gesture and pulls me in close to his side. A gentle, chaste kiss is pressed to my lips.

"Missed you," he whispers, so close our mouths still lightly touch. My entire body suddenly warms, making my fingers and toes tingle. I press one . . . two . . . three more kisses onto him and pull away, dragging my teeth along his bottom lip.

"Missed you too."

"Yeah? I'm not so sure, you may need to do some convincing. . ." he trails off.

Convincing, huh? My hands grasp our wine glasses, leaving them on the kitchen island and out of harm's way.

"However will I do that?" My fingers brush along his shoulders, cataloging each dip and curve.

Instead of an answer, my body is pulled into his and kisses are rained down my neck. My head tilts of its own accord, allowing him access. I want to keep this man. God, please let me keep him. My eyes snap open—when did they close?—at the soft scratch of stubble against my chin. His own eyes are closed as his lips press against mine gently. So gently. It's decadent, addicting, and I refuse to believe I could ever have enough.

"What are we making?" he purrs against my lips, kiss-swollen and aching.

"Right, dinner." I giggle. "I'll show you." We disentangle slowly, and I sway over to the monstrosity that is Ben's fridge, swinging my hips just a little more than necessary. With an *oomph* I pull open the heavy door and take out my bag of ingredients. Ben's hands are on my waist as I put the bag down on the counter.

"I got everything from the farmer's market on Sunday with my dad. Everything should be fresh." I lean back in his arms as I unpack.

"Sweetheart, you're so wonderful." He kisses the side of my head. "Let me pay you back."

"Oh, my dad bought it. He never lets me buy groceries in his presence."

A brush of a sigh ruffles the hair by my ear. "Your dad bought us dinner?"

Oh. Huh. That doesn't sound great now that he's said it out loud. "He really wouldn't have let me pay for it. It's not worth the argument."

"I'll give you some cash next time." Another kiss is pressed to my hair before Ben grabs the wine bottle from the island and refills our glasses.

"Okay," I quietly reply. "Show me to your cast iron skillet."

"How about I put some music on? Let's have a little fun." Ben winks. He points toward a cabinet for me and then heads toward his cellphone on the counter. I pull out the—shit, is that copper?—cookware I need while he presumably sets up a playlist. Hopefully he doesn't only like eighties hair bands or something. I like a good eighties headbanger as much as the next person, but there's such a thing as too much.

"Do you like Queen? Or are they before your time?" He lifts his eyes from his phone and . . . is he blushing?

"Who doesn't like Queen?" I try to be reassuring.

"Thank God," he mutters, turning on the music. It's the first time I've seen Benjamin James flustered.

***

"Dance with me." Ben pokes my side a little while later as the pork chops sizzle on the stove.

"We're cooking! With hot things that could burn us!" I protest weakly, letting him take my hand.

"That's why we move away from the flame." He chuckles, pulling me in close. I side-eye the pork chops, making sure the timer is still going before I turn to him fully.

"I'm not going to impress you with my cooking prowess if you make me burn the food."

He clasps my hand in his and winds his other hand around to the small of my back, then shakes his head with a chuckle.

"Come here, sweetheart." The low timbre of his voice should not cause my entire body to visibly tremble. But it does. "Just a few moments, and then you can return."

I nod and rest my hand on the back of his neck, tangling my fingers in the small hairs there. As the mid-tempo song plays, he leads us in a simple dance around the room, and I drown in the soft blue pools of his eyes.

"Where . . . where did you learn to dance?" I whisper.

"I took lessons. Oh, don't look at me like that! I'm forced to go to an endless amount of charity galas every year as publicity for the company. I was told that I wasn't allowed to look like an idiot. Hence, the lessons."

"Hence the lessons," I repeat with a smile. My head falls, of its own accord, to Ben's chest. Cedar, sandalwood, citrus. I nuzzle slightly into the soft button-down and close my eyes. Do people usually fall this fast? Because it's as if the ground has opened up beneath me. I'm helpless to resist. With a shrill *beep*, the timer goes off and I lift my head. Back to impressing Ben with my cooking prowess. The pork chops—thankfully—aren't burnt. The apple and honey have married together in a sweet, thick glaze over the meat just like in the pictures.

By some miracle, everything is finished at the same time. Ben insists I sit down outside at his ornate glass outdoor dining table so he can plate everything himself. Something about doing his fair share of the work. I let him go as I turn my eyes back to the view. It's sunset now and the water is aflame in oranges and pinks. Only the deep, delicious scent of fresh food is strong enough to pull my gaze. A light tendril of steam wafts from the two plates in Ben's hands as he places them on the table before us.

"This looks wonderful, Darby. Thank you for doing this for me." Ben lifts his glass to me. "I don't relax nearly as much as I should, and I appreciate you wanting to help."

I tap our glasses together with a soft *clink*. "I hope you like it." I anxiously tap my foot as I wait for Ben to slice into his food and take that first bite.

Please taste good, please taste good, please taste good.

"Mmm. Fuck, baby." He groans in the most sexual way I have ever encountered. Has he ever called me baby before because *fucking shit*. I cross my legs to try and stifle the gentle ache that sound caused. "This is delicious. You're amazing."

"I'm so glad you like it," I murmur back. I take a few seconds just to watch his full lips wrap around another bite. God, he really has no idea how sexy he is. Eventually I tear my eyes from the display before me and dig into my own meal. *Delicious*. I'll have to thank Casey for the recipe.

The evening sky is a deep blue, the last vestiges of the day barely clinging on. The only real light comes from behind us in the house, casting a glow on the ground and pool in front of us. Ben and I are tangled together on the outdoor couch, nursing the last of our wine. Dinner was perfect. A soft, gentle flow of conversation that never felt forced or disingenuous. Even now, as my eyes flicker from the water to the pool to the sky, my entire body is warm. Safe. My head is a little light from the wine, but I have full clarity. And I am safe.

"This evening has been indescribable," Ben whispers from where he has buried his face in my neck. "Everything with you is so easy."

"Ahh, so I'm easy, am I?" I say with a chuckle, placing my empty glass on the ground next to Ben's.

Ben lifts his head and holds my gaze. "That's not what I meant."

"I know." I smile. "I was just teasing."

"You are such a wonderful woman, Darby. I'm a lucky man."

"I don't know about that. I think I'm the lucky one." I squirm at the attention.

"Let me compliment you." He presses a single, sweet kiss to the sensitive spot right behind my ear. My entire body melts into a warm puddle of goo.

"Mm-kay," I slur, my eyes closing.

"So sweet." A kiss to my neck.

"So intelligent." A kiss to my collarbone.

"So thoughtful." A kiss to my jaw.

"So beautiful." A nibble to my earlobe.

"So talented." A kiss to my cheek.

"So intuitive." A kiss to each eyelid.

"So honest." A kiss to the tip of my nose.

"So perfect for me." A kiss to the corner of my mouth.

After a few seconds of silence my eyes flutter open to see him gazing at me. My cheeks instantly heat at the intense ferocity in his eyes. He believes what he says, and it's as if he's willing me to believe it too. There is suddenly far too much space between us. My hands make small fists in his shirt and pull him down to meet me. His lips are warm and soft, and I chase the last remnants of wine from them. With a gentle pressure, Ben tilts us down until my back is against the couch cushion and he looms above me. Every single inch of him presses against me in a way that makes my skin tingle.

"How about dessert?" he purrs against my mouth. His body is a warm, solid weight that is steadily making my thoughts more and more cloudy.

"There's chocolate cheesecake in the fridge," I reply.

Ben chuckles, highlighting all the places we're wrapped around each other. "Not what I meant."

"*Oh*." My breath comes out in a whoosh. Do I want to know what it feels like to be this wrapped around Ben without clothes? Abso-fucking-lutely. Am I *ready* to know what it feels like to be this wrapped around Ben without clothes? Eh . . .

"Could we . . ." I gulp down the giant wad of nervousness in my throat. Here goes nothing. "Can we maybe go slow?"

"Yeah! Yes." He coughs. "No pressure. We can just go eat some cheesecake if you want."

"I just . . . I don't want . . ." Fuck, I'm just as inept as my mother says. "I don't want to rush things. But I really like the kissing. The kissing is good."

"Yeah." His eyes drop to my mouth. "It's fucking fantastic."

This man is a goddamn prince.

"More, please," I insist, nibbling the edge of his stubbly jaw.

"Whatever you want."

Rough kisses are rained down my neck and everything I want is right here.

"Maybe cheesecake too?" I ask after the skin of my throat feels raw with a burn that will be very difficult to explain at work.

He barks a laugh into my skin, placing a gentle kiss there. "Of course. Let me go get it."

My eyes follow the lines of his torso as he's slowly bathed in the light streaming in from the open doors to the house. I am so lucky. As he disappears into the house, I turn my gaze to the view.

"I brought a blanket as well." His voice floods over me like the water lapping against the shore. He wraps us up together effortlessly, tucking me under his arm like I've always been meant to be right here. The perfect fit of us is almost overwhelming.

"Open up." A forkful of cheesecake is pressed to my lips, and I open to the sweet treat. I could get used to this so easily.

"Just stay." Ben presses all too persuasive kisses to his now favorite raw spot on my neck. "I won't push you into anything. It's just late and you've been drinking."

"I had one glass—"

"Three glasses."

"Two."

"*Three*."

I give him a hard stare. "Two glasses of wine. And that was hours ago."

"But it's still late." I've never seen a grown man pout before. It's almost too adorable.

"What would you prefer then?" I smile up at him. "What is your plan?"

"You stay the night with me. Preferably in my bed, but I wouldn't complain if I had to make up the guest bedroom. Then you can leave for work in the morning after I've made you an entirely delicious, sugary breakfast."

I raise a brow. "What about Mr. *I go to work before sunrise?*"

"I can go in late. It'll be good for me not to be the first one there for a change. Keeps the employees on their toes," he insists. I've made it to the front door. It would be easy to just walk out and get in my car. But I'm physically unable to make that next step.

"*Ben*." A whine escapes my throat.

"*Darby*." Oh fuck. He's using that deep, growly voice that makes me want to drop to my knees. Wholly unfair.

"That's cheating," I accuse. Still, my fingers wrap around his exposed forearms. His hands are on my face, thumbs running little circles on my cheeks.

"I have no idea what you're talking about. None whatsoever." Despite what he says, the shit-eating grin on his face deceives him.

"I don't have any pajamas."

"I have T-shirts and sweatpants you can borrow." His thumb gently traces my bottom lip. "And before you say it, I have an extra couple toothbrushes as well."

"Ah, always prepared?" How many women does he entertain?

"My sister likes to show up unannounced. If I don't have toothbrushes on hand, she will use mine. Which is disgusting."

I haven't even known him a week. I can't just sleep at his house—in his bed! I can't. I won't allow myself. No.

"Fine. I'll stay." Well, there goes my self-control, apparently. The dimple grin I'm getting makes my decision worth it. I'm pulled into a comforting bear hug that I swear I could get lost in. I snuggle into his warm, soft button-down and breathe a happy sigh. Despite everything, I'm happy I'm staying. I want to spend a night in Benjamin James's arms. Who knows how long I'll have the opportunity? How long will it take for him to come to his senses and find someone worthy of his time?

"Are you tired? Or do you want to watch a movie, maybe?" he asks, tucking my head under his chin.

"It's like nine, Ben." I giggle. "I can stay up a little bit more."

"Movie it is."

Ben leads me into his home theater. I don't know why I'm surprised he has a literal movie theater in his home, considering the size of the place. The enclosed space has no windows and just one door to limit the amount of light. There are multiple plush chairs and two leather loveseats that I'm sure I would just sink into. It's relaxing in here. I could see Ben and I whiling away the hours in each other's arms in this room. It may be my favorite room I've seen so far.

"I picked the movie last time so it's only fair that you choose this time," Ben says, handing me the remote. "I have access to unreleased stuff on Streemz, plus there are some DVDs in the cabinet over there. You're probably too young to know what DVDs are . . . Shit, I'm going to go make us some popcorn."

"Ben, I grew up watching DVDs." I roll my eyes.

He pecks me on the cheek and leaves me to my decision. Should I torture the poor man and choose something deliciously gooey and romantic? Or try to choose something that we both would enjoy? The voice in my head, which sounds suspiciously like Casey, is telling me to torture him. With a flop, I sink into the leather loveseat. Getting out of this is going to be a problem. A few clicks later and I'm hovering over *Pride and Prejudice*. Oh, I shouldn't. I couldn't.

I must.

"What are we watching?" Ben asks, coming into the room with two bowls of popcorn and an extra slice of cheesecake. He knows me far too well.

"I've become one with the couch," I complain, avoiding his question.

"I specifically asked for seats so comfortable I'd never want to get up." He chuckles, placing the food down on the floor in front of me.

"Whoever picked them succeeded. I may never leave."

He wraps an arm around my shoulders and pulls me in. "Works for me."

I hide my smile in his chest. The beginning credits roll and Ben's forehead crinkles slightly in the middle in confusion.

"What is this?" he asks.

Oh my God. "You've never seen *Pride and Prejudice*?"

"No?" His head tilts just a smidge.

A devilish cackle escapes my lips before I can contain it.

"Just watch. You'll love it."

*T*he next time I open my eyes, Ben is stroking my face and the credits are rolling. I missed him watching this movie for the first time. Ugh, I suck.

"You led me to believe you were not tired, my lady." He chuckles.

I lean into his warm, calloused palm. "I lied, good sir."

"I noticed. Ready for bed, sweetheart?"

I nod and let him help me to my feet. The couch put up a good fight, but his warm chest and the promise of bed has it beat. Barely. We ascend the wood and glass staircase and head toward the master bedroom.

"*Oh.*" I gasp when he opens the double doors. I should've known he'd take advantage of the view. The entire back wall of the room is glass, looking down on the backyard and the spectacular view of the water. I tear my eyes away to take in the rest of the room. It's huge, of course. Not that I expected anything otherwise. The bed is no different. It must be a special size or something because it's bigger than a king. Gray sheets lay upon a white platform, and I just want to jump on it.

"Not many pillows?" I turn to face him.

He shrugs. "I don't sleep as much as I should. Extra pillows don't matter to me."

"Hmm." If things continue, I'll be sneaking pillows onto this bed. There needs to be at least ten. Twelve. Fifteen?

"I'm going to grab you some clothes from the closet. Any requests?"

"Soft," I reply with a smile. "Thank you."

He disappears behind another door, and I wander into the en-suite bathroom. This is officially my favorite room. The shower is so large that there isn't a door, just a wall that you follow into its own special space. Multiple shower heads, sprays that come out of the wall, and a digital temperature gauge. I must be in a movie or something. I didn't realize this tech even existed! The tub is a massive, sunken beast that is embedded in the floor. I could spend hours in that tub.

"I warned you that I went a bit crazy with this house," Ben says from behind me. He places the clothes on the counter as I walk over to him.

"His and her sinks?" I ask with a smile.

Is that a light pink flush on his chiseled cheeks? "Call me an optimist."

I kiss his stubbled jaw, all I can reach even on my tiptoes, and decide not to tease him further. "I usually take a shower before bed. Is that alright?"

"Of course. There are some towels in here." Ben opens a small closet behind the door. "You know what? Let me run to the guest room for a second. I'll grab some of my sister's stuff. I'm sure you'd rather use that than my shampoo." Without letting me respond, he dashes out of the room.

I wouldn't have minded smelling like him.

I can only hide in the shower for so long. Despite its downright frightening appearance, the controls are intuitive. So I can't pretend that I'm too confused to get any real showering done. I don't want to focus on how I'm naked just a few steps away from a gorgeous man. I definitely don't want to focus on how he is probably changing and in a similar state of undress. I've felt the strength of his chest under my palms; I know he has to be built like a statue. Why did I sleep over again? I scrub my face, trying to get the image of his naked body out of my head. I have to go in there.

I walk out of the shower area and grab my towel from the heated rack. My shower is going to feel so bland from now on. I've barely tasted decadence and I'm already spoiled. Ben has left a blow dryer on the counter, which I scoff at. Absolutely not. Instead, I tie my hair back into a braid to air dry. Then I pull on my underwear and appraise the clothes before me. The T-shirt he's chosen, boasting a Harvard logo, looks longer than the dress I wore for our date. I'll be practically swimming in it. I pull it on and confirm that, yes, I'm swimming in it. The gray shirt comes down to my knees. I turn my gaze to the pants and shrug. I don't need them, and I'm scared I'll trip and break my face if I wear them. I'm going to be sleeping in the man's bed, after all. A pair of pants isn't going to save me.

"Fuck," Ben utters as I enter the bedroom. He's laying underneath the sheets in a soft white T-shirt, phone in hand.

"Mm?" I smile, doing a twirl. "Do I look fabulous?"

He stands slowly, crossing the room like a primed predator ready to pounce. "I like you in my clothes."

Any retort I had dies the moment our eyes lock. The usual blue is eaten by black pupil. A hand reaches out and drags my body into his, the other running along the skin of my thigh.

"I love your legs. You're so beautiful," he murmurs into my ear.

That breaks the spell.

"My *legs*?" I snort. "Yeah, okay."

"What?" He pulls back and meets my gaze again. Poor guy seems genuinely confused.

"I know my legs aren't my best feature. You don't have to just say things. Compliment my boobs or something. I have great boobs."

"Yeah, you do. But you also have great legs. Why do you think you don't?"

"I . . ." Well, shit. "I have my dad's knees." At least, that's what my mom always told me. The woman downright refused to buy me shorts as I got older.

"Either your dad has some feminine fucking knees, or you're crazy. Those are beautiful, *womanly* knees." With a dip and a squeal, I'm in his arms, bridal-style. "And I like them."

Well, shit. I'm dumped on the deceptively soft bed and a kiss is pressed to each knee.

"You have very lovely knees as well." I smile. He lifts up on said knees to tower above me, and wow I like being under him. His shoulders are so massive he almost blocks out the view behind him. Strong thighs are covered in soft gray sweatpants that are very clearly outlining his dick because he is very clearly not wearing underwear. He's not hard, but the outline itself proves that it isn't just his thighs that are impressive. I now understand the use of the eggplant emoji.

"Thanks for the compliment, sweetheart." He rolls his eyes and flops down beside me. "Let me hold you."

I nod and turn onto my side as he comes up behind me as my big spoon. Strong arms wrap around me and pull me gently to his chest.

Yep, massive dick.

He shuts off the lamps with a click of a button and we're submerged in darkness. My nails make little trails in his arm hair as we soak in the silence.

"Ben?" I whisper, on the off chance he fell asleep while I was caressing him.

"Yeah?"

Not asleep then. "Tell me something about you that I don't know."

"Hmm . . ." He kisses behind my ear. "I hate zucchini."

"So do I!" My voice reverberates off the walls of the silent room. "Sorry."

He chuckles, squeezing me tight. "Now you."

"I've seen every single episode of *The Great British Baking Show*."

"The what now?"

"I'll educate you." I pat his arm. "We'll make a star baker out of you yet."

"I have no idea what that means, but okay."

The room is silent once more, but something's been bugging me.

"Ben?"

"Darby."

"Why did you want me to stay the night so bad?" I mean, if he knew he wasn't going to get laid, wouldn't he rather be alone?

He sighs, pulling me closer. "I got nervous."

"What about?" I try to face him, but his arms keep me caged in.

"We haven't talked about my parents yet. They . . . shit. . ." He takes a deep breath, exhaling against the back of my neck. "They died about five years ago. They were driving home from a date night and got hit by a drunk driver."

I nuzzle my face into the crook of his elbow, kissing the soft skin. "And I'd been drinking."

"And you'd been drinking. I'm sorry if I was a bit too forceful."

"No, no you have nothing to be sorry about. I'm sorry you lost them."

"They would've loved you," he whispers so softly I barely hear the words.

My heart aches at the vulnerability in his tone, in the way he's clenching me just a bit tighter. Even though I know he's wrong. They would've known I'm not good enough for him—just like everyone else does. Just like he will, soon enough.

"I'm sorry."

"Thank you for staying. Let's get some rest."

"Goodnight, Ben," I whisper.

"Goodnight, Darby." He presses a soft kiss to my hair, and I close my eyes.

***

*I know it's a dream, the edges are fuzzy in a way that isn't real. That doesn't change the fact that I can't stop running.*

*"You're so lazy!" a twenty-foot version of my mother screeches from behind me. "You never do anything right! Why are you so stupid?"*

*I just want to wake up. I need to wake up. Wake up! Wake up!*

*"Why do you and your father always gang up on me? Why do you always treat me this way? I hope you have a daughter just like you."*

*Wake up!*

***

I wake, panting to the smell of chocolate-chip pancakes and morning light streaming in through the floor-to-ceiling windows. Thank God Ben isn't here to see me like this. His side of the bed is cool, and I flop onto it to soothe my heated skin. Fuck, I need to get a handle on myself before Ben comes back. I need to get a handle on myself period. Mourning the loss of a comfortable bed, I drag myself to the bathroom. It's a little too obvious that I've been crying. A splash or two of cold water is going to have to do in lieu of concealer. When I make it back to the bedroom, Ben hasn't returned. Thank God. I check my phone almost absentmindedly and find a text from him.

BEN

If you wake up before I get back, stay upstairs. I'm bringing you breakfast in bed.

I don't deserve him. Well, I don't want to disobey orders.

With a shrug I burrow back under the covers and scroll through Instagram.

"Good morning, sweetheart," he calls. I snap my head up to see him coming through the door with a heavy tray. Every ounce of space is filled to the brim with pancakes, fruit, and orange juice. Once again, I don't deserve him.

"Good morning." I stretch my arms up and smile, continuing to laze about. As my mother always said, I'm lazy. Ben delicately places the tray down on the floor at the foot of the bed and comes up to greet me. A calloused hand takes hold of the back of my neck to bring me up for a kiss. There's a safety that I am enveloped in when I'm with Ben. Each kiss makes me feel more at home.

"I brought breakfast," he whispers, not pulling back more than is absolutely necessary.

"Is it you? Because you look delicious." I grin, hooking my hands behind his neck.

"You're one to talk." His fingers tangle in the strands of hair that have come loose. "Looking like that in my clothes."

"I've heard pancakes taste best when they're cold." I shrug. "Might be something worth finding out."

A chuckle escapes him before he presses his lips back to mine. A gentle tug is enough to coax him back onto the bed and on top of me. A playful nip here, a suck there, and sweet morning kisses suddenly blend into deeper temptation. Hands begin wandering, nails dig in, and I lose myself in the pure rightness of it all. I'm falling and I'm falling fast. His hand is slowly, so slowly, creeping up my thigh. It's headed for much more dangerous territory, territory that I had very much planned to be off-limits. A delicate gasp escapes my lips as his fingers brush against my hip bone.

"Darby," he growls in *that* voice. My favorite voice. And I whimper, digging my nails harder into his back.

And then his phone rings.

"Shit." He pulls back and rests his head on my chest. It's now that I realize how heavily we're both breathing, how close we were to more.

How close I am to being fucking late for work.

"It's okay," I breathe. I need more air. "I'll, um, start breakfast."

"I'll be right back," he promises. He gives me one last kiss on the cheek before digging his phone out of his sweatpants pocket. Fuck fuck fuckity fuck fuck. I'm so totally fucked.

## 8

## Fondant Coffee Cups

*M*ust. Resist. Urge. To. Scroll. Ben's. Instagram. He finally added me on his personal account, and I haven't had a chance to snoop yet. However, I know the minute I pull my phone out Mindy will walk through the meeting room door, and I'll end up looking like a moron. But she's fifteen minutes late and I'm just staring at my outline presentation. I pulled up the PowerPoint on the computer in front of me, projecting it on the screen on the far wall. If I'm completely honest, it is more of a first draft, but I'm not convinced Mindy won't hate it. So we're calling it an outline. If there's anything my mother taught me, it's to lower my expectations.

That's not dark at all.

"Sorry, sorry!" She tumbles into the room, coffee dangling precariously from blood red nails. "My other meeting ran late. I'm here."

"No problem." I wince as she spills her drink on the wood table in front of us. It's just a drop or two, but I know how much that little extra burst of caffeine can make all the difference. Coffee wasted is a tragedy.

"Okay, let's see this outline. What've you got for me?" She settles her notebook, coffee, and pen down and lifts her brown-eyed gaze to me.

No pressure. They already think I'm worthless here, I can't disappoint her any further. Right?

"Well, I was thinking we'd use data from the last five years. I wanted a good historical sample, but much longer than five and I run the risk of diluting the current economic influence." I stand, bringing the remote to control my presentation with me.

"So long as you get your point across," she agrees with a nod.

"I found a few places already where we're needlessly over-spending. We could contribute more to charitable giving if we pull back." I click the presentation forward.

"Probably shouldn't call it needless." She sniffs, looking me up and down in the same way my mother used to. "But good."

Shit. "Right, of course. I won't!"

Her eyes give me one last sweep, and with a barely concealed snort she looks down to her phone. "Listen, I've got some things I need to deal with. Email me the presentation and I'll give you notes." She stands as I helplessly gape at her like a fish. "It looks like you're going in the right direction, though. Good job, Clarke."

And with that, she stands and leaves.

That could've gone worse. Could've done without the obvious judgment of my general state of being. But I got a "good job" and a promise to look over the presentation. That's enough for now. Just wait. I'm going to blow your socks off, Mindy.

The walk back to my desk is a long one, despite it being right around the corner. Thoughts of the presentation swirl around, mixed with a desire to snoop on Ben's Instagram. No one pays attention to me in this place anyway. After I send off the presentation to Mindy, I whip out my phone and scroll.

Picture of the sunset behind his house, picture of his food, picture of him with his ex-wife. Wait. I immediately click on the photo and there she is. Blonde waves cascade down her airbrushed face, one single curl falling delicately over her ocean blue eyes. Of course she would look like an actual Barbie doll. I can't understand why he'd post a picture of both of them so recently.

There's no caption.

As if she has some sort of sixth sense, Casey sends me a text begging me to come home as soon as work is done, forcing me to close Instagram. After confirming that her needs are in fact not urgent, I tell her I'll be home at the normal time. While my interest is definitely piqued, this is most likely Casey just being Casey. Which means dramatic just for the sake of being dramatic. The goof.

"The absolute fuck have you been?" Casey demands as I enter our apartment. She's clearly upset because the entire apartment is spotless. The woman is a cyclone, causing mayhem and mess wherever she goes, unless she's upset. Then she cleans like a madwoman.

"I was at work, dumbass," I reply, hanging my coat up. I sniff the air. Why does it smell like chocolate in here?

"Regardless!" She throws her hands up. "I need you right now."

"Well, okay, but I've never been with a woman before. . ." I trail off my joke when I get a glimpse of her face. "Never mind. What do you need? I'm here for you."

"I'm going to propose to Hannah, and I need you to help me. You're all romantic and sweet and junk, and if I planned it, well, it would be some big lesbian disaster. So, help?" She collapses on the couch.

I chuckle, sitting down next to her. "Well, we wouldn't want some big lesbian disaster. Of course I'll help you."

"Thank God. Okay, so, I don't have anything planned."

"Not surprising, considering it's you." I dodge the pillow she throws at me. "First things first: have you bought a ring?"

"Nope."

"Do you know your budget for a ring?"

"Nope."

"Do you know when you want to propose?"

"Nope!"

I sigh, rubbing my temples. "This is going to be a long night, isn't it?"

"Yep! Which is why I baked you double chocolate fudge chip muffins after my shift," she chirps.

"I was wondering what that smell was." I jump up and beeline to the kitchen. "Want chocolate. Give chocolate."

"Okay, you can have one and then you need to help me plan!"

"I can eat and plan at the same time. I'm a fantastic multi-tasker. Now get a notebook and a pen, and I'll get a plate." I smile at the slightly warm muffins. *Mine.* She flutters off to her room as I pick out the fluffiest, chocolatiest one and abscond to the couch.

"Okay, the ring. We need to figure out your budget," I say, taking my first bite. The first of many because, damn, this fucker is good. Layers of fudgy sweetness and rich chocolate chips in addition . . . mmm. Who needs dinner?

"How do we do that?" Casey asks, holding up her notebook and pen. She's poised to take notes, and I feel slightly bad that I was kidding about that.

"Well, it's up to you. The rule"—I finger quote—"is that you use two months' salary. However, this is the twenty-first century, so it's more about how much you feel comfortable spending."

"Um . . ." She blinks. "I don't want to spend too much. I can't spend too much."

"You don't have to tell me the number. Just write it down and commit to it. It's easy to get overwhelmed by all the shiny objects when shopping and forget that there's a set limit to how much you can spend."

"Fair enough." She scribbles down something. "What next?"

After licking my fingers clean of crumbs, I start in on muffin number two. I think I blacked out while eating the first one because I'm not entirely sure how that's already gone. "We have to figure out how you're going to propose once you have the ring. Privately or publicly? Low key or big deal? Getting down on one knee or something else?"

"Hannah would hate something public, she's far too shy for that. But she is a romantic. Something thought out with care would be perfect for her."

"You could make her a romantic home-cooked meal for two." I smirk. That's my go-to idea as of late. "Candles, jazz music, rose petals . . . the whole nine yards."

"That's perfect! It's not so crazy that she'll get embarrassed, but it's still romantic and personal. I'll make her favorite things!"

"Now that we have a plan in place, all we have to do is

execute. Do you want to go ring shopping alone? Or do you want me to go with you?" I stick my thumb in my mouth, sucking off a bit of melted chocolate. Should I get one more muffin? Did I just question that? Third muffin now, please.

"Oh, you're not getting out of this. You're coming with me to the ring shop." She nods, writing down her last few notes. Her tongue pokes out of the side of her mouth in concentration.

Deny myself the opportunity to pick out an engagement ring when I'll probably never wear one myself? Fat chance. "Of course. When?"

"Can we go on Saturday? I want to go as quickly as possible before I psyche myself out."

"Saturday I'm yours."

It takes an extra week, and a lot of nagging, for Casey to pluck up the courage to go ring shopping, despite her saying she would be ready during our planning session. Not that I mind very much, considering it gives me more time with Ben. I haven't trusted myself to sleep over again since our deliciously heated make out. I've known him for barely a month, and I don't want to jump in any faster than I'm already falling.

"What about this one?" Casey asks, pointing at the thirteenth ring in the last five minutes. I counted.

"Case, babe, you have to relax." I smile, running a comforting hand over her back. "Whichever one you pick will be the right one, and Hannah will love it."

"May I help you ladies?" An older gentleman slides over to us behind the glass counter. The shop is a small, family-owned operation that is exactly Hannah and Casey's speed. Not that my happily-ever-after-obsessed ass has a catalog of all the best jewelers in the city and surrounding areas. Nope. Not me. I wait for a beat to see if Casey will speak up, but the silence persists.

"Yes. My friend here is searching for an engagement ring for her girlfriend," I reply.

"Ahhh." He smiles. It's a big, toothy grin as if his teeth are too big for his face. "Do you have an idea of the shape? Size? Carats?"

Casey turns to me, her eyes as big as saucers, and I'm just going to have to take over until she's ready. Thank God I have days' worth of time logged into Pinterest crafting the perfect weddings. Plural. The odds of me walking down the aisle may be one in one thousand, but it doesn't stop me from hoping.

"We're open to multiple options. This is our first trip, so we're trying to get a feel for what we like." I sling my arm around Casey's shoulders.

"Then how about I pull a range of different types for you so you can see everything? We can then narrow down your favorites and focus on those shapes and sizes. Would you two like to sit at our display area while you wait for me?" He steps out from behind the counter and guides us over to a small sitting area. There is a large red couch and a table with specific lighting units.

"My name is Greg, by the way. And you two?" he asks as we sit.

"I'm Darby and this is Casey," I reply, shaking his hand.

"Lovely to meet the two of you. If you need anything to drink, please let me know." And with that, he walks back to the display cases.

"I feel like my tongue is stuck to the roof of my mouth," Casey mumbles, her head falling into her hands.

"I get being a little nervous, but you seem terrified. Are you okay?" I rub her back in what I hope is a soothing manner.

"I want Hannah forever," she says firmly. "Hannah is my person and I choose her. But what if she realizes that I'm an obnoxious, loud, sarcastic woman that has blinded her with my fantastic tongue?"

"I'm going to ignore that last bit, because *ew*. I don't need to know about your sex life. But, Case, Hannah thinks you hung the moon and the stars. That woman adores you."

"She's too good for me. What if she knows it and just hasn't left me yet?"

"She is too good for you." I laugh. "But you're the best couple in the world. I promise you she will say yes. If anything, she'll say that it's about damn time."

"Here we are!" Greg animatedly announces as he arrives with a tray full of glittering diamonds. "Plenty of different sizes and cuts for you to peruse." He places the tray down on the table and adjusts the lamps so that they light up the rings.

"This one," Casey states with a confidence that makes me smile. "I don't need to see anything else. I want this one."

"Ah, the edgeless pave." He lifts the ring from its place. "This one in particular is a white gold featuring a diamond knot halo."

Casey takes the ring, examining every inch of the shiny surface. The way her face lights up as she smoothes her fingers over it definitely doesn't make a tear come to my eye. Absolutely not. It's not like my best friend is getting married or anything.

"Wipe your eyes, you big blubber baby." Casey sniffles, smacking me lightly on the arm with her free hand.

"You're one to talk!" I smack her back.

"Would you like to look at any of the others?" Greg asks, stopping us from starting a war.

Casey shakes her head before Greg can finish speaking. "No. This is the one. I know it."

"Then we can move forward. You've picked a beautiful ring, Casey. I'm sure your beloved will be ecstatic."

"Hannah is going to adore it," I agree. "It will look gorgeous on her."

"Will you try it on so I can see how it looks?" she asks, turning to me.

Say what now?

"Oh. . . um . . . no. I don't think that's a good idea." I may have just shut down my one opportunity to see myself with an engagement ring on. But Ben will see the light eventually and move on, and I can't have the image in my head.

She shrugs, turning back to Greg. "I'll take it."

$\mathcal{I}$t's not my fault that I can't stop blabbering about ring shopping with Casey all throughout dinner with Ben.

"I'm just so honored that she brought me along," I continue, waving my fork around. "I can't wait for their wedding."

"Doesn't Hannah have to say yes first?" Ben says with a smile. He's all-powerful grace tonight in his suit, leaning back in the booth as if he owns the place. For all I know, he probably does.

"Oh, that's a given." I wave him off. "Hannah and I talk about it all the time. I'm just not allowed to tell Casey because Hannah didn't want to pressure her."

Ben laughs, shaking his head. "Poor Casey. Proposing is

hard enough, but she doesn't even get to know she has a guaranteed yes."

"It's character building. Casey needs a little struggle." I take Ben's hand on the small red table. "But I've been going on and on, haven't I? How are you?"

Ben's arm comes to wrap around my shoulder where we sit together in the booth. We're in the back of the restaurant, all snuggled up in some deep, dark corner. "I'm good now that I'm with you. Seeing you is always the best part of my day."

"Well aren't you charming?" I grin, leaning into him. Seeing him is the best part of my day too.

"Speaking of, there is something I wanted to talk to you about." He strokes his thumb across my cheek.

"Yes?"

"I . . . fuck, I haven't dated in so long I've forgotten how to do this. Darby." He clears his throat. "I don't want to see anyone else, and I was hoping you felt the same. Do . . . do you?"

I can't resist teasing him. Must tease. "I was under the impression we weren't seeing other people. Are you seeing someone else, Ben?"

"No!" The pure terror in his eyes is priceless. "No, I'm not seeing anyone else. Only you."

"Neither am I. Only you." I kiss the very tip of his nose.

"So you're mine now?" He growls, leaning in close to my ear. A single shiver travels the length of my spine. I was always his, from the moment I met him, but I certainly can't tell him that.

"Mm-hmm," I manage instead.

I don't bring up the fact that he's posted another picture of him and his ex on Instagram. I don't bring up the fact that I stared at it for two seconds too long. And I don't bring up the fact that I can't get her perfect face out of my head.

*A* present arrives the next day. Okay, so it's like seven boxes all beautifully wrapped with my name on them. They come while I'm out with my dad, so Casey is the one who accepts them.

"Open them! Open them! Open them! Open them!" Casey chants from the couch the moment I get home. She gave me some warning in the form of a text, but I didn't realize she and Hannah would be sitting there *waiting*.

"If you want to open them privately, we'll go into Casey's room." Hannah smiles as I hang up my coat.

"No we won't! I've been sitting here in anticipation for hours and I want to know!" Casey whines, flopping into Hannah.

"You didn't think that would work, did you?" I smirk, grabbing some scissors from the kitchen.

Hannah shrugs. "I figured I'd try."

"Just open them!" Casey continues, practically flailing at this point. I swear, she's like a toddler sometimes. I sit down on the floor in front of the tower of presents and grab the smallest on top.

"Wait." I pause. "Was there a letter? Or a card?"

"I forgot! I hid it from Casey." Hannah stands, making Casey roll fully onto the couch with a groan. She goes into my room and comes back with an envelope. "Here."

"Thanks." I take it from her and tear open the note quickly as Casey pouts.

*My sweetheart,*

*I wanted to let you know how special you are, and how I think of you always. I hope you enjoy everything.*

*Yours,*

*Ben*

Heat floods my entire body, making my cheeks flush. Ben. How sweet of him.

"Is it Ben? I told Hannah it was Ben. It has to be!" Casey blabbers.

"It's Ben." I pick up the scissors to hide the, no doubt stupid, grin on my face. Picking up the smallest gift on top of the pile, I tear into it carefully.

"We should place bets on what's in each box!" Casey exclaims, clapping her hands.

"Stop it." Hannah shushes her. Casey pouts but snuggles up into Hannah's embrace anyway. "I am feeling the anticipation, though."

I roll my eyes at the two of them and focus back on the white box in front of me. I lift the lid to find a pair of diamond earrings. They're round studs, simple but elegant. And huge. Gasping quietly, I lift one, feeling the heavy weight.

"Well, fuck, that's a great start," Casey breathes, sliding onto the floor and crawling over to me. "Those are stunning."

"They are," I reply, my eyes transfixed by the flickers of light bouncing off the hard angles.

"Open more!" Casey insists, shoving another box in my hands.

My hands tremble as I fiddle with the wrapping on the next box. I've never been showered with gifts before . . . at least, not unless it was a holiday. The lid opens to reveal a dozen cupcakes with mini coffee cups made out of fondant on top.

"Coffee cups?" Casey picks up one cupcake and inspects it.

"We met downstairs in the coffee shop," I murmur.

"Oh that's so sweet," Hannah gushes, leaning over the arm of the couch. "I never knew he could be like this. He's always so professional at the office."

"He's wonderful," I reply, bringing the cupcakes into the kitchen. I don't want them getting destroyed. While there, I shoot a quick thank you text to Ben. I'm sure I gush a little too much, but this means a lot to me.

"You only got through two out of seven! Hurry up!" Casey calls, snapping me back to the current situation in my living room. If I don't open all of these gifts in the next five minutes, I think Casey may just have a panic attack. I sit back down and allow Casey to hand me the next box. The impatient cow.

"*Oh,*" I breathe, pulling out a new, expensive set of paints and paint brushes.

"He knows you." Casey nods.

"I briefly mentioned painting on our first date. I can't believe he remembered. . ." I trail off, slowly running my fingers along the brush handles. A soft thumb brushes the side of my face and I lift my gaze to see Casey smiling at me. I wipe the rest of the tears—not sure when that happened—away and focus on the next box.

Eventually all the boxes are opened, and I'm surrounded by extremely personal items. Earrings, cupcakes, paint brushes, a brand-new romance novel, a cook book written by Paul Holly-wood, and more. How he even knew to buy these . . . It's obvious that he's been paying attention to me. Much more attention than I thought. Hannah helps me gather the items and bring them into my room before she and Casey sequester themselves in the other room. I appreciate the space. I didn't expect to get so emotional. But no one treats me like this other than my dad. No one gives me attention and gifts without wanting something in return. My phone buzzes. I've just been sitting here on my bed for who knows how long.

BEN

No need to thank me. You deserve everything in the world, and it's my job to make that happen.

ME

I don't know what to say. Thank you.

How does he expect me not to fall head over heels in love with him when he treats me this way? How can I keep pretending like I'm not already in love with him? I'm pretty sure I fell in love with him the moment I flung chocolate onto his chest when I met him.

"Knock, knock," Casey calls from behind the door. When I don't respond she opens it a crack. "Hey, you okay?"

"Yeah, more than," I reply with a smile. "What's up?"

"I'm, um, well . . . I'm thinking tonight is going to be the night. You know, *the* night. Would it be weird to ask if you could stay at Dad's or Ben's? I'd like to have Hannah all to myself," Casey whispers, closing the door behind her.

"Oh! Oh, absolutely!" I jump up and run to hug her. "Case, she's going to love it! And she's going to say yes!"

Casey rubs the back of her neck. "Yeah, yeah, well I hope. If she says no, you'll have to come back and talk me off the ledge."

"Casey."

"Kidding! Mostly . . . Anyway, I appreciate it."

"I'll be out of your hair in a bit." I give her another hug, holding her tight. "I'm so proud of you, Case."

"You're getting all mushy. I'm leaving." Casey sniffs and

walks toward the door. "Thanks, Darbs." As she leaves, my phone buzzes again.

BEN

You deserve everything, sweetheart.

God, could he be any sweeter?

ME

How do you feel about another sleepover?

My heart pounds as I press send. Yes, I could've easily stayed at my dad's. I'm always welcome there. But I have someone who loves taking care of me. Why shouldn't I let him? Either way, I need to beat cheeks out of here, so I start pulling together an overnight bag.

BEN

I'm stuck in an awful meeting. But why don't I give you the code to the front door? You can let yourself in and I'll pick up some dinner for us on my way home.

ME

Sounds perfect.

## 9

# A Jar of Nutella

can't sleep. Ben, the demon, is wearing boxer shorts and a tank top to bed. A skin-tight tank top. Despite the actual size of the bed itself, every single movement I make somehow brings us in contact. Whenever sleep is within my grasp, the gentle rasp of his leg hair or a brush of his arm sends a jolt of electricity along my skin.

The snores escaping him prove that I am alone in this predicament.

I am the only one plagued with the image of more deliberate contact, of what exactly we could be doing instead right now. Of what we would be doing instead right now if I didn't know in my heart that I'm a worthless piece of crap.

Nice, Darby. It's just impossible not to beat myself up apparently.

With an unintended sigh, I roll away from Ben and curl into myself, willing sleep to overtake me.

*I* wake up the next morning to about seventy texts. Ben is already in the shower, unfortunately, so I start scrolling through. Surprise to no one—Hannah said yes. Of course. I send separate congratulatory texts to Casey and Hannah. I'm happy for those two idiots. Putting my phone down on the bedside table, I take a second to focus on the fact that Ben is completely naked in the next room. It would be so simple to just get up, walk in, and join him under the warm water. But my legs feel like lead. I can't get up. With a dramatic sigh, I bury my face in his pillow. I want him. Of course I *want* him, but I . . . I don't know. Does he want me? Or does he want the woman he thinks I am? If he even knew half the shit my mother put me through, what I put myself through . . . fuck. I don't know anything at all.

"Good morning, sweetheart," Ben calls from the bathroom.

I lift my head up from the pillow to Ben walking into the room with just a towel around his waist. Good *Lord*. He is built just as I thought he would be. Broad chested and sprinkled with dark hair that thickens as it travels down carefully structured abs. He's thick and muscley and my mouth is dry.

"Darby?" he calls again after I don't respond. My gaze is firmly latched onto his thick thighs, but I pry myself away to look him in the eye.

"Morning," I rasp. Jesus, I sound like a smoker. I clear my throat, embarrassment raising my temperature.

"Listen, I have to run. I swear, it's like no one can function without me," he continues, oblivious to the white-hot ache that has settled in between my legs. "But you are in no rush to leave.

Stay as long as you want, eat whatever you want, do whatever you want."

"And if all I want to do is call off work and lay about in bed?" I tease.

"Then I will be disappointed I can't join you." He walks into the closet and, from the sounds of things, starts rummaging through his clothes.

"Unfortunately, I have that big project I was telling you about. I'll be leaving not too long after you," I admit, pulling myself out of bed. I'll miss you, soft sheets. And the two pillows I snuck with me.

"You could always come back tonight," he calls.

I walk into the bathroom with a sigh. I need to get a handle on myself and what I want. Any more of Ben half naked and I'll jump him without thought.

"I can't!" I yell over the sound of running water. "I'm training for another race in a few months, and I want to get some overtime in on this project." Which isn't a lie.

"Well that fucking sucks," he says, moseying into the bathroom as he pulls his suit jacket on. God, does the man fill it out. His suit is navy blue with a crisp white shirt underneath. He's not wearing a tie, but he has a white pocket square neatly tucked in.

"Indeed." I spit out my toothpaste.

"If you change your mind, you're always welcome here." He wraps his arms around my middle from behind, forcing me to gaze at our reflections in the mirror. Even with my hair a complete mess, my brown eyes are bright, and I can admit I look happier than I have in a long time.

"Thank you," I whisper, turning in his arms and burying myself in his chest. Sandalwood, cedar, and citrus. Home.

$\mathcal{M}$y thoughts tumble around like clothes in a dryer all throughout my workday. Not even the now regular "'sup Clarke" is enough to break me out of my own inner monologue. I need to figure out how to clear my head or I'm going to flop this presentation. Or end up unemployed. Maybe my run tonight will help me get my head out of my ass. I always relax when I run. Something about the rhythmic thumping of my feet against the pavement soothes me. I'll create a to-do list and think about Ben and organize my life once more.

"Okay, so, what kind of tricks are you whipping out in the bedroom?" Casey demands the moment I return home in the early evening.

"Hello to you too." I close the door behind me.

"I'm being serious." Casey crosses her arms as I put my stuff down.

"And I have no idea what you're talking about."

"That." She points to a few boxes on the coffee table. "He sent you more."

"Oh." Well, shit. I approach the table as if the boxes will jump up and bite me.

"I mean, you deserve to be pampered—duh. But I'm genuinely curious as to how you've got this man whipped so fast." Casey's face breaks out in a massive grin.

"I have no idea, trust me," I reply. With delicate movements, I open the top box to uncover brand-new running shoes. Does he have supersonic hearing? I'm pretty sure he was miles deep in the closet when I mentioned my run.

"Hmm. Well, despite Daddy Ben demanding your attention, I need you. Hannah wants to have an engagement party and as my maid of honor you're on deck to help. Lord knows I'm shit at anything but food." Casey flops on the couch.

"We'll address the Daddy Ben comment in a moment." I give her a look. "But did you just ask me to be your maid of honor?"

"I didn't realize I had to ask. I figured that was a given." She shrugs.

"Right." I smile. "I'll be happy to help Hannah."

She lays back and closes her eyes. "She shouldn't need too much help. She's got her own maid of honor, and you know how involved her parents are going to want to be. Despite living so far away, they always seem to be involved."

"Have you texted Dad? He was just asking me about you and Hannah."

"Duh. He congratulated me and suggested Hawke as the ring bearer. I told him that mutt would somehow ruin the whole wedding." She smirks.

"Sounds about right. Tell Hannah to text me with whatever she needs. I'm going for a run."

"Okay. I'm working tonight and then crashing at her place, so I guess I'll see you later."

"Congratulations again. I'm glad you two are getting married." I take her hand in mine and give it a gentle squeeze. "You're perfect together."

"You are the mushiest person ever. Stop it before my allergies kick in and my eyes start watering."

After a short drive, I'm in Marymoor Park with my headphones in and my brand-new running shoes on. The best way to break them in is to pound them out on the pavement. Double socks and Band-Aids on my ankles just in case, though. I'm not trying to get blisters. I, of course, sent a thank you text to Ben after I opened them and the other gifts. Although I appreciate them, I'm not sure why he's showering me with so much attention. It's not like I've done anything particularly wonderful to deserve them. After a quick stretch, I focus on my to-do list and getting my laps in.

First, I need to figure out this work project. Mindy's notes have been positive, I guess, but not very encouraging. I need to come up with something special. It's a presentation about financials, which is enough to put anyone to sleep. I need to figure out how to make it interesting enough that the higher ups understand that I am intelligent. If I can do that, I can save this job. I can force myself out of the coffee bitch persona I'm getting boxed into. I can make her proud of me. And have the authority to get that asshole Jason to stop "'sup-ing" me. I hate when he "'sups" me.

Second, I need to make myself available to Casey and Hannah for their wedding planning. Which will be much easier when this project is over. Regardless, whatever they want, they get.

Third, Ben. My feet almost stop at the thought of him. Ben. Benjamin James. I'm over my head with this one. Every time I see him my heart pounds so hard I swear it's going to leap right out of my chest. It doesn't seem fair to continue this relationship without being completely honest about me and my past. But at the same time, how can I know that he won't leave? Telling him that Mommy was mean to me just makes me sound like a whiny brat. I don't know how to explain something I've never been able to talk about. Maybe it's best to just leave the past in the past. Tell him she's gone. My shoe catches on a crack in the sidewalk and I stumble into a tree to keep myself from falling. I wipe the sweat from my forehead and, fuck, I'm crying. I bury my face in my hands and just try to breathe. In and out. I'm a goddamn mess. Ben doesn't deserve this. My mom always said that I was more trouble than I was worth. Maybe she was right after all.

If it wasn't enough that I cried in public, I also got drenched in a random downpour. You have to love Seattle's rain. By the time I make it back to my apartment I'm soaked, depressed, and starving. Leave it to my mom to fuck me up even when I haven't talked to her in years. Shivering, I peel the clothes from my body and rush into the warm shower. Ben's shower is much nicer than this, with all its buttons and settings. I shake my head. No point in drawing comparisons between our homes; it'll just make me feel worse. I need all of the cupcakes Ben bought me in my mouth right this minute. All of them. Every single one. Within a half hour I'm at my desk, laptop open with the box of cupcakes beside me. I will nail this project if it kills me. That is, if the sheer volume of cupcake intake doesn't kill me first.

HANNAH

Casey said you'd be willing to help with the engagement party! Mom is insisting we have it as soon as possible. My best friend lives back home in Wisconsin and so do my parents. Do you mind?

Hannah texts about two hours into me hitting my face against my desk trying to come up with anything to make this presentation interesting. Considering I'm dangerously close to giving myself a bruise, I deserve a break to text with Hannah and make myself some dinner.

ME

I don't mind at all. Just tell me what you need and I'll make it happen.

It's not every day your best friend gets engaged, after all. I bring the empty cupcake box with me and throw it into the garbage. They didn't survive very long.

HANNAH

> Maybe we could get lunch this week? I think it'd be easier to plan in person.

ME

> Yeah, sounds good. How about I come by the office tomorrow and pick you up?

Maybe I could also sneak in to see Ben for a few minutes. Opening the fridge, I pull together ingredients for a sandwich.

HANNAH

> Perfect! This means so much to me, Darby. Thank you.

I smile at my phone. Hannah is one of the good ones.

***

*"Darby, why haven't you cleaned the dishes?" Mom asks, her face darkening as she walks into the living room.*

*"I was going to do it after dinner," I reply, not looking away from the TV I've been glued to since I arrived home from school.*

*"If you cleaned them when you dirtied them, they wouldn't pile up, and I wouldn't have to look at them," she snaps.*

*"Or you could just avoid the sink," I mutter.*

*"Excuse me?" She walks in front of the TV, forcing me to meet her gaze.*

*"I said, you could just avoid the sink. I'll get to it, I always do." I cross my arms over my chest. "I deserve to take a second and relax."*

*"Oh, you deserve to? You were at school, Darby, not work."*

*"You weren't at school or at work, so I'm not sure what your*

*point is."*

*"Go to your room!" she screams, pointing the way with her freshly manicured nails.*

*"Fine! I do my chores, so I don't understand why you're always screaming at me about them!" I yell back as I stand.*

*"Oh, you don't know why I always yell? Don't you? You finish them because I yell. You're lazy and ungrateful! You aren't even doing your homework while avoiding your chores. That's why you get such mediocre grades. Laziness. Then you try to make me the bad guy when I'm trying to make you succeed. You're a disappointment, Darby."*

*"I'm a disappointment? Well, you raised me, so what does that say about you?"*

*My face stings before I can register the slap that preceded it. Instantly my own hand is on the hot skin of my cheek.*

*"Shut up and go to your room," she slowly snarls. "Now."*

***

I wake to find I fell asleep on my laptop. My entire cheek is stuck to the keyboard, and I slowly peel myself free. Mom didn't hit me often. She knew her words were more damaging than anything she could physically do. But sometimes I pushed a little too hard or said exactly the right thing, and she snapped. Most parents slap their kids, though, so it's not that big of a deal. Some kids get spanked, some kids get slapped. Anyway, she's out of my life. I don't need her, and I don't need to think about her. Despite whatever my subconscious has decided. What I do need is to work on this project. While I relish being busy, I'd much rather be doing research on venues for Casey and Hannah's engagement party. I walk into the kitchen and pull out a jar of Nutella and a spoon. Let's kick this presentation in the ass.

# Chocolate Cake, Part One

Okay, dress? Check. Hair styled? Check. Makeup on? Check. Shoes? Check. Purse? Check. Date? Uncheck. Ben has still not arrived to take us to the engagement party. It's not as if he's meeting my friends and family for the first time or anything! A good impression doesn't matter! Oh God, I need champagne. Or cookies. Having essentially planned this event with Hannah and Casey, I stocked it with baked goods. Why did I agree to show up early to help set up when Ben has been working harder than ever? Maybe I should just text him and tell him to meet me there. A knock to the door snaps me out of my thoughts.

"You are so . . ." I swing the door open, fully prepared to berate Ben for how late we are going to be. That is, until I get a good eyeful of him. He's *stunning*. Wrapped up in a midnight black tuxedo, which is cut impeccably to emphasize the width of his chest and shoulders. I didn't realize black tuxedos could look this good in real life. Apparently all one needs is an exceptional tailor.

"Late? I know, I'm sorry." He hands me a bouquet of roses

that slightly reduces my annoyance. "You know how much pressure I've been under."

"I do. But you promised you'd be here on time tonight. This is important to me," I insist, turning to put the flowers in some water. There's no point in letting them wilt while we're gone just because I'm not happy. I bury my face in the roses and inhale. Mmm, my favorite.

"I'm sorry, Darby. And, hey, I'm not that late. We'll still be early!" He takes a small step into the apartment. "Please forgive me?"

Fluffing the blooms in their new glass vase, I turn to him. His shoulders are hunched in that kicked puppy kind of way.

"Yes. Like you said, we'll still be early." I sigh. At least he's here.

"You look magnificent tonight, sweetheart." He envelops me in his strong arms. "You're beautiful."

My eyes drop to the black dress I'm wearing. It's your standard, basic dress. Knee-length, flared skirt, round neckline, and sleeves that stop at my elbows. Nothing special. Certainly not anything like what his ex would wear to a party. Yes, I'm still hung up on those pictures.

"Thank you," I reply, instead of fighting him.

His calloused hand comes up to cup my face. "I missed you."

I breathe deeply, melting into his embrace. "I missed you too."

"I know this night is important to you. I'll do everything I can to make sure you enjoy yourself. I'm looking forward to meeting everyone." He presses a light kiss to my cheek. "Whatever you need tonight, just let me know."

"I will."

The restaurant is almost silent as Ben and I walk in. We are still, thankfully, early enough to help set up. Casey, Hannah, and Hannah's parents, here all the way from Wisconsin, are the only occupants at the moment.

"Hey!" I call. Casey and Hannah snap their heads toward us, a frightening grin forming on Casey's face.

"Well, looky who we have here," she says with a tone that promises mischief.

I throw her as menacing a glare as I can muster with Ben beside me. "Casey, Hannah, this is Ben."

"It's nice to meet you, Casey, and . . . wait a minute." Ben's grin grows. "Hannah! You work at Streemz in HR, right? You're the one who handles most of the new hires."

"Oh!" A light flush graces Hannah's cheeks. "Yes, that's me. It's nice to see you, Mr. James."

"Congratulations to you both!" His arm winds around my shoulders. Look at him, making an effort. I didn't even need to tell him that Hannah works for him—he just knew. Granted, I wouldn't be surprised if Xavier gave him a heads up. But it's the thought that counts.

"Thank you, Mr. James," Hannah responds.

"Ben," he corrects. "I'm just Ben."

"Ben," Hannah slowly repeats.

"So!" Casey interrupts, leaning on the nearest table. "My best friend's boyfriend and my fiancée's boss . . . that's quite a resume you have."

"Darby, do you mind helping me finish up the centerpieces?" Hannah asks, taking my hand.

"Lead the way," I agree. I kiss Ben's cheek and smack Casey's arm for good measure on the way over to the table covered in decorations. Casey is going to completely eviscerate him, but I'm hoping she does so nicely. Can someone be nicely eviscerated? Here's hoping.

"Don't worry, she won't go overboard," Hannah whispers once we're far enough away. "She doesn't want me getting fired, after all."

Jesus, this is awkward. "He would never . . ."

"I know," she interrupts, lifting her hand. "Of course he wouldn't. But if it helps Casey behave, then I'm not going to tell her otherwise."

"Oh. That's not a bad point." I chuckle, grabbing one of the mason jars from the group in front of me. Three white daisies and a light pink ribbon make it a centerpiece.

"Are you excited for tonight? You look beautiful," I say, picking up another jar. Hannah is wrapped up in a strappy, sparkly green dress that pops against her dark skin.

"I am. I haven't seen Taylor, my maid of honor, in far too long. I'm so glad she was able to come out for this," she replies.

"I'm excited to meet her."

"Shut up!" Casey screams from across the room before doubling over in a fit of giggles. Ben is chuckling next to her, his face contorted into a guilty-child-just-did-something-wrong way.

"Huh." Hannah smiles. "Apparently we had nothing to worry about."

"Who would've guessed?"

I'm forced to pry Ben and Casey apart as guests are now arriving. They bonded over some meme or something and are now best friends.

"You'll come over one night, I'll make dinner, and we'll play

Mario Kart or some shit," Casey promises, taking Hannah's hand in hers.

"You're the hosts, go greet people!" I insist, pushing at Casey's arm.

"We'll make a date," Ben agrees as if I'm not even here. Casey glares at me playfully before allowing herself to be pulled toward the door.

"Having fun?" I cock my head at Ben.

"Absolutely. Casey's a fucking riot." Ben lights up with that two-dimple smile that always gets me. "Let's go get a drink while they do their thing." Ben lowers his hand to the small of my back, directing me through the room to the bar. I never expected him and Casey to click so quickly, but I don't hate it. The thought of all four of us hanging out makes a warm, happy glow settle in the pit of my belly. Normalcy. Could I have normalcy? A partner, a best friend, a life I don't deserve but somehow still get?

"Thank you for making an effort with Casey," I say, turning to face him. "I can't express what it means to me."

"Trust me, I'd do just about anything for you. And I meant it, Casey is hilarious. I genuinely like her."

"Hmm." I nod. "Well, that's one down, one to go."

Ben smiles, ordering us each a glass of wine. "Nervous about me meeting your parents?"

My entire body freezes.

*Parents?* As in . . . plural? I must've explained something, said something, right?

"Uh . . ." I swallow down the lump that tastes a lot like fear. "Just my dad."

"Oh. You just mentioned once that Casey was always at your house growing up. I figured even if your parents split that they'd both show up for her." He eyes me.

"No." I wring my hands together to keep them from shaking.

"Hey." His hand comes down in a gentle hold on both of mine. The action slows their movement. "Whatever it is, it's okay."

"Later," I croak. "We can talk about it later."

"Okay, sweetheart. Whatever you want. I'm looking forward to meeting your dad. You always say such wonderful things about him. Plus, I owe him for that dinner he bought us." Ben catches my eye, smiling in a way that I expect is meant to be reassuring.

"He won't let you pay him back," I reply, trying to find the floor that came out from under me. I can do this. I can be here for Casey and Hannah tonight. I have to. I can't let *her* ruin an event like this when she isn't even here.

"I can be very persuasive," he replies, lifting my hands up to kiss them. You poor man. You don't deserve half the shit I'm going to unload on you.

"Kiddo!"

I turn at the sound of my dad's voice. He hasn't noticed me and Ben yet as he is currently wrapped up in a giant Casey-filled hug.

"Dad!" Casey squeals in that beautifully unique Casey way.

I take a big gulp of my wine and set it down on the high-top table in front of me. "Well, you ready to meet Dad?"

"Isn't that Casey's dad?" Ben cocks his head.

"Nope!" I pop the *p*. "He basically raised us both, so he's *our* dad."

"You're kind to share him."

I wave to my dad, who makes his way over. "I'm not kind. My dad is kind for treating her like his own." Before Ben can inevitably fight back, Dad weaves his way through the group of people between us and the door. His girlfriend, Lisa, in tow.

"Hey kiddo." Dad throws his arms around me for a big bear hug. You're never too old for a bear hug from your dad.

"Hey Dad." I squeeze him right around the middle just to hear his "oof" in return.

"Darby, good to see you," Lisa says pleasantly, giving me a quick kiss on the cheek. Her perfume smacks me in the face, as usual.

"Dad, Lisa, this is Ben. My boyfriend." I step back, gesturing to Ben. I don't think I've ever called him my boyfriend. Hmm, does this mean we're going to prom together now?

"It's nice to meet you, Ben." Dad offers his hand for a shake.

"It's nice to meet you as well, Mr. Clarke. Your daughter speaks highly of you," Ben replies, not missing a beat. God, he's always so levelheaded. Can't relate.

"You can call me Ted, Ben." Dad smiles. "Unless you hurt my kid. Then it's Mr. Clarke."

"I have no intention of doing that, Ted," Ben replies confidently. He wraps an arm around my shoulders, squeezing me.

"That's what I like to hear. This is Lisa," Dad says. Lisa and Ben nod at each other before Dad suggests we all head to the bar for drinks. I've lost sight of my wine, so I follow along. I may need a few more glasses to get through this night.

*** 

"He gets along with everyone he meets, doesn't he?" Casey asks, coming up behind me. Dad and Ben have been giggling like teenagers while talking about cars for the last half hour.

"It's a gift." I shrug, taking a huge bite out of the thick

chocolate cake I had special ordered. "He's just likable. Which . . . can't relate."

Casey snort laughs into her old fashioned. "Right? People tend to hate me as quickly as they love him."

"We're weird people. Normals aren't prepared to handle us."

"I do like him, though. I wasn't expecting him to be so laid back, you know considering how stupidly fucking rich he is. I should've known better. You're picky as hell. You wouldn't date just any old schleb."

I roll my eyes dramatically. "Yeah, yeah. Why aren't you talking to all of your guests?"

"All of these people are here for Hannah. You know me, I don't have anybody in my life except you guys. Some people from the restaurant, sure, but I'm happy with the few people I have," Casey says, swirling her drink around in the glass.

Grabbing her tightly, I squeeze until she yelps. "I love you."

"Ugh. Shut up, you mushy weirdo." She bats her hand at me until I let her go with a laugh. "You looked a little off earlier, you okay?"

"Me?" Shit. "Yeah, I'm fine."

"I'm not going to pretend I believe you. Tell me what's up," she insists.

"Ben. He assumed my mom would be here since I mentioned you were basically raised at my house."

"Ahh. I don't blame him. It's a pretty normal assumption to make. What'd you say?"

"I told him we would talk about it later." I down the rest of my wine and sweep the restaurant for a waiter. I need another. Or two.

"What do you think you'll say? I mean, you've barely even talked to me about it. I just know what I saw."

"I don't know."

"Good luck. And just let me know if you need me."

"I will." Fuck, why does this topic keep coming up? Booze, where is the booze? With the next inhale I calm immediately. Cedar, sandalwood, citrus. Ben.

"I abandoned you, didn't I?" Ben whispers in my ear, hugging me from behind. "I'm sorry. I made the mistake of telling your dad about my classic car collection."

"Don't worry about it. You guys were having fun," I reply, snuggling into his embrace.

"Yeah, we were. You were right, he's a great guy. Makes me wish my parents were still around." Ben sighs, tightening his arms.

"I'm sorry," I say, kissing his cheek.

"What happened to them?" Casey interjects with all of her usual tact.

"Car accident about five years ago," Ben replies, his body going slightly rigid.

Casey hisses, scrunching her face. "That's awful. I'm so sorry. I wish things like that wouldn't happen."

"Me too." He exhales. "What about you? I don't see your parents here."

"Ah. Jeff and Mary are still very much alive. They're just very Christian and opposed to my entire 'lifestyle,' as they call it. They're able to stomach two visits a year at Easter and Christmas, but that's it." She flips her strawberry blonde hair with practiced ease. She's gotten used to telling people, but I know how to spot the wobble in her stance.

"A toast then, to orphans." Ben raises his glass to Casey.

"To orphans." Casey smiles, clinking their glasses together.

***

After being reminded of Ben's parents' accident, I don't

touch alcohol again. I'm not driving tonight, but he reminded me that a clear head is always better. Especially when Hannah surprises me and announces that I'm giving a speech tonight. Apparently it's a thing the maid of honor does. Hah. Fuck my life.

Using a spoon, I clink it against my glass of Coke until the room dies down. Well, here goes nothing.

"Thank you all for coming tonight to celebrate the engagement of Hannah and Casey." I pause for a few whoops and applause. "For those of you who don't know me, I'm Darby, Casey's maid of honor. And best friend . . . and roommate, but who's counting, right? I've known Casey since we were in diapers, and I'll be the first one to tell you that I didn't think she'd ever get married."

"Watch it!" Casey snaps, tightening her grip on Hannah's waist.

"It's your engagement party, I'm supposed to embarrass you." I smile. "Anyway. It's not that she doesn't deserve happiness, I can't think of anyone who deserves it more. I just never thought she'd meet anyone who could keep up with her. And then Hannah showed up. Hannah with her sweet smiles and shyness somehow was the perfect fit. Casey brings out Hannah's joy and excitement, while Hannah allows Casey to slow down and savor life's greatest moments. There are no two people better suited for each other than you two. I'm honored you've let me watch you grow as a couple and as individuals. I love you both. I wouldn't leave Casey with just anyone after all."

"God, you're such a dope." Casey sniffles from beside me. She buries her face in Hannah's neck when the room laughs.

"No, you're the dope. And you're my dope. You're stuck with me Casey Fairbanks, and by association that means you're stuck with me too, Hannah. I hope you both know that. If everyone could raise their glasses." A pause. "To Casey and Hannah. The most beautiful couple I've ever had the pleasure of knowing. May your wedding be gorgeous, your marriage be long, and your lives be full of love and happiness."

The room takes a collective sip, and before I can raise my own glass to my lips, I'm enveloped by Casey. My arms wrap around her and we both squeeze. When we were kids we used to each squeeze each other as hard as we could, trying to get the other person to admit defeat. I always won.

"I love you. You're the worst for making me cry in public, for making me cry period, and I'm going to get my revenge. But I love you," she whispers.

"I love you too."

# Chocolate Cake, Part Two

The drive back to Ben's house can only be described as safe. It's as if I'm in a warm, protected bubble of love from the evening. Despite a few hiccups, it was a reminder of how much love I have in my life. Casey, Hannah, Dad, even Ben. I'm a lucky woman no matter what.

Ben is uncharacteristically quiet, but I can't blame him. Tonight was a lot even for me. He probably needs time to decompress. Maybe he's realizing how much less complicated his life would be without me. Ha . . . ha . . . God, I hope not.

"I'm thinking we should eat some cake," I babble. So much for feeling safe. "Thank goodness Hannah and Casey let us bring home some leftovers."

"Sure," Ben agrees, parking the car in his oversized garage. Ben wasn't kidding when he said he had a collection of classic cars. It's more like a fucking fleet in a massive concrete underground bunker.

"You . . . you okay?" I ask as we both get out of the car. With a reassuringly gentle smile, Ben walks over and presses a soft kiss to my forehead.

"I'm great, sweetheart. I just worry about you. Sometimes you just seem like you're holding so much back." He grabs our things, and the cake, from the backseat and heads toward the door, leading into the home.

Well, shit. "I do?"

"Listen, I know you said we'd talk." He walks through the dark hallway, flipping on lights as he goes. "But I'm not going to force it. I hate that shit. If I don't want to talk about something and someone starts pressing me about it, it just pisses me off. So I'm here when you're ready."

"It's not . . ." Fuck, words are hard. "I've just never—I've never talked about it." I'm trailing behind him like a lost child.

"Let's just take some cake upstairs, get in some comfy clothes, and put on a movie. I'm sick of the tux." He kisses the top of my head. "I'll get some forks. Why don't you head upstairs?"

"Okay," I mumble. As I take each step I'm disappointed for some reason. Was I hoping he'd push me? Was I wishing that someone would force me to open up and talk about this ridiculous shit I've been burying for so long? Or do I just want to get the inevitable over with? Do I want to spew all of my crazy at him at once so he can leave me before I fall too much in love? I don't know what I want.

"Need help with your dress?" Warm hands take hold of my shoulders, and wow . . . I've just been standing in his bedroom ruminating in my own bubble of self-pity.

"Mm-hmm." I smile, lifting my hair out of the way of my zipper. He tugs the metal down until it reaches the small of my back. A kiss is pressed to the nape of my neck, and this is all so domestic. Like we've been doing this for years.

"I'll let you change," he murmurs. I turn just as he walks into the closet, presumably to get rid of his tux.

*I*t's dark. The lights in Ben's bedroom were turned off long ago, and the movie has ended. With Ben's arms around me and a belly full of cake, I'm unable to sleep. My eyes are glued open and I'm staring at the bedside table in front of me. He may still be awake. His breathing is even on the back of my neck, but that doesn't mean anything.

"She was horrible," I whisper into the silent space.

"Who, sweetheart?" Ben mumbles, nuzzling into my skin. Not asleep, but not all the way awake either.

"My mom," I reply. It's like I'm a bomb just waiting to explode. All of this tension has finally bubbled over and I need to speak.

Ben's arms tighten around me, not forcing me to roll over or move at all. "I'm sorry."

"It was different. It wasn't just awful, it wasn't normal." I bury one of my hands in my hair. I'm not saying it right. "I never . . . fuck, I never felt safe."

"Sweetheart," he coos, now nuzzling against me. His fingers rub against my skin in a way that would be soothing if I wasn't so numb.

"My dad loves me more than anything, and I know that. He tried so hard to shelter me from her, and I don't know how to thank him." I sniffle. "I know he tried so hard, but I was still alone with her. And . . . and I don't know how to explain her or what she did to me. Nothing sounds right."

"You don't have to explain anything. Only say what you want and nothing more," he promises.

"She never made me feel like enough. She never made me feel worthy of her love and kindness, so I never received it."

"Darby, sweetheart, come here." He releases me so I can turn in his arms. A calloused thumb comes up and rubs at the tears on my cheek. "You're enough. You're more than enough. If she couldn't see that, it's her problem and not yours."

"Can we sleep now?" I'm suddenly exhausted. I haven't said much. I know that, but it's more than I've ever said.

"Yes, thank you for telling me. Come here." He pulls me to his chest, settling his head on top of mine. "Sleep, sweetheart."

"Thank you."

***

*"Go upstairs and change," Mom insists the moment I step into the kitchen. I look down at my outfit and frown. I'm wearing a crew-neck pink T-shirt and jean shorts.*

*"What's wrong with my outfit?" I ask. Her gaze lifts from the plate of scrambled eggs in front of her to lift a single eyebrow at me.*

*"Your shorts. They're too short," she replies as if it were obvious.*

*"They're almost at my knees." I cock my head. It's the middle of summer, any longer and I'll be far too hot. "I'm supposed to meet Casey in the front yard soon. We're going to play outside."*

*"Trust me, honey," she says in a syrupy-sweet way that makes my toes curl. "You don't want to go out like that. Not with how your thighs look, and your father's knees . . . I'm just trying to help you."*

*"Oh . . . okay . . ."*

*"You used to be so skinny. Could've been a model . . ."*

***

I blink my eyes open to the sensation of slightly calloused fingers running along my arm. Not light enough to tickle, but not heavy enough to drag me out of sleep if I wasn't already waking up.

"Hey you," Ben rumbles in that I-just-woke-up voice that makes me tremble.

"Hey," I croak in a much less sexy fashion. I clear my throat and turn to fully face him. "How long have you been up?"

"Not long." He shifts, sneaking his arm underneath me to wrap around my shoulders.

"So, what, you've just been staring at me all this time?"

"Maybe."

"You're lucky you're hot." I smile, leaning up to kiss his stubbly cheek.

"Yeah? I'm hot?" He waggles his eyebrows.

"You won't be if you keep acting like a goofball."

His grin turns evil. "You sure? Because I think you like it." His fingers wiggle at me coming closer and closer.

"Nope. I've changed my mind and will be leaving forever."

His fingers stop and pull back just long enough for me to open my mouth to apologize. At my hesitation, he descends. I'm suddenly batting away tickling fingers that are attacking my belly and arms. Taking heaving breaths between giggles, I beg for an end to the insanity.

"Only if you apologize," he insists with the biggest grin on his face.

"I'm sorry!" I cry, continuing to try and free myself.

He stops the tickling and goes back to running his fingers along my skin. His nails lightly scratch along my exposed belly as my shirt has ridden up in the excitement. "You're forgiven."

"Thank goodness," I murmur, relaxing into the attention.

In the merriment, his body now presses up against mine and his face hovers so close. We would be gazing right into each other's eyes if he wasn't staring so intently at the patch of skin his fingers are dancing along. Why *is* he staring so intently at my belly? Is he noticing that there is some stubborn fluffiness I haven't been able to get rid of? He hasn't seen me with my shirt off yet. His head drops to press a firm kiss to the area he was caressing.

"You're so beautiful, Darby," he growls.

"*Fuck.*" My breathing speeds up. I didn't even mean to vocalize that, but . . . *fuck.*

"I mean . . ." He nibbles at my belly button. "If you want to."

Oh, I want to. I *really* want to.

"I know you want to wait. No pressure," he promises, his head still hovering over my belly. "But I'm ready whenever you are."

"My mommy issues aren't scaring you away?" I chuckle. I'd rather know now if he doesn't want to be with someone as broken as I am.

Slowly, he climbs up my body until his nose is pressed against mine. "I'm not going anywhere."

"*Oh.*"

Could he be telling the truth? He's still here after all. Is it possible that maybe—just maybe—I could give my heart to this man and he wouldn't run? That I could have some semblance of happiness? Is he the one I could let down my walls for?

It's like we've been staring at each other for hours, not mere seconds. In one breath there is anticipation, in another I've dragged him down. With each kiss I try to convey that for the first time in my life, I feel safe. That *he* makes me feel safe. Ben has created a home for me here in his arms, and it's all I've ever wanted.

"I want to," I whisper against his lips once my own are spit-slicked and swollen. "I want to."

"Yeah?" is his eloquent reply. Lust-blown pupils search my face.

"Uh huh." I nod, pulling him back for more. We've been separated for too long. I need to feel his skin against mine. I pull roughly on the hem of his shirt, trying to somehow get it off him without disconnecting from the kiss.

Our lips part as he sits up and pulls the shirt off. "Yeah? You sure?"

My eyes roam the miles of skin before me. The perfectly sculpted bear of a man that looms over me like a predator. I've never wanted to be wrecked so bad.

"Mm-hmm," I repeat, making little grabby hands at him.

The devious grin I get in response is delicious. Ben dives in to nibble at the sensitive spot on my neck as his hands roam over my clothed skin. Clothes, too many clothes. Ben seems to agree as he starts yanking up the shirt I'm wearing, bearing my chest to the cold morning air. I lift my arms to assist him and lay back as my shirt is thrown to the abyss.

"Baby," he groans. "You're so gorgeous." Calloused fingers trail along my collarbone, taking in the new territory.

"I should mention . . ." I trail off as he lays kisses along the same trail his fingers took.

"Mm?" He responds, mouth quite occupied.

"I'm a virgin."

Well, I could've been a bit more eloquent about that. Especially since the kisses have stopped. Why have the kisses stopped?

"You've never done this before?" he clarifies, picking his head up.

"Uh, no," I whisper. I'm going to regret telling him, aren't I?

"And you're sure that I'm the one you want?" His gaze bores into me as if he's begging for me to tell the truth.

"Yeah," I reply. "If you're okay with that."

"Of course I'm okay with that." He nods vigorously. "Definitely okay with that."

"Good." I smile, tangling my fingers into his short, brown locks. "I believe you were in the middle of something?"

"My tactics have changed." He sits up, breaking my hold on him to straddle my legs. "I have new information. Now I need to . . . take my time."

"*Ben*," I whine. The grabby hands have returned. "Come back."

"*Baby*," he admonishes with a fond smile. "Let me take care of you."

I pout in response but make a show of laying my hands down on the bed.

"Good girl," he purrs. "So good for me." The weight of his palms settles on my waist and my eyes flutter closed. Apparently I have a praise kink, if the warmth flooding my core is any indication. A gentle, stubbly kiss is placed on the tender skin right above my belly button.

"Promise me you'll tell me if anything's wrong or if you want to stop," he murmurs.

"I promise."

I'm fighting to keep my eyes open as kisses are rained down on my thighs. The sight of Ben down there is mesmerizing, but overwhelming.

His long nose nuzzles against my clothed wetness, and I involuntarily jolt toward the unfamiliar feeling.

"*Behave.*"

I ferociously shake my head. "Don't wanna."

"Darby, god damnit, I want to make this good for you."

"Yeah?" I sneakily shift my hand down and stroke along the rock-solid hardness. "Maybe I want this to be good for *you*."

Ben lets loose a shuddering breath that turns into a deep groan. "Darby."

"I'm a grown-ass woman, Ben, and I want you to ruin me."

His eyes snap open as he stares me down. "Yeah? That what you want?"

"Oh, fuck yes," I whimper, trying to rub my legs together.

His grin is shark-like as he wraps his fingers around the band of my underwear. I let out a sigh of relief as he pulls it away from my skin, which turns into a squeal as he snaps it.

"Careful what you ask for."

Before I can reply, he's wound his fingers back around the band and has whipped them off.

"Look at you," he says, running one single finger along the wetness that has gathered. "All this for me?"

He's trying to break me. And he's succeeded. Any verbalization skills I may have had are long gone as I nod at him.

"Such a good girl," he says to my pleased whimper. "Yeah? You like when I tell you how good you are for me?"

My nodding is so insistent I may end up giving myself a headache.

"You like it when I'm in control, don't you, baby? You just had to tell me what you needed, huh?" He drags his wet fingers along the inside of my thigh. "I'll give you whatever you need, whatever you want. All you have to do is ask."

"But . . . you. . ." I attempt to reply. I need him to get what he needs. I don't know what I'm doing . . . How can I please him? What if I'm awful?

"Shhh." He smiles. "Let me wreck you."

Before I can protest, his mouth is on me and my back has bowed. Those big, plush lips are doing things I didn't even know were legal. Maybe they aren't. My fingers clench in the sheets below me, practically tearing into the expensive fabric. I have no idea if I'm quiet or the blood rushing in my ears has blocked out all sound. With an expert suck and a flick of his tongue, I tumble over the edge embarrassingly quickly. Waves of warmth and pleasure shudder through each inch of my limbs until my body lies limp below him.

"Wow," I whisper. So that's what all the fuss is about. That makes sense now.

"Yeah?" an arrogant voice asks from above me. I crack open my eyes to meet completely black, lust-filled pupils. His chest is heaving in deep breaths as he holds his weight above me on his forearms.

"Yeah," I muster.

"Need to stop?" he asks.

"No." I clear my throat. "I want this." And he has to get something out of this too.

"I do too." He sits up again and pulls off his gray boxer briefs to reveal the most massive thing I've ever seen. How in the royal fuck is that going to fit? They can't possibly make condoms that big. As if it has a mind of its own, my hand reaches toward him.

"Mmm . . . may I?" I ask, embarrassment running hot in my cheeks.

Ben chuckles. "Whatever you want."

I want to touch it. Duh.

I slowly reach out and brush my fingers against the warm skin. Much warmer than I expected. Soft too. Tentatively, I wrap my hand around it. Oh, wow, my fingers don't touch. I asked to get ruined, and I have a feeling that's what's going to happen with this massive thing. I may never walk again.

"Still okay?" he asks, snapping me out of my trance.

"Yeah." I glance up. His face is strained, like he's clenching his teeth. I must be torturing him. Okay, Darby, time to pull it together. I have to be good at this or else I'll lose him. I slide back down on the sheets with what I hope is a confident smile. "Do I need to beg?"

"We can play with that later," he promises. "For now, I'm all yours." *For now* being the operative phrase. With a distracting kiss, his fingers find my wetness again, pressing inside and gently stretching me further. While I appreciate the gesture, I just want him to hurry up.

I nip his bottom lip. "Come on."

"Impatient." He chuckles. "I want to make this good for you."

"Just stop. I'll be fine." I huff. Not that his fingers don't feel lovely, because yeah they do, but I've been the focus of all the attention. He needs some too.

His eyebrows furrow as he gazes at me, eyes searching for . . . something. "Are you sure you're okay?"

"Yes, I promise. I'm just impatient and horny and can you just please stick that massive dick in me?" I regret the words the minute they leave my mouth.

"My what now?" Ben snickers, burying his face in my belly. "God, you're something."

"Did I ruin everything?" I bury my face in my hands. I should never be allowed anywhere to do anything ever again.

"Hey." He pulls my hands away. "I wouldn't change a thing about you."

"Really?" There's no way he's being honest. Even Casey would change things about me if she could. Even my dad.

His lips are soft and sweet. "Really. I'm not going to let you live that down. But I'm also still hard as a rock, so what does that say about me?"

"Bad things." I smile, winding my fingers into his hair.

"Come here." He pulls my lips back to his. And just like that, I'm back in the moment. I'm here with him, focusing solely on him. Ben. I love you. I love you, Ben. I love you more than anything, but I am way too much of a chicken to say it yet.

I'm utterly fascinated watching him roll on the extra-large condom. Apparently, they do make them in extra large. Who knew?

"Let me know if it hurts," he says as he lines himself up.

I nod, unable to trust my own voice. I'm nervous as fuck, but I also want this. I want to make love to the man I'm head over fucking heels for. I want to share love with him, even if it's only for a little while.

It stings. It's a big stretch, even with all the prep and the earlier orgasm. But there's something inherently right about the ache. Like he's meant to be with me, and we're meant to share in this moment together.

"Alright?" he asks as he bottoms out.

"Mm-hmm. Just wait a sec?" I reply, my voice shaking. I will not cry during my first time having sex, I will not cry during my first time having sex.

He nuzzles into my neck, finding all of his favorite places to kiss and nibble as I try to adjust.

"Okay . . . s'okay." I grasp his forearms with my hands. Gently he drags back and then slides back in, the movement easier than before. It still aches, but with each movement of his hips it becomes a good ache. An ache I can appreciate, an ache I may learn to crave.

"Oh!" I cry, my nails digging in just as he hits a spot that I've heard Casey gossip about.

"Good? Bad?" He stops, restraint visible in his clenched fists.

"Good! M-more?" I gently lift my legs and wrap them around his waist, bringing him that much closer.

"I can do more," he growls, picking up his pace.

This feels fucking amazing.

I've never felt closer to someone in my entire life. Our eyes meet and I don't even need to orgasm at this point. My heart is connected to another person—it belongs to him. The sight of his muscles flexing, his hot breath fanning my face, his grunts and moans filling my ears . . . it's a symphony of the senses. Despite it all, my heartbeat picks up speed and my breaths come out as fractured moans. The end is approaching, I'm careening toward it like a freight train off the rails.

"Ben, I'm . . . I'm gonna . . ." I squeal, toes curling as one of his thick fingers sneaks down and rubs.

"That's it. Such a good girl," he praises, picking up speed even more. "Come for me, baby."

"Ben!" Stars burst behind my eyelids as a dark, heavy pleasure soars from the core of my body to the tips of my fingers. It's deeper and richer than anything I've ever experienced, but I force my eyes open. I want to know what Ben looks like when he loses himself. I want to know what he looks like when he's lost to the pleasure he's just given me.

"Darby," he groans, hips erratic in their thrusting. Finally his head dips and his body slows as he keeps himself buried inside me.

Am I breathing? I must be because I'm not dead. Yet. Ben rolled us over onto our sides, but my leg propped up on his hip is preventing us from disconnecting. I want to live inside this moment for as long as I can.

"How you feeling?" Ben breaks the silence, his fingers trailing up and down my arm.

"Can't describe it." I bury my face into his chest. "But it's good."

"You're indescribable." He huffs a chuckle. "More than that. I don't think I've ever felt this way about someone."

"Really?" I lift my head to meet his gaze.

He gently cups my face. "Of course really. I don't just say that. I knew you were something the moment I met you."

"I don't deserve you." I smile.

His face falls. "Why would you say something like that?"

"I . . ." I'm speechless.

"We deserve each other. We're good for each other, okay?" he insists, not allowing me to duck my head.

"Okay."

"How about we go take a shower and clean up a bit?" he says, all sternness gone from his tone.

"In a minute. I'm basking." I smile, rubbing the tips of our noses together. He chuckles and gives me a quick peck on the lips.

***

The shower, thanks to my puppy dog eyes, turns into a decadent bubble bath in his giant sunken bathtub. This may be the longest I've ever seen him go without his phone and I'm delighted. How long can I push this?

"This is the laziest Saturday I've had in years," he says. He's leaning against the edge of the tub, arms splayed out in perfect relaxation. The scent of roses wafts up from the bubbles as I run my toe along his thigh. Let it be known that I had no idea I had a thigh kink until I watched him fuck me into the mattress.

"I'm happy I was able to facilitate this for you." I giggle.

His head lifts lazily so he can give me a cheeky grin. "Have an ulterior motive I should know about, sweetheart?"

"No," I reply with a gentle lilt. "I just love seeing you relaxed. You work so hard."

He sighs, laying his head back down. "This acquisition is

tough. No one seems to have their head screwed on straight. I'm hoping things will die down soon."

"Me too, if only because I want to spend more time with you."

"You can spend all the time you want with me." His hand finds mine and links our fingers together. "You're always welcome."

"Well, I have this project, and the wedding coming up, so I'm going to be busy. But I wouldn't say no to some Ben time in between cake tasting and planning."

"And now I know how to get you relaxed." He turns his head to grin at me.

"Stop!" I giggle, splashing some warm water at him. The bubbles catch in his stubble, making him resemble Santa Claus.

"I see how it is," he growls, dunking his head under water. In a moment he's gone and in the next he's snapped up right beside me covering me in water and bubbles.

"Ben!" I try to get away to retaliate, but I'm locked in his strong arms, squirming against wet skin.

"No, no, you wanted a water fight." His eyes sparkle. "So you're getting a water fight."

The air is thick with laughter and weak protests, the scent of roses increasing as the water is disturbed. This is perfection. If it's up to me, I will happily spend the rest of my life this way.

## Chocolate-Covered Raisins

*M*y eyes burn as I stare at my laptop screen in front of me. I'm a masochist. An absolute masochist. I have about seventeen different tabs open at once. Five for the wedding, another seven for my work project, and the remaining few are possible MBA programs. Why do I do this to myself? With a dramatic sigh I thunk my head against the desk. How is one human supposed to handle all of this? Must rest eyes. Must . . . rest . . . eyes . . .

***

*"Ted, you completely missed dinner!" Mom practically stamps her foot in annoyance. I'm hidden behind the railing of the stairs, called down by the sound of Dad coming home.*

*"I told you before that I'd be late all week. It's been insane at the firm." Dad sighs, placing his briefcase down. "Is Darby asleep yet?"*

*"She should be, but considering she stays up all night reading books . . ." she trails off with a scoff.*

*Dad beams with his back turned to her. "We should count our blessings there. Staying up all night reading is the least awful thing she could do."*

*"Stop trying to distract me. You're late. Again."*

*"I told you, Marie, it's been super busy. You remember that new closet you wanted? And those clothes you needed because you lost ten pounds? And those pieces of sterling silver jewelry you had to have?"*

*"Just what are you accusing me of?"*

*"I'm not accusing you of anything. I'm just saying that if you want to live like that, I have to work all night." Dad ambles over to the wine rack and picks up a bottle of red. There's exhaustion in every single movement.*

*"You're probably cheating on me," she snaps.*

*"Probably." Dad snorts. "Probably."*

***

My eyes snap open. Fuck, how long was I out? An hour . . . shit. I should eat something before getting back to work. I stand from my desk and twist my face in disgust as seemingly every single bone in my body cracks. I would work on my bed, but then I know I'd fall back asleep. I wander into the kitchen and rummage through the fridge. Casey, the absolute saint, has left me a decadent lasagna. Her lasagna is always at least seven layers and filled to the brim with sauce and full-fat ricotta cheese. My mouth waters as I lift the pan out of the fridge and onto the counter to cut myself a slice. The scent of basil, oregano, and cheese wafts up at me as I lift the tinfoil. Get in me.

That's what she said.

***

Thirty minutes and a full stomach later my phone rings just as I enter my bedroom.

"Ben!" I exclaim, smiling to myself. I haven't seen him since last weekend.

He chuckles. "Hey, sweetheart."

"I miss you," I reply, plopping onto my bed.

"I know, I'm sorry." The sound of rustling papers filters through. "I'm up to my eyeballs in legal bullshit. I think I've been home for six hours over the last few days."

"The world will continue to turn if you take a break, you know," I say, leaning back.

"Hah, I wish." He exhales. "For now I'm stuck at work. How are you? How is everything going? Still trying to plan a wedding and slam dunk an entire work project on your own?"

"Maybe. I accidentally fell asleep and then fed myself, so I was about to get back to it."

"Well, before you get too involved, your doorbell should be ringing in about thirty seconds."

"My what?" I stand and cross the apartment, heading toward the door.

"Your doorbell," he repeats, a smirk in his tone.

"Did you . . .?" Was he lying? Is he here to see me? Seeing Ben would be the best distraction. A small bit of my heart throbs at the possibility. The doorbell rings and I steel myself. I will not cry if he has romantically surprised me and showed up to my apartment.

"Surprise!" he calls into the phone as I open the door to see . . . a stranger.

"I don't understand." I smile at the man in front of me who is definitely not Ben.

"This is Taylor, my personal masseuse. He is the best in the business. I figure you're stressing yourself out and could use a bit of relaxation!" Ben explains.

"Oh!" I muster up some excitement. "This is so sweet." It's not that I don't appreciate a personal masseuse being sent to my house. Especially after that impromptu nap on my desk. I guess it makes me naive to have expected him to be standing there.

"Nothing is too much for my girl," Ben says. "I'm going to let you go and enjoy. I'll text you later, okay?"

"Oh, okay. Thank you, Ben."

He hangs up before I can get his name out.

Within moments of allowing him into the apartment, Taylor has set up a table, offered me a robe, and insisted I go change.

"You carry so much tension in your shoulders," he says as he rubs my back.

"Doesn't everyone?" I joke.

"No," he snips, pressing his hands harder into my back. Okay, no joking with the masseuse.

"So, um, you've known Ben a long time?" I remark after a few moments. I can't just sit here in silence with this guy.

"His assistant, Xavier, have you met him? Well, he called me about three years ago to come in and help. I was Xav's roommate in college one year and he remembered how wonderful I was at massages," he explains, kneading at some entrenched knots. "I had just gotten my license and Mr. James insisted I be on call for him right after our first session."

"Wow. Does he call often?" I am useless at conversation.

"You don't have to talk with me, honey, just relax." Taylor chuckles, pressing into a knot that causes my entire body to go limp. *Oh my damn* that's good. Of course he's a wizard with his hands; Ben wouldn't use anyone but the best. Does it make me selfish that I still wish it were Ben instead? He did this sweet thing for me because he knew I'd be stressed. I couldn't ask for more. No matter if all I want is just him.

I'm practically asleep by the time Taylor packs up and leaves. I lose the battle.

"**I**'m going to get fired!" I exclaim as I open my front door.

"No you won't, you absolute drama queen." Casey snorts from the kitchen. "All your boss's notes have been positive, you haven't told Jason from HR to fuck himself yet, and you have weeks before the presentation."

"But!"

"You always do this." She rolls her eyes.

"Casey!" I whine, throwing myself at her. Gracefully she catches me in a hug, far too used to me by now.

"Stop it," she scolds. "You have to stop being so hard on yourself. Now buck up and eat this." She picks up a fork-full of some ridiculous-looking pasta thing and pushes it at me. My trust in her skills is the reason I open my mouth.

Holy shit. It's like walking through my mother's old herb garden in the middle of summer. "*Casey.*"

"I know, right? It's amazing what some fresh veggies, home-made pasta, and a splash of olive oil can do."

"More," I demand, opening my mouth again.

She giggles as she spoons another helping into my mouth. "Heathen. Shouldn't Ben be doing this?"

My smile falters. "Yeah. He should."

"Uh oh. Spill." She sighs, cocking her hip.

"What?"

"You used your 'I'm perfectly fine, but no I'm not' voice. Spill."

I sigh, sliding onto the black leather barstool at our counter. "Nothing is wrong, per se. I just haven't seen him in a little while and I miss him."

"Awwwww," she coos. "Little antisocial Darby is falling in *love.*"

"I'm not in love!" I wince as my voice hits an awful pitch.

"Ha! That's the 'I'm lying' noise! You love him," she teases, stuffing her face with noodles.

"Shut up! Do you think he misses me?"

"Probably. He was all goo-goo eyes at you during the whole engagement party. He's lucky I liked him, or I would've teased him the whole time."

"He had goo-goo eyes?" I smile despite myself.

"You're going to be such an annoying in love person, aren't you?"

"Consider it payback for all of the years I've had to listen to you wax poetic about Hannah."

"Hannah deserves to be talked about. She's a perfect human." Another bite of pasta. "So when are you seeing him again?"

"Saturday. He promised to make time for dinner."

"Make time? Ugh." She rolls her eyes. "Is he actually that busy or just being a dick?"

"Trust me, he's that busy."

"Fuck."

***

THE MOM-STER

**It's your birthday soon.**

> You're going to be twenty-six, but it feels like just yesterday you were learning to talk. Your first word was mama.

> You know what you're doing to me is wrong. I know you know it, honey. I would never poison you against your father. Why have you let him do this to me?

> No one ever loves you like your mom, and one day when you're a mom you'll finally understand that.

The woman is always more aggressive as it gets closer to my birthday. She probably thinks the guilt will overwhelm me. It used to. Doesn't anymore. Nope. I delete yet another text as I blow dry my hair for my date with Ben. He's barely had time to even text me over the last couple days, and my entire body is thrumming at the very thought of seeing him. I'd rather we didn't even go out to dinner. I just want to lock him in his house, wrap myself around him, and never let go. But he is insisting we do something nice.

*Knock, knock.*

There's no way he's here three hours early. I straighten my sweatpants and meander to the door.

"Special delivery for Darby?" a small woman says as I open the door. She's holding a long, black garment bag with a hard to pronounce French name embroidered across it.

"That's me," I reply, taking the bag. She hands me a letter and smiles before leaving. Maybe I should've tipped her. Ugh, I'm so woefully unprepared for this kind of treatment. I lay the bag on my bed and tear open the note.

*You deserve the world, sweetheart. I can't wait to see you tonight.*
*Ben*

Oh look, my heart has melted onto the floor. I've been needing to mop anyway.

I place the note onto my bedside table for safekeeping and slide down the zipper on the garment bag.

Oh . . . *oh my.* It's a midnight blue dress with spaghetti straps and a deep V-neck. It looks tight and sexy and expensive. My fingers trace over the smooth fabric and a sigh escapes me. It's exquisite. Blinking away the few tears swimming in my eyes, I rush to the vanity in my bathroom to finish getting ready. I will look worthy of a dress that gorgeous if it kills me.

Although it just might.

"**F**uck," Ben breathes when I open the door. The dress rests on my shoulders, hitting right above my knees. It fits perfectly, of course, not that I would've expected any different.

I twirl in front of him. "You like?"

"I'm speechless." His hands grab for me, taking hold of my hips. "I'm in awe."

"Flatterer." I smile, heat rising to my cheeks.

"Who? Me?" He grins back, coming in close to bump my nose with his. "I would never."

Whatever quip I may have dies on my tongue at the fire in

those bright blue eyes. Maybe a night in isn't out of the question.

"Thank you for the dress." I lean closer, brushing our lips together with each word.

A large hand comes up to hold my cheek. "It looks beautiful on you."

"It'll look even better on your floor."

"Are you trying to kill me?"

My fingers walk up his suit jacket. "No. Just thinking maybe we could skip to the second part of the evening."

"Xavier spent the last week on the phone helping me get everything perfect. If we skipped it, he may quit on me."

I sigh. "Well, we can't have that. Then I'd see you even less."

"I'm all yours tonight," he promises. "Yours."

I smile at the conviction in his tone. I wish he could be all mine all the time. My hands curl in his lapels and pull him into a sweet kiss. Hopefully the first kiss of many tonight.

The hot-rod red shiny electric BMW slides in front of the Ledgewater Hotel in downtown Seattle. The valet attendant opens the passenger side door for me to exit and take in the stunning fireplace entrance to Eight Nine Ten Restaurant. I'm speechless. A pleased Ben takes my hand and guides me through the doors and into the dimmed light of the restaurant. Throughout the main dining area, the columns are made to look like trees, with branches cascading from them over the tables. The glass windows look out over the calm Puget

Sound, but not even that is what has my attention. The entire patio, of which we are headed, is empty. On a beautiful evening such as this, nobody in their right mind would eat inside.

"I reserved the patio so we could have our privacy. Only the best for you," Ben answers my unasked question.

Still stunned to speechlessness, I turn to Ben and kiss his cheek. I'm sure if I open my mouth, blubbering and whimpering will emerge.

"Welcome to Eight Nine Ten, my name is Jessica. I'll grab you both some water to start, but is there anything else I can get you?" an annoyingly breathtaking blonde woman asks once we sit at our table. It doesn't help that I know he likes blondes. Married a blonde. Still posts pictures with a blonde.

"I'll need a moment with your wine menu. Would you like anything, sweetheart?" Ben asks, oblivious.

"I'll join you in whatever wine you choose," I reply, trying not to shrink into myself. Ben went through a lot of trouble planning tonight, though I'm not sure of the occasion. I won't let my insecurities ruin it.

"I'll give you a moment." Jessica departs. Are her slacks super tight or is it just me?

"How would you feel if I ordered champagne? We are here to celebrate, after all." Ben extends his arm and takes my hand in his.

"I feel like I'm missing something." I smile. "What are we celebrating?"

"You. You're working so hard. I just wanted to have one night that's all about you."

My insides turn to goo once more. "That's so sweet, Ben. All of this is incredible."

"You deserve it."

"Still, I . . ."

"Have you decided what you'd like to drink?" Jessica asks,

popping up out of nowhere. Her entire body is turned toward Ben, as if I'm a ghost.

"The nicest bottle of champagne you have. We're celebrating," Ben replies, squeezing my hand. He's perfect, isn't he?

"I'll be right back," she says, all but fluttering her eyelashes as she leaves. The last time I checked, I was, in fact, corporeal. I'm not a figment of Ben's imagination.

"To you! For being an amazing maid of honor, a kick-ass woman, and for nailing your presentation in a few weeks! I can't wait to see all that you accomplish." Ben raises his glass. The bottle is chilling in an ice bucket close to the table as the sun sets to my right. Our glasses clink and we both sip the bubbly liquid. It's like I've eaten a bunch of popping candy. The bubbles explode on my tongue in a whirlwind.

"Thank you, Ben. If it's okay with you, I'm going to freshen up in the restroom. I'll be right back." I stand. Ben rushes to my side to finish pulling out my chair with a smile.

"I'll be here," he whispers, tucking a lock of hair behind my ear. With a gentle peck on the lips, I'm off to find a bathroom.

Ben's on his phone when I return. Not that I expected much different.

"Hey," I call as I sit, as he hasn't seemed to notice my arrival.

"Oh! Shit, hey." He practically drops his phone, placing it beside his plate on the table once he recovers from his fumble. "I ordered some crab cakes as an appetizer. Is that okay?"

"Yeah, that's great. I'm starving," I reply, taking up my menu.

His eyes snap to his phone once. *Buzz.* Twice. *Buzz buzz.* A third time.

"Is everything okay?" I ask after another *buzz.*

"Just work shit. . ." he trails off. *Buzz buzz.*

"Do you need to get that?" I ask. I don't want him to get it, obviously. I haven't seen him in forever. But what if it's serious? I don't want him to resent me for asking him to put me first above a work emergency.

"I . . ." *Buzz, buzz.* "Fuck. Five minutes, okay?"

"Oh, okay."

With a crooked dimpled smile, he snatches his phone and stalks off toward the other end of the patio. Who works on a Saturday night? Acquisition or not, people take breaks at some point. I mean, maybe not when you're the CEO of the largest digital streaming service in North America and Europe. Maybe you don't get weekends then. I nibble on a breadstick from the basket that must have been placed while I was in the restroom.

I turn my head to the setting sun and sigh, resting my face in my palm. The water is so clear and undisturbed. It's a mirror of the sky above it. Oranges, pinks, yellows, and purples swirling together in a perfect marriage. If only I could be so calm.

"I'm sorry! Someone threatened to leak the acquisition before we were ready to publicly announce it. It's a cluster-fuck." Ben collapses into his chair, startling me from my appreciation of the view.

"I understand," I reply. A successful man like this needs someone supportive, and I don't want to lose him.

"Let's just continue our evening." He takes a big gulp of his champagne. "Tell me what's going on with everything."

"Well, the project is going okay so far. I feel confident, but my boss, Mindy, is so hard to read. I can't tell if she's happy or annoyed half the time. And then Casey has been talking about catering for the wedding. She's thinking that we'll go try one of the places for my birthday dinner . . ."

"Your birthday's coming up? Darby, why didn't you mention it?" he interrupts, a kind smile belaying his words.

"Oh! I didn't think about it. It's in two weeks."

"We should do something fun with everyone. A party. Do you have Xavier's number? Either way, I'll send him yours and have him coordinate."

"Okay!" I'm practically wagging my tail like an overeager puppy. "Casey, Hannah, and Dad were all invited to the birthday dinner. I'm sure they'd be happy to see you again."

"I'll host something at the house for everyone. Get it catered and all that jazz. Let me shoot Xav an email while I'm thinking about it." He winks and scoops up his phone again.

That dreaded phone. It may be a little irrational to hate an inanimate object.

"Are you ready to order?" Jessica asks as she approaches, gaze fixed on Ben.

"Go ahead, sweetheart," Ben says, not looking up from his email.

"Um, I'll have the pork chops." I hand her my menu.

"Excellent choice," she snaps, snatching my menu away with her perfectly manicured nails. "And you, sir?"

Is she? Yep, she's using my menu to try and lift her boobs up. Not that they need the help.

"The scallops, please." He lifts his menu, eyes still glued to his phone. "Thanks."

"Perfect. Oh! Here are your crab cakes." She gestures to a male waiter who places the warm plate down between us. "Enjoy!"

***

He still hasn't looked up from his phone. It's been, like, ten minutes of me awkwardly eating this fucking crab cake and he *hasn't looked up*. What am I supposed to do? Call him out on it? Tell him to stop? Ignore him? Let him do what he needs to do? I sip my champagne. Am I overreacting? This is supposed to be a celebration dinner for me, right? I didn't fucking ask him to make me the focus. I would've been happy with a regular night in! He's the one who insisted we do some big date night to celebrate me.

Maybe I'm more like my mom than I thought. Am I really so self-centered that I need to have all eyes on me at all times? He has important business to take care of, much more important than me. The sun dips below the water, and we are now bathed in the light of the moon and the artificial lights of the restaurant.

Despite everything, it is beautiful.

"Let me take that for you." Jessica scoops up the empty plate in front of us. Hope he didn't want any. Because I ate. All. Of. It. And most of the bread.

"Thank you," he responds. Well, at least he's polite to wait staff.

"Thank you," I mumble as well. It's not her fault she's been flirting most of the night. He looks like, well, *him* and he's been on his phone the whole time. She probably thinks he's bored with me. We had sex . . . maybe he is bored of me now.

No! No, Darby, he isn't like that. God, all I want to do at this point is just retreat to my bed and hide under the covers with my stuffed beluga. Screw the main course.

"Are you still thinking about going for your MBA?" Ben asks, placing his phone back down. The moment it's gone I feel foolish for being upset. He gazes at me like I'm the only human being in the world. He's just busy. It's something I need to get used to.

"Well, I haven't applied anywhere yet." I smile. "But I have to admit that I've been looking into a few programs."

"Yeah?" He lights up. "Tell me everything."

Here we go. Darby and Ben back on track.

"I hope you enjoy your meal." Jessica tips her head as her

server places our main courses in front of us. With a thank you from both of us, she sashays away. Hips don't need to move *that* much, okay?

*Buzz, buzz.*

You've got to be kidding me.

*Buzz, buzz.*

Ben, don't do it.

*Buzz, buzz.*

Please, don't.

*BUZZ, BUZZ.*

"Shit," he whispers, eyes glued to the ringing phone.

"Go." I sigh. I don't have any other choice.

"Five minutes," he promises, snatching up the phone. "Jennings, what the fuck?" He walks back to his spot in the corner of the patio.

Guess it's back to a romantic dinner for one. I snap a picture of the pork chops for Casey and then dig in. Thankfully, it's one of the best things I've ever tasted. The silver lining of this date. The chops are soft and warm, melting like butter in my mouth. Despite how good they taste, I just want to go home. I turn my head and Ben is still on the phone, having a very animated conversation. It doesn't look like he'll be done any time soon.

***

I'm finished with my meal and his has long since gone cold by the time he returns. His face is scrunched up and he runs a hand through his hair. Does he realize how much time has passed? I have.

"Hey," he says as he sits down.

"Hi," I reply. I don't mean to come off snappish, but the wince I get in reply proves I didn't succeed.

"Would you like dessert?" he asks, a hopeful smile pulling at the corners of his mouth.

"No, I'm fine. I'm getting pretty cold, and I think I'm just ready to go when you are," I say as nicely as I can. This may be the first time I've ever said no to dessert.

"They're supposed to have an amazing lemon and ricotta cheesecake. We could get it to go?"

He's making an effort, I *know* he's making an effort. My entire body is screaming at me not to fuck this up. He's perfect and goddamnit, I love him. But, I . . .

"No thank you. I'm tired from work and everything, and I think I'm ready to just go home and get some sleep."

His face falls a bit. Fuck. "Okay, sweetheart."

I force a smile in response. So much for our perfect date.

We're quiet until we get in the car. Jessica even sends me a pitying smile as we leave. Jessica. The woman who was literally pushing her boobs into my boyfriend's face feels bad for me. What the fuck. I must be even more pathetic than I thought.

"Are you okay?" he asks as we drive through the lights of downtown Seattle.

He didn't just ask that.

"Yeah." I don't move my gaze from the window. Twenty minutes. Twenty minutes and I'll be home with my beluga and my feelings. I can get over this alone and then we never need to talk about it. He never needs to know how pathetic I am.

Despite not facing him, I can practically hear the wheels turning in his head. Please let it go, please let it go, please let it go.

"I fucked up, didn't I?"

So much for letting it go.

"It's fine," I insist. Let. It. Go.

"This night was supposed to be about you and . . . Was I on my phone too much? Can I make it up to you? Let me take you back to the house. We can watch a movie, spend some time together? I'll leave my phone in another room and I won't look at it until tomorrow. Please?"

An ache settles in the very center of my chest. Pushing it down forces my vision to blur as little tears form in my eyes. Why am I like this? He had to deal with work and my self-centered ass can't handle it. I have no idea if I'm right to be upset or not. I don't trust my own feelings and what the fuck is up with that.

I clear my throat. "Okay. Yeah, let's spend some time together."

His smile lights up the entire car. "Thank you, sweetheart. You won't regret it. I'll make you popcorn and candy. I got Xav to buy a bunch of stuff to refill my stash!"

A startled laugh escapes my lips. His hand comes up and strokes my cheek as I settle into the embrace. We can turn this around.

He doesn't need to know.

True to his word, Ben's phone is placed on the charger in the kitchen far away from us in the theater. In an attempt to make me gain forty-thousand pounds, Ben produces multiple bags of every single kind of candy that has ever existed.

"You made Xav shop for all this?" I laugh, looking at the pile strewn on the counter at the back of the theater.

"I mean, he never left his desk, so . . ." His fingers scratch through his stubble. "No? Someone else did?"

"You are ridiculous." I roll my eyes. To be so rich you don't even know who bought your candy. What a life.

"In a good way?" He smiles, inching toward me.

I pick up a box of chocolate raisins. "Yes, in a good way."

His grin grows as he envelops me in his arms, bending to bury himself in my hair. It's a stretch with his height, but he somehow manages it.

"You pick the movie," he insists, the sound muffled.

"You sure? I picked *Pride and Prejudice* last time," I remind him.

"Absolutely. I don't plan on watching anyway," he growls. The vibration of his chest against mine should not do unspeakable things to my sanity. But, to my credit, it's been about a week since I've seen this man, and I want to jump his bones. Remind him why he should stay with me. Why I'm worthy of his love. Of his time and attention.

"Yeah?" I whisper. "What do you plan on doing instead?"

His head lifts and he meets my gaze, staring right into my soul. "Celebrating."

Fuck. Me.

With a tilt of his head, he directs me to the remote. It's a silent command and there's no way in fuck I'm disobeying.

***

It's difficult to focus on any movie when the man you're head over heels in love with has insisted on keeping his head between your thighs for the length of the film. Without so much as a pillow for his knees, he sank down, yanked my dress up, and has been bathing me in attention ever since. I don't even want to think about how his jaw must feel right about now. Rough stubble rasping against my skin, a surprisingly nimble tongue drawing all sorts of moans and gasps from me . . . pleasurable torture.

"Fuck," I groan as he denies me pleasure once more. I've been on the edge for what seems like hours, and I swear I'm going to die. Why, oh why, did I try to watch *Pride and Prejudice* with him again? I couldn't have picked anything shorter?

"Need something?" He hums, eyes lifting to meet mine. My legs are draped over his shoulders, fingers clenched in the couch . . . Isn't it obvious?

"Please?" I squeak, the sound high pitched and whiny enough to make me wince.

"Such a good girl. I'll give you whatever you want, you just had to ask." He winks. I just had to . . . this fucker.

"You . . ." My protest dies in my throat as he returns to his ministrations. *I love you.*

## Brownies

"So, we, uh"—Dad clears his throat—"haven't talked about this boyfriend of yours."

It takes all of the strength in my body not to thunk my head against the table in front of me. No, Dad. This is Daddy-Daughter Sunday brunch at 7720. Do not want to talk to you about boys.

"We really don't have to." I smile. Where are my pancakes? If I stuff my face, then I don't have to answer any questions.

"He seemed nice," he continues as if I didn't say anything. "A little older than I would've liked. But nice all the same."

"I'm . . . glad?" Even Hawke finds this awkward. He is refusing to look at either of us. He rolls on his back, letting the late spring sun warm his belly.

"I'm just saying that I approve. Seems like a good guy. You don't have to act like I'm pulling your teeth out." He rolls his eyes with a smile.

I settle in my seat with a relieved exhale. "Thanks, Dad."

Our conversation is put on hold due to the arrival of a,

frankly exquisite, tower of chocolate chip pancakes. All for me. *Mmm.*

"So what would you like to do for dinner on your birthday? I was thinking maybe sushi?" Dad asks a little bit later, after the wafting scent of pancakes has dissipated from the air.

"Oh! Ben was talking about hosting a catered dinner at his house. Would that be okay?"

"Oh *really?*" Dad's smile turns sinister. Shit. "So he's serious enough about you to throw you a birthday party with all your family and friends?"

"It's not like he hasn't already met you," I grumble.

"But this is personal, kiddo." The joking tone disappears. "He's opening up his home to the people you care about to celebrate you."

I didn't think about it like that.

"I guess." I shrug.

"Does he . . ." Dad looks at his plate of eggs and toast. "Does he know about your mom?"

Ugh. "To an extent."

"You know whenever you're ready to talk about it that I'll be here, right? I know we've never really gone into it."

"I don't want to go into it. I'd prefer we just leave the past in the past, okay?" I force a smile before shoving too much pancake in my mouth.

"Okay, kiddo. Whatever you want."

He's too understanding. Sometimes I wish he would push, even if it didn't help. It feels like I'm constantly on the edge of a cliff, only I'm blindfolded, and I don't know where the ledge is. Backwards or forwards.

According to Xavier, the details of my party are a surprise, and I'm not allowed to know. So I'm forced into giving up cell phone numbers for my dad and Casey so they can all gang up on me.

"This group text is fucking fire." Casey cackles from the couch.

"Don't tease me, it's rude," I whine.

"Who taught Dad emojis?" she continues as Hannah giggles next to her.

"Who's even in this group text anyway?" I ask from where I have been shunned. I'm not allowed to come anywhere near the couch when "party business" is being discussed.

"Me, Casey, Xavier, your dad, and Ben. Although Ben doesn't reply much," Hannah supplies.

I snort. "At least it's not just my texts he never replies to."

"He's busy." Hannah smiles. "He almost never comes out of his office anymore. Poor Xavier's been running around like a chicken with his head cut off."

"Wait, I have a meme for that." Casey dives back into her phone. All her long limbs are wrapped around Hannah's tinier frame.

"Can I just have a clue about what is in store for me because I'm concerned?" I beg. Who knows what nonsense Casey is up to, especially if Ben isn't toning her down.

"You should be." Casey smirks, not looking up.

Hannah slaps Casey's calf. "Stop that! Darby, Ben and I would never let anything go wrong."

"True."

"I've been leashed," Casey promises. "They wouldn't let me get a bouncy house, though, so I mean . . . who's really missing out here?"

"Us! Who doesn't love bouncy houses?" I smile, reclining back in the chair.

"That's what I fucking said!" She snorts. "And they called it dumb."

"Do you actually want a bouncy house? Because we could . . .," Hannah says.

Casey and I burst out laughing at the pure look on her face. She's too good for us. We don't deserve her.

"I hate you both."

"Clarke!" Mindy screeches so loud I jump in my chair. Uh oh. I just sent her my newest draft of the presentation. There can be good screeching, right?

"Yes?" I school my features as I enter her office.

"This new draft is excellent," she praises. "You're doing a great job."

I just barely stamp down the excited squeal threatening to rip its way out of my throat. She's proud of me.

Calmly, Darby.

"Thank you, Mindy."

Nailed it.

"Johnson!" she yells, holding up one finger at me.

Wally Johnson, one of the other finance underlings, comes ambling into the office. He's all long limbs and angles that I'm sure he expected to outgrow as an adult. Not that I feel bad for his predicament, considering he's one of the men in Jason's group of man boys. I swear if I hear another "'sup" from their general direction I'm going to tear my hair out. Or their hair out. What would they put a disgusting amount of gel in then?

"Yeah, Mindy?" he asks, nodding in my direction.

"Get us some coffee. And not too much sugar!"

Am I no longer the coffee bitch? Am I no longer the *coffee bitch*? Fuck. Yes.

A full day of work combined with Mindy actually praising my work efforts. This calls for a huge brownie and sugary drink from Starbucks. Because consuming mountains of sugar before an evening run sounds like an amazing idea.

*Buzz, buzz.*

BEN

I know I've been terrible at responding to texts. Sending over a gift.

Is that an apology? I guess. Honestly, I don't need any more gifts. At this point it feels like I've gotten something new every other day. I shrug my shoulders and go for the coffee and brownie before going home.

ME

Thank you, but I don't need anything more. My apartment is full of gifts.

By the time I get in the elevator to go to my apartment, I still haven't received a response from Ben. Maybe he got offended? I don't want him to think I don't appreciate his efforts. I consider juggling the coffee and brownie to whip out my phone until someone calls my name.

"Hey!" Xavier is standing at my door.

"Oh! Gosh, how long have you been standing there?" My

cheeks heat. I should've gone straight home after Ben's text. Fuck.

"Not long. How are you?" He smiles, holding the door open for me once I turn the key.

"Good! Not that I'm not super glad to see you, but it's a bit of a surprise. What's going on?" I ask, putting my treats on the coffee table. They can wait a moment. Even if I can smell the chocolate from here. Yum.

"Ben sent me." He rolls his eyes. "Apparently he's decided that since he can't see you this weekend that you need a girl's day."

"With you?"

"I'm flattered. But no. I have to work too. For you and Casey and Hannah. He says, and I quote, go out with your girls and get some great food. Go see a movie and buy some outfits for your birthday party."

"I mean, that's sweet but—"

"It's on him." Xavier whips out the shiniest, thickest, heaviest looking black credit card I've ever seen. For a moment I just stare at it. I've only read about these things. I didn't think they were real.

"I can't accept that," I breathe.

"Honey, take the black card," he says, empty hand on his hip. "Not everyone has a boyfriend who can give them anything."

"I don't need anything!" I step back and run a hand through my hair.

"Listen." Xavier sits and pats the spot next to him on the couch. He waits until I join him to resume speaking. "Ben means well. He's a good guy. I wouldn't still be working for his workaholic ass if he wasn't. He's just . . . not always available."

"I'm starting to get that."

"I have to go. Ben needs me back at the office. But you can

text me anytime you want to check up on him. And if I ever think he's going too far, I'll have you come and get him, okay?"

A smile breaks on my face despite the lump that's formed in my throat. "Deal."

"Adios, love." He kisses my cheek. "And have fun."

*Fun.* I'm supposed to have fun with my rich boyfriend's credit card . . . minus the boyfriend. This just doesn't compute. Does he think I'm dating him because of his money? Why does he keep throwing presents at me like he's Santa Claus? I'm not a child. The black card still sits in my palm like a brand. If I use it, does it mean that he'll keep sending it to me? If I don't use it, will it offend him and make him think I don't appreciate his acts of kindness? I'm in over my head here. I need Casey to come home. I need a fucking voice of reason before I run myself ragged.

***

"He . . . llo?" Casey walks in to find me sprawled on the floor. The remnants of my brownie strewn across my face.

"Hey," I reply, unmoving.

"You, uh, want to talk about it?" She cautiously approaches.

"Yeah, I do," I reply.

"Save any brownie for me?" She sits beside me.

"How did you know about the brownie? Are you a brownie whisperer?"

She snorts. "Yeah, the brownie crumbs all over your cheeks tipped me off. So, any left?"

"Nope."

"We'll discuss your glaring lack of friendship and respect later. First, what's up?"

"I'm feeling . . . conflicted."

"About?"

"Ben."

Her eyebrows lift. "The perfect, sexy Daddy Ben? Do tell."

"I told you not to call him that," I whine. I would very much like to smother myself with a pillow right now.

"And I ignored you. Come on." She pokes my thigh. "Tell me what's up."

I sigh. "He's wonderful. He's so kind and thoughtful . . . when he's around."

"When he's around?" she repeats, shifting to get comfortable.

"When he's around. Which is becoming less and less. He's going through a ridiculously busy time at work right now, which I'm not allowed to talk about because of corporate secrets or something. But it seems like he's just never available. And when he is, he's on his phone."

"Huh."

"And I won't see him this weekend. Again. And to make up for it he sent his credit card and told me to *have fun?*"

She snorts again. "Nice."

"Am I crazy here or do I sound more like a prostitute than a girlfriend?"

"I mean, honestly? I think calling yourself a prostitute is a bit much. But throwing your credit card at someone is pretty bitchy." She shrugs. "I think you guys care about each other, but it's obvious you're not on the same page."

I turn my head to face her for the first time since she arrived. "I think that much is obvious. But you really think I'm overreacting?"

"I'm not going to lie, you've got major trust issues."

I roll my eyes. "Thanks."

"But, like I said, you two aren't on the same page. I think you're going to have to talk to him about it."

Talk? Like an adult? A loud groan escapes me.

"What?" She stands. "You asked for my opinion and I gave it."

"Remind me not to do that again." I smile. Regardless, I do feel better. Venting to Casey always helps.

"So are we going to use that credit card and go get some fancy-ass food? Or are you going to take a moral stance against it and eat the brownie crumbs from your face?"

That's the question.

"What do you think I should do?" I ask, despite telling her I wouldn't ask her opinion ever again not five seconds ago. Hypocrite.

"It's up to you. If you think he sent it from a good place, then let him treat you. If you think there's some creepy ulterior motive, then don't." She leans against the wall. "But let me know soon because I'm hungry as fuck."

"Ben's not an asshole. He's a good person, Casey, and I . . ." Whoop, not going to let the L word slip just yet. "I care about him. I need to trust that while he's not being awesome to me right now, he's not actively trying to be an asshole."

"Look at you! My baby is all grown up and trusting people." She fake sniffles.

"Shut up or I'm not bringing you with me."

"Consider me silenced."

The night sky is pierced by high rises from the rooftop bar in downtown Bellevue. Casey, Hannah, and I are huddled together on a black couch in the corner. From up here, the world seems a little less complicated.

"To kicking ass at work!" Hannah lifts the pinkest little cocktail I've ever seen in a toast.

"To getting married!" I smile, lifting my own drink.

"To us!" Casey finishes. We all take a nice long sip and allow the alcohol to fight off the barest chill.

"How is wedding planning coming? What do you need me to do?" I ask, relaxing back. Ben told me to have a fun night out with my girls, and I plan on enjoying it. No more fixating.

"You'll need to come dress shopping with each of us! We aren't allowed to see each other in our outfits until the big day," Hannah replies.

Casey rolls her eyes. "I don't understand why you're insisting on that. It's so archaic."

"It's tradition!" Hannah says.

"You're marrying a woman, babe. I think traditional is out." Casey snorts.

These two. "I think it's sweet. And I'll accompany you both on your separate trips."

"Thank you, Darby." Hannah pointedly stares at Casey. "For being so kind."

"Whatever makes you happy." Casey grins. "Happy wife, happy life, right?"

"Exactly." Hannah sits back and takes another sip.

"So what about other stuff? Venue, date, theme?" I dig further.

"I booked a little winery in Woodinville for six months from now. They had an unexpected cancellation and we decided to jump on it," Casey says.

"Six months!?" My mouth drops open. "Is that enough time?"

"Well, my maid of honor is a certified badass, so I'm banking on her doing most of the work." Casey winks.

"Thanks," I deadpan.

"Don't worry!" Hannah chirps. "I've had my wedding planned since I was six. It'll be a piece of wedding cake!"

"You're so fucking adorable." Casey sneaks a quick kiss from Hannah. "Like, honestly, you're the cutest thing I've ever seen."

"Stop." Hannah giggles.

"If you were anyone else, I'd gag." I smile into my drink. Strawberry alcohol burns my throat as I swallow. Are Ben and I that sweet when we're together?

"You love us," Casey replies, confident as ever.

"Meh." I shrug. "I'll love you if you let me go cake tasting with you."

"Actually!" Hannah's eyes light up. "That would be wonderful! I was thinking of having a small cake, and then doing a full dessert table. Cupcakes, cookies, candy . . . the whole shebang!"

"Are you sure you want to marry Casey, because I'm pretty sure I just fell in love with you."

"Mine!" Casey cackles, wrapping her arms tight around Hannah. "Get your own!"

"Working on it," I reply. I glance down at my phone. Zero texts. Fuck.

*∗*

"We should see a movie!" Hannah claps, bumping into Casey. Somehow, drunk Hannah is just as endearing as sober Hannah. Maybe even more so.

"Babe, it's eleven at night. They're all closed." Casey smiles at her. The arm around Hannah's waist tightens.

"Boooooooo!" Hannah cries. "Dumb!"

"Absolutely. So dumb," I agree, leading the way to the driver of our ride share.

"Do we have candy at your apartment? We should go there and watch a movie! CANDY!" Hannah continues, stumbling just a tad on her heels.

"Of course I have candy, babe. I live with Darby for fucks' sake." Casey smiles. We both help her into the car and share a passing grin as she keeps babbling. No one has any right to be this adorable. Maybe it's the fact that I'm buzzed.

"Darby!" Hannah yells once we're all settled.

I chuckle. "Yeah?"

"Do you miss Ben? I miss Casey when I don't see her for, like, an hour. And you haven't seen him in . . . a week? *Two?* Darby, that's like *forever.*"

"You're telling me," I reply, turning toward the window.

"You should call him and tell him you miss him and you want him to come over and eat candy with us!" She lights up as if she's thought of the greatest idea ever.

God, this is killing my buzz. I need more alcohol. "I don't think that's the best idea."

"It's girls' night, babe. He can join us another night." Casey swoops in for the rescue. God, I love her.

"Okay," Hannah agrees, laying her head on Casey's shoulder. Placated for now.

***

I don't remember who started the drinking game, but I've never been so drunk in my life. Drunk. Dr . . . unk. Funny word. The rules are, you take a shot whenever someone says "under baked", "soggy bottom", or "proof" on *The Great British Baking Show*. A double shot if Paul Holly-wood gives someone a handshake. He got me drunk as *fuck*. At least, the room has definitely been spinning for at least an hour.

"It's *stodgy*," Hannah mimics, giggling at the screen. "*Stodgy.*"

"What does that even mean?" I ask, throwing a piece of popcorn at Paul Hollywood's stupidly perfect blue eyes, which don't remind me of anyone.

"It's English slang. Means super heavy," Casey supplies. She's the only one who can hold her alcohol and it's rude.

"Stodgy," Hannah repeats. "Stodgy."

"Yes, baby, stodgy." Casey caresses Hannah's hair.

"Why isn't Ben here? You should call Ben!" Hannah's eyes find mine. Did she already suggest that? I don't remember. . .

"Yeah! I should!" I agree. Ben is good. Miss Ben. Ben. Where is phone? It's as if my hand is trying to push through thick pudding as I grab for the device.

"Oh this shit is going to be good. Put it on speaker phone," Casey insists, an evil smirk on her face. I glare at her as I fumble around with my phone. Why is this so difficult? Why are there two sets of screens in front of my face?

*Ring.* We all giggle as the call tries to connect. *Ring. Ring.*

"Sweetheart? It's after one in the morning, are you okay?" Ben's voice floods the apartment.

"Ben!" I cheer. "You're there! I'm here, but you're there!"

A chuckle is my response. "Yeah, sweetheart. Did you have some fun tonight?"

"Yeah, but not like I'd have with you. I miss you," I croon, laying down on the floor next to my phone.

"I miss you too, sweetheart." He sighs.

"Can you come over?"

"I can't. I'm still at the office. You get some rest tonight, drink some water, and I'll text you tomorrow, okay?"

"Will you really? Like *actually?*" I whine, rolling over onto my side.

"I promise. Are you alone? Are you in the apartment?"

"I'll take care of her," Casey pipes up. "She's got water in her system, and I've already got some pain killers prepped in the kitchen for the morning."

Ben releases an audible breath. "Thank you, Casey."

"He's not coming!" Hannah whisper-yells, getting on the floor and crawling over to me.

"I know. He never does," I reply.

"Bye, girls. I'll talk to you tomorrow, Darby. Sleep well."

***

*"You have the prettiest blonde hair," Mom coos as she rips the brush through my tresses. "Anyone would kill to have hair like this naturally."*

*"Mom, it hurts," I reply, fighting off tears.*

*"It's not my fault your hair is so tangled. I have to get them out. No one is going to appreciate this gorgeous hair if you don't take care of it."*

*"But shouldn't people like me for me?" I ask, meeting her disapproving gaze in the mirror.*

*"Your hair has more personality than you do." She pauses. "Kidding! But looking good is important. This hair will take you places."*

***

It wasn't too much after that when I bought my first box of black hair dye. It hasn't been blonde since.

Ugh, my head hurts. Why am I awake? Blearily, I rub my eyes and take in the bright sunshine. So it's daytime. Fabulous. I lift my phone, which has somehow become seven thousand pounds heavier. Noon. And one text from Ben. Memories flash in my head. Did I call him last night? I'll deal with that after coffee and pain meds. All the pain meds. But first, I must pee.

"Good morning, sunshine," Casey chirps as I stumble into the kitchen.

"Why?" I glare at her. "Why did you let me get so drunk?"

She shrugs, leaning her butt against the counter. "It was funny."

"I hate you."

"I have double chocolate chip pancakes on the stovetop, pumpkin spice coffee just brewed, and pain killers on the counter." She points. Her ability to buy, and horde, pumpkin spice coffee year-round is legendary. And appreciated.

"Oh my God, I love you."

"That's what I thought." She smirks.

I grab a plate and drag a large stack of pancakes onto it. "Where's Hannah?"

"Still asleep. She deserves to sleep it off a bit."

"So did I," I grumble, downing three pills in one gulp.

"You're the dumbass that got out of bed." She snorts. "How are you feeling?"

"I've felt worse. How are you? Chipper and unaffected as usual?"

"Yep! Did Ben text yet?"

"I was hoping that phone call was a dream." I rub my eyes. "I'm sure he is super impressed with me right now."

"He seemed more amused than anything, maybe a little worried. You were pretty cute, though."

"Ugh. Guess I should check the damage." I cringe, pulling my phone out. I open his text and brace myself.

I miss you too. Every day. Things will get easier soon, I promise. I hope you sleep well. Text me when you wake up so I know you're ok.

"Oh God," I breathe.

"What? Is he pissed or something?" She leans to peer over my shoulder.

"No. He's perfect and understanding, and I'm the worst girlfriend alive," I whine.

"You're so dramatic." She sighs, returning to her position.



I'm okay, just embarrassed! I'm sorry I drunk dialed you. I hope you got some rest last night, you were working late.

"So, anyway." I return my focus to the delicious pancakes. "Thanks for last night. I really needed that."

"Anytime. Watching you two drunk is pretty amusing." Casey smiles.

"Oh my God." Hannah groans as she shuffles into the kitchen. I've never seen her hair look quite like *that* before.

"Good morning, my love!" Casey bounces over, kissing Hannah's cheek.

"Did you attempt to wrap my hair?" Hannah lifts a brow.

"Yeah. I know how important it is to you, and you were so out of it. Did I do okay?" Casey asks. I've never seen Casey blush like this.

"I love you. You're sweeter than anyone I know. But please, *never* do it again." Hannah grins.

It takes five whole minutes for me to stop cackling.

# Raspberry Chocolate Cake

By some miracle, my birthday falls perfectly on a sunny Saturday.

THE MOM-STER

> Every year on your birthday I pray that you'll call me. I pray that you'll see how wrong you are and give our relationship a chance.

> I'm doing well. Your stepfather, who you've never even tried to meet, just got promoted. We're loving living in Virginia. It's such a beautiful state. You'd love it here.

> I don't know if you even get these messages. I wish you would call me.

Despite the barrage of birthday related messages from *her*, I refuse to linger on them. I'm spending the evening with my family, my friends, and the man I love. The man I love who I have not seen in weeks . . . nope. Not going there. It's my birthday and I refuse to wallow.

Casey's mouth is agape from the moment we drive through the gate, all the way until we reach Ben's home. She's speechless as we step out of the car and walk up the long driveway, my dad coming up behind us.

"Hey guys. Come on in!" Ben greets, swinging the front door open wide.

"Well f—" Casey breaks off before she can swear, eyeing my dad apologetically. "Wow. Wow, this place is ridiculous."

"Yeah." Ben scrubs his stubble. "This is home. Welcome!"

"May I offer you a drink?" A waiter approaches, several glasses of champagne on his tray. We each take a flute as Casey continues drooling. I don't blame her. I acted the same way when I first came here. The waiter retreats outside, where I assume the rest of the staff is waiting.

"Hi!" Xavier appears from the living room. He kisses Hannah and Casey on both cheeks before shaking Dad's hand. "And the woman of the hour! Happy birthday, Darby."

"Thanks, Xav." We quickly hug. "You haven't been waiting too long, I hope?"

"Oh, not at all! Just had to get here early to help with catering. You are going to love the food; it is to *die for*."

"I picked it," Casey says as we move through the home. "Pulled a few strings, promised a few favors . . ."

"Stop it, you!" Hannah giggles. "Just let her enjoy!"

Xavier lifts a brow at Ben, who nods his head just a touch. What is going on there?

"Who wants a tour?" Xavier chirps, already herding everyone but Ben and I further into the house. Their chattering gets further and further away until Ben's body visibly relaxes.

"Alone," he coos, scooping me into his arms. Suddenly, I'm at his height and being twirled around in a circle. "Fuck, I missed you."

You could've seen me . . . No, Darby, he's being sweet.

"I missed you."

"C'mere." His arms encourage me to wrap my legs around him and he swoops in for a kiss. I'm going to have stubble burn. I'm going to have bright-ass red stubble burn and I could not give less of a fuck. Not when he tastes like champagne and *Ben.* I'm deposited on some sort of surface, which I don't feel very inclined to check as it has allowed his hands to roam. Big, calloused fingers spread over every inch he can reach. One hand is all over my thigh, just barely underneath my dress, and the other is on my breast, squeezing. Must be closer. I push at the hem of his sweater trying to get it off. Off!

"Baby," he rasps, mouth moving to my neck. "We can't right now."

"Why? Now is good," I demand, going for the button of his slacks instead.

"Your family is around the fucking corner," he reminds me.

Right. *Right.* "I forgot they existed."

I forget about everything when you kiss me. I'm so head over fucking heels for you that the whole world melts away. And I want to tell you.

"Xav can only keep them occupied for so long. But tonight" —he pulls himself from my neck—"tonight you're all mine."

"Is that a promise?" I ask in the sexiest voice I can muster. It must do something because Ben's response is a groan and a hard kiss.

"The things you do to me."

"What do I do to you? Show me." I raise a brow.

He takes my wrist and very gently presses my palm against the thick length straining against his slacks. "How am I supposed to be around your family now?"

I shrug, ignoring the onslaught of nervous excitement that action produced.

"Not my fault."

"Absolutely your fault. Your. Fault."

"And this is the dining room!" Xav calls from another room in the house. Ah, so I'm sitting on the dining room table. Right. I should take the warning. With a helping hand from Ben I hop off the table and smooth out my dress. He readjusts himself in his pants and *how* does he make even that simple action mouth-watering? This is going to be a long night.

***

Miraculously no one knows about the interlude between me and Ben. Or, at least, no one has said anything and thank fuck for that.

"Keep your eyes closed!" Ben's hands are over my face, so it's not like I can see anyway. Casey is leading us all outside to enjoy dinner.

"Is it a bouncy house?" I joke to Casey's giggles.

"Told you," Casey snarks. "I told *all of you*."

"Okay, open!" Ben's hands fall and I blink open my eyes.

*Oh*. The backyard is lit up by the setting sun and about three thousand twinkly lights. They cover the table, the ground, and are strung up over our heads like stars. Two waiters hang back close to the house with drinks on their trays, chatting amongst themselves. The table itself is set up with mountains of sushi that make my stomach practically leap toward it of its own accord. They did all this for me? *He* did all this for me?

Maybe he loves me too. Maybe if I said it, he'd say it back.

"Oh my . . ." I turn toward the lawn and . . . wait. "Is that a *band?*"

There's maybe six of us here, we really don't need a band.

"Dancing!" Hannah supplies, clapping her hands. She is practically jumping with excitement.

"I can't believe you all did this for me. It's beautiful." I turn to my people. How did an absolute loser like me get so lucky?

"Anything for you, kiddo." Dad smiles. "Lisa is running a little late, but she said to start without her. She'll be here soon."

Right, Dad's girlfriend. Is it awful that I forgot she exists? "Are you sure? We can wait." I gaze longingly at the food.

"No waiting!" Casey insists. "We're digging in! And just wait until you see dessert!"

"Casey!" Ben admonishes, hand on my shoulder.

"Right, not saying anything else. Eat! Go! Drinks! Band start playing! Focus on something other than me!" Casey blathers.

"Keep your secrets, I just want that sushi." I smile. I'm being pulled in with invisible ropes. Must have sushi. Must eat all of it.

I have become a snake. With each sushi roll I practically unhinge my jaw and just engulf it in one bite. Ben has hardly touched his food, he's just staring at my mouth. I'm unsure if this is a good thing or not. Casey has said on more than one occasion that the way I eat sushi is inhuman.

"Ben, I hate to ask, but Lisa seems to be having a little trouble at the gate," Dad says not too long after we sit down.

"I'll go give them a call." Ben smiles. He squeezes my hand as he stands, and I do not watch his ass as he walks into the house. That man fills out a pair of slacks like nobody's business. The things I want to do to him right now. . .

"So, Ted, what is it that you do?" Xavier asks, taking a dainty sip from his glass. His fluffy brown curls are in full force, artfully styled as post-sex bed head. Either that, or he just had sex. I'd believe either.

"I'm an accountant at Carver's over in Tacoma," Dad replies. "I take credit for getting this one into math."

"Credit . . . blame . . ." I grin.

"Ugh, math!" Xavier squirms in his chair. "Just awful."

"Not good at it?" Casey smirks.

"I never said that, darling. I just said it's awful."

"Hi everyone!" Lisa walks up, kissing Dad on the cheek. "I'm so sorry I'm late. Happy birthday, Darby!"

"Thanks Lisa." I crane my neck to find Ben.

"Ben said he'd be along shortly. He got an important sounding phone call," Lisa explains as she sits.

Xavier catches my eye and sends me a reassuring smile. It's just one phone call. How long can that take?

***

Twenty-five minutes. Ben still hasn't returned after twenty-five minutes. My disappointment must be obvious as Casey hasn't stopped chattering at me. She talks a lot naturally, sure, but this is her "I'm concerned" level chatter.

Was it naive of me to think he would put down the phone today of all days? Am I being selfish for wanting him to just focus on me today? I'm so foolish. Here I was practically planning to tell him I love him, thinking this party meant something. And he chooses the phone yet again.

"I'll be right back," Xavier murmurs, rising from his seat and crossing the lawn. The sun has set completely now, the moon rising over our heads casting a cold glow on the evening.

"And then Chef Sandra said that I'm next in line for a promotion. I hope she wasn't just saying that to make me feel better, because I've been at the restaurant now for almost four years. And . . ." Casey is still chattering. I tune it out for now, having already heard about this conversation.

Thirty minutes. *Fuck.*

"I'm sorry!" Ben walks up with his hands in the air. "Phone is gone for the night and another business crisis has been averted."

"Good," I reply. A bit too firmly if the raised eyebrows I receive in reply are any indication.

"Do you want dessert, sweetheart?" Ben's hand comes up, thumb stroking my cheek. Yes, of course I want dessert. But what I really want is to know how you fucking feel about me.

"Okay," I agree, fingers wrapping around his wrist. No way am I letting him go get it. Nope. I've learned my lesson.

"Xav! Bring it out!" Ben calls into the house. Xavier walks in front of two waiters carrying a large tray. Xavier moves out of the way, just as they set it down before me.

"Oh my God." I practically drool all over the table.

Before me sits a masterpiece the likes of which I've never before seen in person. A hard chocolate shell, roughly the size of half a yoga ball, shines under the twinkling lights. Beside it is a marble gravy dish filled with steaming red sauce. The air smells of chocolate and raspberries.

"Is this a chocolate dome over a cake like they did on the *Great British Baking Show*?" I shriek as my senses return to me.

"Yep!" Casey claps once. "And you said you needed it."

"I did. It's true. I need it. Can I?" I reach for the sauce.

"Go for it." Ben chuckles.

With a trembling hand, I lift the gravy dish and pour it over the structure. The sauce melts the milk chocolate ball to reveal raspberries. There must be a hundred of them perfectly nestled on top of a thick single-layer chocolate cake. It is an exact replica of the raspberry chocolate cake on the title screen of the show.

"I hate all of you." I sniffle. Cool, I'm getting emotional over a fucking cake. I'm the worst.

"Love you too." Casey smiles, wrapping me up in a big hug.

"If Paul Hollywood comes out of that kitchen, I may faint," I say as I pull back.

"Well, he's old and pretty so he's definitely your type." Casey cackles.

Dad's face scrunches up so tight it's as if he sucked on a lemon.

"Fuck," Ben says under his breath, hand ruffling through his hair.

"I'm too old for this," Dad murmurs.

"Don't you dare," I snap as Casey opens her mouth. "Don't."

***

I have never, and I mean *never*, been this satisfied by food in my life. I may never walk again, but it's worth it. So, so very worth it.

"Having fun?" Casey asks. Ben, Dad, Lisa, and Hannah all went to look at Ben's car collection while I try to digest my feast. Xavier is flirting with the band. The entire band.

"Yeah. I'm pretty fucking lucky I have all of you in my life, honestly. I'm not sure how I got this lucky." I smile at her, laying my head on her shoulder.

"Because you deserve good things, dumb nuts. You're pretty amazing." She wraps an arm around my shoulder.

"No, you're the amazing one. Some of your amazingness just rubbed off on me by association."

"Duh." She snorts. "Honestly, though, Darby, you deserve good things."

I snuggle into her and ignore the comment. As lovely as this is, and how grateful I am, I've never felt more unsteady with Ben.

I shake my head and point, using the band warming up as a distraction. "Do you think Xav will go home with any of them?"

"By the looks of it, he may be going home with *all* of them." Casey chuckles. "Ah, to be young and single."

"Were you ever single? I feel like you and Hannah have been together for a decade."

"Six years isn't a decade, but no I never got to have that crazy single phase. We met when we were nineteen, for goodness' sake."

"Do you regret it at all?"

"Not even a second. Hannah is the best thing that has ever happened to me, and there's nothing in this world that would make me give her up."

The conviction of that statement stuns me into silence. Casey is very rarely so serious, but it's in these moments that I find myself closest to her. For a few seconds all that can be heard are guitar twangs and haphazard drumbeats.

"Your wedding is going to be beautiful." I sigh with a smile.

"Yeah, it is."

***

"Would you dance with me?" My eyes lift from where I was watching Casey, Hannah, and Xavier doing some sort of ridiculous three-person dance. The alcohol has been plenty this evening.

"Ben, I'm not even sure if I can stand," I reply, resting my hand upon my forehead for added measure.

"For me, sweetheart?" he asks, bowing at the waist. Well, damn.

"For you," I agree, taking his outstretched hand. He pulls

me straight up and into his arms, almost every single inch of our bodies pressed together. The space between our mouths suddenly seems so small as each breath he makes fans across my face. My fingers bunch up in the fabric of his sweater at his shoulders, digging in just a touch too rough. The action makes his grip on my waist tighten, my breath catching. He's going to kill me. Him and those perfect blue eyes of his. The music fades, the laughter and noise filtering down until all I can hear is each deep breath he takes.

In.

Out.

In.

Out.

The words dance on the tip of my tongue again, threatening to burst. *I love you.* I love everything about you. It's like I've loved you for my entire life.

"Ben, I . . ." My mouth opens.

"Kiddo! They're playing 'Hotel California'!" Dad calls, snapping me violently out of my trance.

"Coming!" I reply, smiling at Ben before I practically run away from him.

Oh my God. I'm not even sure how he feels about me, and I was about to spill my guts? Put a lid on it, Darby, or you'll lose him. That is, if he isn't already pulling away.

"Darby!" Xav catches me by the elbow right as I reach the group. "You are so good for Ben."

Well. Okay then. The alcohol has been flowing a bit more than I thought.

"Thank you, Xav."

"You really are. You're an absolute sweetheart." He smiles, giving my arm a squeeze.

"Is that why he still posts pictures of his ex on Instagram?"

Okay, so I'm feeling a little passive aggressive after that phone call.

Xav snorts, hiding his giggle behind his glass of wine. "Let's fix that, shall we?"

"Wait what—"

"Ben! Come here!"

Fuck.

"What's up?" Ben smiles as he approaches. Dimples and all.

"I'm going to need you to stop posting pictures of your ex-wife on your socials. You're going to give poor Darby the wrong idea," Xav says, pushing a strand of hair behind my ear.

At least the image of Ben's eyes bugging out of his face is amusing.

"I didn't . . . Did I?" Ben seems to mentally picture his Instagram as his finger scrolls through the air. "Oh fuck. That's just . . . That's nothing. It was when we went to Italy, and I loved the view of the hills in Florence in the background."

"Don't tell me! I'm not the one you're doing the nasty with!" Xavier twirls on his heel and heads back for the band.

"I didn't mean—" Ben starts.

"I know," I interrupt. "It's okay."

So, no, I didn't know. But it's enough, for now.

"We'll put our daddy-daughter day on break for tomorrow. You've had a big day; you deserve to sleep in," Dad says as he and Lisa gather up their things. They're the first to leave.

"You sure?" I ask.

"Yeah. Just relax. There's always next weekend." He smiles, going in for a big hug. My arms wrap around his waist, and I breathe in deep. Raspberry and chocolate. I blame the cake.

"Thanks for today, Dad. I love you."

"Don't mention it. Heck, Casey and Xavier did most of the work anyway. He and Ben are good people . . . work a bit too much, though."

"And you would know nothing about working too much, huh?" I eye him.

"I was guilty of it for ten years, kiddo. I know it when I see it." He winks. His smile falters. "Just . . . be careful. I've seen how working too hard can ruin a relationship."

That's not ominous at all. "I will, Dad."

"Congratulations again, kiddo. I am incredibly proud of you."

"Thanks. Drive safe, okay?"

"Always."

Dad says quick goodbyes to the rest of the group before leading Lisa out with an arm around her waist.

I'm still stuck on what my dad said. Every time Ben chooses the phone over me, I feel that much farther away from him. Is my dad right? Could this ruin us?

"You okay, sweetheart?" Ben asks, coming up behind me.

"Mm-hmm," I respond, squashing the thoughts in my head. I want to remember this night forever. "Let's dance."

Xavier is the last to leave. He suspiciously follows the band's van in his car all the way until they're out of sight. Ben closes the door for the night with an audible sigh.

He turns with a smile. "Did you have fun?"

"Mm-hmm." I nod, snuggling into his warm chest. "Best day ever."

He tangles one hand in my hair and then presses a kiss to the top of my head. "Good. You deserved it."

Ruin a relationship. Work can ruin a relationship. I've seen it *ruin a relationship.*

"Come with me," I whisper, grabbing his hand. Without a word I lead him up the stairs, down the long hallway, and through the double doors into his bedroom. Ben's head is cocked in confusion like a puppy, but he doesn't fight me as I push him to lay down on his bed.

"Are there more pillows?" he asks, twisting his neck to look behind him.

"Shhhh," I scold him, sitting on his lap. If he keeps talking I'm going to lose all this false confidence I've built up. His gaze snaps back to me as I run a hand down his chest and tangle it in the waistband of his pants. A pair of ocean blue eyes are glued to each movement of my fingers as I unbutton him and then slide down the zipper. I lift to pull his pants down to his shins before hopping off the bed to remove them the rest of the way, along with his shoes and socks.

My hands instantly find his powerful thighs. This man before me is so beautiful, so sexy, and I will do everything I can to keep him.

I've decided.

I will suffer through unending phone calls, numerous emails—whatever I need to. He'll know exactly what he has to come home to. I may not be confident enough to tell him how I feel, but I can push through this. I don't want to lose him.

My fingers dance up his sides and underneath his sweater, bunching it up until he sits up to pull it off. The motion seems to break him out of his trance as he starts reaching for me, for the zipper on my dress.

"No." My hand in the middle of his chest pushes him back down. "Let me?"

He falls back, crossing his arms behind his head. "What're you up to?"

"Saying thank you." I smile.

"Darby, you don't—"

"Let. Me." I stand again, undoing my dress myself. The fabric slides to the ground with a soft whoosh and I'm left in my bra and panties. With one more movement his boxer briefs are gone and he lies naked before me. Very slowly I climb back onto his lap, allowing his hands to slide onto my thighs.

"I want you to vocalize. Can you do that for me?" I ask, pressing fleeting kisses onto his chest and stomach.

"*Fuck, baby,*" he breathes. "Whatever you want."

"Thank you," I reply, inwardly cringing. Thank you? Jesus, Darby, get a fucking hold of yourself. "I want you to tell me what you like, how you like it, and if I'm doing something right." Because I have no idea what I'm doing.

I press more kisses onto his abs and make my way lower. His cock is half-hard and warm as I press one kiss to the tip. It's just a blowjob . . . how hard can it be? I trail the tip of my tongue up the side as he takes a shuddering breath.

"You, uh . . ." His voice is shaky, but still strong. "You know you don't have to, right?"

"I want to." I want to keep you, I want you to love me, I want us.

"*Baby,*" he groans minutes later, the hand tangled in my hair tugging up until I pull off his cock with an audible pop.

"Is everything okay?" I ask, trying so hard to hide my nerves. I've never done this before and I hope it's not obvious.

He huffs a laugh. "More than. Jesus, yeah. C'mere." He guides me to sit astride him again, sitting up himself. "That's not how I want the night to end."

*Oh.* "How did you want it to end?" There are the nerves. I knew they'd surface eventually. The fuckers.

"How about I show you?" He arches an eyebrow.

Give up control? Yes, please. "Okay."

"Let me take care of you," he murmurs, hands now unrestrained in their movement across my skin. "Let me thank *you*."

"I—"

"Shhh." He smiles. "Not your turn."

He pulls me in for a deep kiss and I twist my fingers into the few gray hairs at his temples. My favorite. Gentle fingers unhook my bra and rip my underwear off. Apparently his patience is gone for the evening. He lifts my bottom and lines himself up, sliding me down. The pain from the first time is all but gone, just an aching stretch left now as I settle fully on his lap once more.

"You're beautiful," he says. "More than I could ever deserve."

"N-no." I shake my head.

He kisses the very tip of my nose. "Yes, baby. Let me show you."

# Cinnamon Buns

"*Mama!*" *I run into the house, all flailing limbs and joy.* "*Mama!*"

"*What?*" *my mother asks, coming into the kitchen. She's been looking through recipes in her big recipe book.*

"*I got an A- on my spelling test!*" *I reply, slapping the piece of paper down on the countertop. Now. Now she'll be proud of me. An A. She must be proud.*

"*Oh. That's good, honey,*" *she replies, looking it over.* "*Could've been an A+, though, couldn't it?*" *With one more smile, she heads back into the living room to her book.*

*It's like the floor has been ripped out from underneath me. At ten years old I realize that maybe, just maybe, I'll never be enough for her. She'll never be proud of me. No matter what I do.*

*The paper floats to the ground.*

***

Done! I narrowed down my choices for an MBA program

to three, and before my date with Casey at the dress shop. I am a powerhouse today! I am radiant! Okay, maybe not radiant, but at the very least I am productive as fuck. And that deserves homemade cinnamon buns.

"No!" Casey yelps the moment I step out of my room. "You aren't allowed out of there until you've finished doing whatever you told me to make you finish!"

Ugh, I love this buffoon. "I did finish. I narrowed down the programs."

"You're not just lying to get at this deliciousness?" She cocks a brow.

"I did my job, now give me the goods," I demand, walking into the kitchen.

Casey is wearing a "fuck me I'm Irish" apron and has frosting stuck to her strawberry blonde locks. The entire room smells like cinnamon and sugar and I just want to wrap myself up in it. Eating the treats will have to do.

"Okay, I'll believe you for now. You may have some of this Paul Hollywood-worthy perfection."

"Thank *God*!" There they sit, all stuck together and frosted like little perfect bites of heaven.

"My Chelsea buns." Casey bows.

I stare at her for five whole seconds and then stick out my hand to shake hers.

"I got a handshake!" She cackles, running around the room.

"I'm surprised we aren't single." I smile, tearing away my first bun. My first of many hopefully. Because the best decision is to get hyped up on sugar before dress shopping.

THE MOM-STER

I heard Casey is getting married. You must be
so excited. Call me.

*A*h, yes. The "I know what's going on in your life because I care" text. Her way of pretending she's a good mom while simultaneously trying to make me feel guilty for ignoring her. Is it acceptable to throw your phone at the wall in public? I'm guessing it's frowned upon.

"Everything is ruffly!" Casey exclaims, emerging from a sea of wedding dresses. "I feel like I'm in a potato chip commercial."

I wrinkle my nose at her. "That was a stretch, even for you. Should've gone with a frosting joke."

"I feel like we've been doing far too many baking references. It's becoming our brand."

"It's always been our brand, dummy." I flick through the gowns before me. "Look, this one isn't too intense."

Casey slides up beside me to get a look. The dress is pure satin from head to toe with a high-neck, cross-back detailing. It seems to be floor length.

"This could work." She nods, pulling it off the rack. "It's not too crazy, but still . . ."

"Elegant?" our sales assistant, Chloe, supplies. She has been flitting around the room like a fairy, pulling dresses to put in Casey's room.

"Uh-huh," Casey agrees, rolling her eyes once Chloe's back is turned.

Chloe takes the dress and allows us to peruse the shop a bit more. Nothing else seems to catch Casey's eye or adhere to her set rules. No lace, no crochet, no tulle, no glitter, no feathers.

"Alright," she breathes, staring down the dressing room door. "I'm going in."

"I'll be here, dork." I giggle. Chloe leads me to the room of mirrors and a long white couch.

"Champagne? Water?" she asks once I sit. Well, fuck.

"Uh, water please," I reply. It is far too early in the day for booze.

"I look like a feathery goose!" Casey shrieks from behind closed doors.

Maybe it's not too early for booze after all. My eyes trail along the dresses on the wall. I can't lie to myself and say I haven't picked out a few favorites. My heart aches just a little at the thought of walking down the aisle to Ben. It won't happen, but *God* do I want it. I want it more than anything.

Casey is refusing to come out for the first few dresses, so I'm stuck staring at my phone. More specifically at the text from my mother that I haven't deleted yet because it seems I like pain. It's not like Casey's engagement is a secret or anything, but I wonder sometimes who she talks to. Who she gets her information from. If she knows about Ben . . . Nah, if she knew about Ben she'd show up at my door. There's no way she'd let that kind of money go without trying to get a piece of it. Because that's all people are to her. Tools to exploit. Fuck. I'm deleting this shit. No more torturing myself.

It doesn't help that I haven't seen Ben in two weeks. Two weeks since my birthday party and I have barely anything to show for it. Four text messages and another offer of his black card, to be exact. At least he asked this time and didn't send Xavier to my apartment to assault me with it again. Is it too late to ask for that champagne?

"Okay, I'm coming out!" Casey announces.

Right. Need to be here for Casey and her big moment. Cannot wallow in my own shit.

"I thought you already came out when you got caught making out with Chrissy Sanchez under the bleachers!" I reply.

"You're just jealous I got some ass in high school!" She chuckles, stepping into the room. She's wearing the dress I picked for her. The skirt is slim but doesn't stick to her form as it slides across the wood floor. The sleeveless top shows off her arms and comes up to just the bottom of her neck.

It's *perfect*.

I'm suddenly bombarded with memories of us playing in the grass as kids, learning to drive together with my dad, obsessing over college, and staying up all night the day she met Hannah. My best friend, my *sister*, is getting married!

"Oh my God. Stop!" Casey stomps her foot.

"What?" I sniffle, reaching for a tissue from the strategically placed box next to me. Chloe must have a sixth sense for the weepy ones.

"You're not allowed to cry! You promised!"

I wipe my eyes with a fresh tissue. "I promised no such thing. You should just be happy Dad didn't come; he would've been blubbering from the moment we got here."

She nods. "Facts. But that doesn't mean you're allowed to make up for it by making me cry!"

"Shut up and twirl for me," I whimper. I'm in no position to stop crying now. It's happening.

She rolls her eyes but does as asked. The back of the dress has a cross-back, her skin peeking out in certain areas.

"So?"

"Your ass looks so cute," I sob.

"Goddamnit, Darby."

Fifteen minutes and twenty-two tissues later, Casey makes an announcement. "This is the winner."

"Well, you only let me see this one, but I agree. You do look stunning." I smile. "Does it feel right?"

She wiggles a little. "Yeah. It does. It feels like the one."

"Shall we try it with the veil?" Chloe asks from the corner. She's done a beautiful job replenishing my tissue supply.

"A veil?" Casey turns to me. "Do I have to?"

"I mean, you don't *have* to. But what's the harm in trying it? If you don't like it, don't buy it. You only get married once," I reply.

"Alright, alright. Veil me," she concedes, situating herself in the middle of the mirrors.

Chloe brings up a shorter veil with small diamonds along the edge. There's no lace, no frills, and no feathers. Casey should be pleased. Without further ado, Chloe places the veil on Casey's head, securing it in the back with a bobby pin.

"*Oh*," Casey breathes, gazing at her reflection.

"You look perfect, Case," I whisper, a few lingering tears slipping down my cheeks.

"I'm getting married," she whispers back, her own eyes threatening to overflow.

I rise, crossing the room to her.

"You are." I wrap her up in my arms. "I love you."

"I love you too."

*N*ever before has a salad tasted so good. This is because salad is usually disgusting.

"How do you make lettuce taste like . . . not lettuce?" I ask.

I'm sitting on a little chair next to the counter in Casey's kitchen at work.

"Salt." Casey chuckles. "So much fucking salt. You should see a doctor."

Huh. Salt.

I nod. "Worth it."

"So why did you follow me to work anyway? Shouldn't you be whisked away on a private jet to Paris for dinner or some shit? Daddy Ben slacking?" she continues, preparing some sort of soup. The pot is so big I'm certain Casey could never pick it up on her own. In fact, I think I could hide inside it.

"He, uh, he hasn't texted today. The acquisition, y'know?" I smile.

"Do we even know what he's acquiring? This has taken like seventy years."

"No, I'm not allowed to know. Corporate secrets and all that."

"Maybe you should just call him? Take initiative! Stop waiting for that workaholic to put you first. Make it happen!" she yells. All seven people in the kitchen turn to us. Luckily they're used to her and return to work.

"You're right?" I chew on a bit of tomato. Maybe she's right? Maybe? One phone call isn't too annoying.

She snorts. "Of course I'm right."

Well, now she's staring at me, so I pull out my phone.

"Is it ringing?" she continues, staring me down. Can someone menacingly stir soup because it's happening.

"Darby?" Ben answers.

"Hey! I, uh . . ." Darby, you've been dating this man for months. Stop acting nervous. "I missed you and I just wanted to say hi. See how you are."

"I miss you, too, sweetheart. Unfortunately, I can't talk

right now. My sister showed up at the office unexpectedly and I'm stuck at home with her. Can I text you tomorrow?"

"Oh, um, yeah. Sure."

"Thank you! I'll talk to you tomorrow."

I stare at my phone for a few moments in pure shock after hanging up.

"Well?" Casey prompts, still aggressively stirring. It smells like tomatoes.

"He's home with his sister," I reply.

"Okay, wait a minute." She turns to me. "This guy who hasn't seen you in two weeks is at home? Presumably just hanging out with his sister? And he didn't invite you? And he's met your entire family and friend group? He didn't even offer a fifteen-minute meetup?"

"Maybe she's going through something. Do you want to meet your brother's new girlfriend in the middle of a crisis?"

She shrugs, turning back to her soup. "Maybe. But doesn't she live in the area? Seems weird he hasn't mentioned you meeting her at all."

"I don't know where she lives," I admit, eyes focused on my salad.

"Listen, I don't mean to pry . . ."

I glare at her.

"Okay, so I do mean to pry. But it's because I love you. You need to stand up for what you want. I know conflict is your worst nemesis, but no one is going to stick up for you in your relationship. You have to be able to communicate your needs, or he'll unknowingly bulldoze right over you."

Fuck. "Sometimes you hit the nail on the head a little too hard."

I ignore the seven heads that bob in agreement.

One more program eliminated, so I'm down to two. With how well things are going at work, I may not even need the MBA. But it's good to be prepared. Although now I have nothing to distract myself with.

Why are there no baked goods in this house? I really wish I didn't give the rest of the buns to Hannah. That's my own damn fault. Starbucks is still open, but that would require I put on real pants. And I have no interest in putting on real pants. Maybe Paul Hollywood will cheer me up. I meander out of my bedroom and flop on the couch. Ugh.

*Ring, ring.*

"This is the sultan of swing, how may I help you?" I answer without looking.

Ben's chuckle floats through the phone. "You're adorable."

"Ben!" I leap up.

"Hey, sweetheart. I felt bad about hanging up so quick earlier. How are you?"

Am I purring? "Better now. How are you? Is your sister okay?"

"What? Oh, no, she's fine. She just shows up sometimes. I'm sure I mentioned that."

Yeah, you did. But I was kind of hoping she was having an emergency and that's why you didn't invite me over to meet her. Work with me here!

"Uh-huh. Well, I'm glad she got you out of the office."

"She dragged me, sweetheart. It was awful. She's tough to deal with, just be glad you didn't have to." He sighs.

"I wouldn't have minded," I reply.

"Anyway. I'm out of the office, and she is, and I quote, getting fucked up out at some club before going back home to Bainbridge Island. So I was wondering if you may be free? I could order some takeout and we can snuggle up in the theater at my place?" Oh cool, she lives a ferry ride away. Nope. Burying that disappointment.

"Yeah! I'll be right over!" I jump off the couch. Seems I will be putting on real pants tonight, but it's worth it.

"And that's Prue. She's the other judge, and much sweeter than Paul on the surface. But they're both very fair and no nonsense in their judging," I explain, shoving another handful of popcorn in my mouth.

"Why is it called *The Great British Baking Show* in the United States and *The Great British Bake Off* everywhere else?" Ben asks, absentmindedly rubbing my shoulder with his thumb.

"Something about licensing." I shrug. "It is what it is."

"Hmm. And why is everyone so obsessed with Paul Hollywood?"

"I don't think most people are. I'm pretty sure I'm just strange." I smile.

He shrugs and snuggles deeper into the couch. This. This boring little moment of domesticity is all I've ever wanted. To be with someone vegging out and relaxing. Just *being*. I curl tighter into his side, each tightly wound muscle turning to goo with each passing moment.

"*Ben! Bennnnnnnn! Benjamin Alexander James!*" a slurred

female voice calls from the hallway. "Benny Ben, where are you?"

"Fuck, I thought she was going to go home tonight." Ben leaps up, jostling me in the process, and walks toward the door; however, it bursts open before he can reach it.

Inside the doorway stands Ben's sister, there's no doubt about it. From the long brown hair to the blue eyes and the dimpled smile . . . it's obvious.

"Benny!" Her eyes are glassy as she wobbles into the room. "I didn't know you had a girlfriend!"

A giant stone falls into my belly. Not only did he have no intention of introducing me to her, but he didn't even tell her I exist? After *months* of dating? Jesus Christ.

Ben is frozen. There's no other way to describe it. It's as if his brain has completely turned off and there's no hope of him coming back online. His sister's eyes keep darting back and forth between Ben and me as each second ticks by.

Come on, Ben . . . say something. Tell her that yes, you have a girlfriend and yes, she's right here. Introduce me. Introduce her. Do something!

The silence is deafening. Nothing is happening, and he couldn't look more panicked.

Fuck it.

"I'll, um, let you guys talk," I say, fighting the prickling sting in my eyes and standing from the couch.

"Well, this is fucking awkward," his sister remarks, crashing into the wall as she makes room for me to leave.

"Shit, wait Darby!" Ben reanimates. A few moments too late for me to actually listen. I keep moving and make it all the way to the front door before he catches me.

"Sweetheart, I'm sorry. I just . . . My brain short circuited. Chelsea can be a lot," he rambles.

I open my mouth, but no words come. I'm speechless.

Am I so unimportant that the mere idea of introducing me to his sister never even crossed his mind? Am I so much of a throwaway that I'm not worth this interaction? I shut my mouth and turn back to the door. I need to get out of here. Now.

"Please don't leave," he whispers, grasping my hand in a gentle hold. "Let me explain."

My vision is blurring the longer I stand here staring at his front door. No. No, I will not cry in front of him. I refuse. I shake my head and open the door. My fingers slip through his.

"Sweetheart!"

Of course he's following me outside. He couldn't possibly let me leave with whatever dignity I have left. Nope. He wants to see tears and screaming and whatever else is threatening to escape me.

"I didn't mean for this to happen. I was planning on calling Chelsea when she woke up tomorrow and I was going to invite her for lunch on Saturday. It was going to be planned and not when she was drunk or in the middle of whatever work drama she's sucked up in this week. I promise!" He keeps following. Why does he have such a long-ass driveway? Fucking rich people.

"You can ask Xavier! I had him put it on my calendar!"

That does it. "Why does Xavier know more about your plans for our relationship than I do?" I whip to face him. I have no idea how this man feels about me and, yet, Xavier does? Really?

He's not two feet in front of me now, but I have never felt more distant.

His face falls. "That's not . . . he doesn't . . ."

"I'm . . ." Is there even a word for what I am? "I'm not able to discuss this rationally right now."

"Yell at me. Hit me. Do whatever you need, whatever you

want. Just don't leave." He reaches for me but stops just before making contact. "I don't want you to leave."

"I didn't want to be humiliated like that," I whisper, the tears falling. "We don't always get what we want."

"I never meant to embarrass you, I never meant to hurt you. You are the most important thing in the world to me." His thumb brushes away the fresh tears on my cheek.

"Doesn't feel like it," I mumble, sniffling.

"Come inside. I'll introduce you to Chelsea, even though she's probably passed out by now, and I'll make this up to you."

I break eye contact to gaze at my car. It'd be so easy to leave. But if I did, I don't know if I'd ever be able to come back. "I don't know."

A breeze whips past us, ruffling the leaves on the trees overhead as I turn back to him. The clouds break allowing the moon to shine on his face. His broken, anguished face.

"Please?"

"Okay."

Chelsea is passed out, just as Ben had guessed. Thank God. I'm not sure I'll ever be able to face her, let alone right now. Ben leads me upstairs and into his room, sitting us down together on his massive bed. I've managed to sneak twelve pillows onto the bed since we've started seeing each other, and I have another two in my car.

"Explain," I say. I'm still halfway to running home.

He sighs, scrubbing a hand over his face. "I didn't mean for this to happen. I was . . . I just . . . *fuck*."

Every bone in my body is screaming that I'm not good enough. That he didn't want me in his life like this because I'm disposable. That if he introduced me to his sister I would be harder to get rid of. And it makes me want to run.

"It's hard for me to explain. I don't let a lot of people into my life. It's not something I'm good at."

I hold his gaze, willing him to give me something. Some kind of hope that he cares.

"I haven't introduced anyone to Chelsea since Jennifer. Listen, I planned to do it this weekend. I never meant to push it this far. But with everything going on, it just got away from me."

"Oh," I murmur. I don't know if this is enough. I don't know.

"It was never about you. Do you understand?" he asks, meeting my eye.

No. No, I don't, but the thought of losing him is too much for me to bear.

"I guess."

"Do you forgive me?" His fingers wind through mine, squeezing.

"Okay." I nod.

Despite forgiving Ben, I can't shake the tension rolling off me in waves. I'm unable to get comfortable; I just keep squirming.

"Do you want to take a bath? Relax a bit? Maybe I could order some cake while you rest?" Ben follows me around the house as I pace like a kicked puppy.

"Ben, it's past midnight. Where would you find cake?" I try to joke.

It falls flat.

"If you want cake, I will find you cake. I don't care what time it is," he replies, eyes glinting.

He's trying. It's obvious that he's trying.

"I'm not going to have you annoying the entire city in the middle of the night for cake." I roll my eyes.

"What *can* I do?" he begs.

"You can relax." You can leave me alone for five seconds.

"Just breathe. And if you really want to, yes, you can draw me a bath."

"Awesome! I'll do that!" He rushes to the bathroom, giving me some peace.

What a night. And the cherry on top will be breakfast tomorrow with his hungover sister. Maybe I should send him out for cake.

"Huh, I thought you were a drunken mirage," Chelsea announces, waltzing into the kitchen in the morning. The sun is high in the sky and Ben's personal chef has bacon, eggs, and toast sizzling. Butter wafts in the air.

"Chelsea." Ben's voice booms across the room. Even the bacon stops sizzling for a moment.

"What?" She winces. "I was just making a joke." She heads straight for the coffee pot.

Why did I ever think this would be awkward? Ha . . . God, someone just kill me now. Put me out of my misery.

"You—" Ben starts.

"It's okay," I whisper, stopping him with a hand on his arm. "It's okay."

He clears his throat. "Right. Well, Chelsea I have someone I'd like to introduce to you."

"Is it the chef?" she snarks with a wink at me.

"Surprisingly, no." He glares. "This is Darby, my girlfriend. Darby, this is my sister Chelsea."

"Hi." I smile. If the Earth could just swallow me whole, that would be great.

"Hi! I was wondering when he'd introduce you. I've known about you for a while now." She sits at the island with us, right next to me.

"I thought last night you said you didn't know?" I ask.

"Oh no, I knew. I was just pretending so Ben wouldn't feel bad about not telling me himself." She takes a large sip of her coffee. "Xav spilled the beans while planning your birthday party. He wouldn't give me any details though or else I would've made a spectacular entrance."

Thank God for small miracles. This is awkward enough without this happening in the middle of my party. I can't imagine Casey being here too.

"Remind me to fire him," Ben grumbles into his coffee.

"You wouldn't survive an hour without him. The only reason he even mentioned it is because he thought I'd been invited. You fucking stepped in it this time." She leans closer. "I know he fucked up. But he probably has a good reason. He's the good sibling after all."

"Oh my God." Ben shudders.

Okay, so maybe he wasn't exaggerating when he said she was a lot. She's like Casey . . . if Casey were even more aggressive. Which, yeah, I did not think was possible.

"Anyway." She relaxes back in her chair. "Tell me everything about you. I want all the sordid details and *don't* skip anything. I plan on stalking your socials later, so I'll find out either way."

"Or you could go to work," Ben interjects.

"I don't start for another two hours, Ben. The beauty of afternoon shifts." She smiles. If people had venom, it would be dripping from her teeth.

"Doesn't it take at least that long to get home on the ferry?" he snaps.

"It's fine. There's not much to tell," I say before they can get into some sort of snapping match. "I work in finance."

She winces. "Ew. Math. I bet you guys stay up all night talking about business and numbers."

"What can I say? It's what gets me off." I shrug.

She snorts into her coffee. "Nice. Okay, I'll back off. For now." She stands and grabs a piece of bacon off the freshly placed plate. "I'll be following you on all social media by the end of the day. We'll talk."

With that, she blows Ben a kiss and stalks out of the room.

"Still like me?" Ben asks, shoveling food onto his plate.

Do you still like me?

"Yes, I still like you."

"Thank God."

## Apple Fritters

"We need to talk."

Nothing good ever comes from that statement. I lift my eyes from my laptop to Casey standing over me.

"Okay?" I put my laptop on the coffee table and pause my show as she joins me on the couch.

"So you know how Hannah and I are getting married in a few months?" She picks at her nails.

"No!" I exclaim, pressing my hand to my chest. "You're getting married?"

She glares at me until my smile falls.

"Case, talk to me. What's up?"

"Hannah and I have been talking about our living situation. Her place is cute, but it's a studio, and the kitchen is non-existent."

Oh.

"I didn't think we'd keep living together once you got married. You and Hannah will be newlyweds. You won't want your spinster best friend hanging around. Did you guys decide you want this place?"

"You're not a spinster! And no. Hannah and I want to start looking for a home to buy. The market out here is fucking bananas, though, and if we find something we love we'd need to move on it immediately. Is . . . is that okay? I won't leave you high and dry! I'll pay a bit of rent or something until you figure things out."

I place a reassuring hand on her knee. "I'm proud of you guys. I'm *happy* for you two. Do what's best for you. I'll figure out my end. If I have to live with my dad for a few months and look for a smaller place, it's no big deal."

"Are you sure?" She meets my gaze. "I don't want to leave you hanging."

"I'm good. Now go scroll some real estate website before I get mushy and make you snuggle."

"Eek!" She squeals, leaping up and running to her room. "Not snuggles!"

I snicker at her retreating form. I'm the first to admit I'm not the best at change, and this is *change*. Casey and I have lived together since we were eighteen, have done everything together. All our major milestones were accomplished together. It's weird that she's going off to live a life that will be entirely her own. It's for the best, and I didn't lie when I said I'm happy for her. But what if we grow apart? I can't make new friends. I suck at it.

No. I shake my head and pick up my abandoned laptop. Casey and I will be sisters forever. No matter what. Fuck, I need to plan this bitch's bachelorette party.

***

Halfway through planning a bachelorette party to kill time before my date with Ben—finally!—there's a knock on my door. Let it be known that my door was never knocked on before I started dating Ben. This is the twenty-first century, we are supposed to be past this behavior.

I open the door to see a delivery woman with rosy cheeks of exertion.

"Darby Clarke?" the woman asks.

"Yes."

"Who is it?" Casey screeches from her room.

"You'd know if you got off your butt and walked ten feet!" I call back. I turn back to the woman with a guilty smile.

"I have a package for you; please sign." She produces a clipboard for me. As I take it from her, she walks a few feet out of view and returns with a dolly filled with boxes.

"I, uh—" I chuckle. "Thought it was *a* package. Not *many* packages."

She doesn't respond, just pushes the dolly into my apartment. After unloading the five—*five*—boxes, she snatches the clipboard and leaves without even a goodbye.

"Thank you!" I call after her anyway.

"Daddy Ben has struck again!" Casey cackles, pleased with herself.

"How long did it take you to come up with that one?" I reply, fetching the scissors from the kitchen drawer.

"Not as long as you may think, but longer than I'm proud of. Rhymes aren't my forte."

Walking back into the living room, Casey hands me a note that had been taped to one of the boxes.

Sweetheart, I'm sorry, but I have to cancel our date tonight. One of the company's investors came to town, and I have to entertain him. Please enjoy and know I'll be thinking of you!
Ben

"Huh," Casey remarks from over my shoulder. "So he basically just sends presents whenever he cancels on you."

"He's sent them without a reason before," I argue, stuffing the note in my pocket.

She snorts. "Not in a hot minute. Okay, let's open up these bad boys!"

The scissors slice through the packing tape of the top package. The moment the seal is broken, the scent of cinnamon apples fills the room.

"Dear God," Casey moans, sniffing at the air like Hawke in the park.

"Keep your pants on," I snark, already salivating.

Apple fritters. Big, thick, doughy, hot apple fritters. The man knows the way to my heart. Not that I've been at all secretive about my downright obsession with baked goods. It helps that he shares the obsession.

I pull out the finely decorated box containing the fritters and place them on the coffee table.

"He needs to cancel on you more often."

"No. No, he doesn't."

I open the second box and notice an envelope with my name written in flawless calligraphy.

"Another note?" Casey asks, fingers already in the fritters. "What's this one say?"

I read aloud. "You are cordially invited to the 53rd annual Seattle Whales Preservation Society Charity Gala."

"Someone is going to get to buy a pretty dress," she sing-songs. "When is it?"

"About a month from now," I reply, checking the date.

"Wonder if you'll see him before the event. How long has it been since you met Chelsea?" she asks, leaning against the wall.

"A week. I hope it's not that long. . . ." I trail off. Five weeks without seeing each other? Why do I believe that's possible?

"This is getting depressing!" Casey whines. "Open the presents!"

"Fine, fine," I grumble, digging into the box. Underneath where the envelope used to be is a velvet box. I open it to reveal a long diamond necklace.

Casey whistles from her perch, the lights above us reflect off the gems in rainbows.

"Wow," I breathe.

"That will go with anything you could pick. Hell, you could wear just that and it'd probably be okay."

"Let's not find out."

To my dismay, there is no actual dress anywhere to be found in the packages. So I guess he means for me to pick out my own? Ha! And I thought dressing for our first date was hard. A fucking charity gala? Yeah, I'm not just out of my league, I'm playing an entirely different sport. I'll have to enlist Xavier's help or else I'll look like an absolute idiot. I'll probably still end up looking like an idiot. *Oof.*

I'm about two and a half apple fritters in before I send Ben a thank you text. And a reminder for the billionth time that I don't need extravagant gifts. Apple fritters? Acceptable. Necklaces that are worth more than my life? Gorgeous, but unnecessary.

Of course what I'd prefer is the date that he cancelled. I

have no idea where his head is at and it's making me unsteady. My own thoughts sound whiny and insecure and I just . . . *ugh*.

I need to get my mind off all this. Without further ado, I pull out the paints and easels Ben sent over a while back. I'd go for a run, but I'm not even partially done with these fritters. Maybe tomorrow.

"Well that's depressing as hell."

Casey's voice makes me jump in my seat. Fuck, I forgot she was home.

"What's depressing about it? It's just a sunset," I grumble. I glance over my painting, looking for whatever she sees. It's the view from Ben's bedroom just before the sun dips below the glassy surface of the Sound. Water and sky are perfect mirrors of each other, with a few hints of color. All of it is blue. Shades of dark blue in the night sky.

"Darby, honey." She shakes her head. "When most people paint a sunset, they use the opportunity to indulge in color. Reds, oranges, yellows, pinks, purples. Hell, I've seen people use green. But this. This is dark, dark and anguished."

"Casey, it's a painting. Stop psychoanalyzing me." I roll my eyes.

She puts her hands up in surrender. "Fine, fine. But all this shit you're repressing? It's not healthy."

With that, she sashays to the door. I didn't even notice she had her uniform on. Once she leaves, I take another glance at my painting. Is it depressing? I cock my head. Just because I chose to mute the color, that makes it depressing?

Nah. Casey's just being Casey and looking for issues where there are none.

"*A*w, it sounds like you're excited about going for your MBA, babe," Xavier coos from outside the dressing room. I picked my favorite program and he's been grilling me about it ever since we arrived at the dress shop.

"I am!" I reply, trying not to yank the precious material too hard over my hips. "I think it's the perfect next step for me professionally."

"You know, I'm sure a recommendation letter from Benjamin James would charm all their little skirts off," he sing-songs. "Do you need help in there? Why is this taking so long?"

I huff. "I'm being careful! This dress is expensive! And I'm not going to exploit my relationship."

"You're so honorable."

"Thank you." I step out of the dressing area. "Well?"

Xavier's mouth drops. Like, actually drops.

"What?" I prod him, turning to get a look at myself in the mirror. The dress itself is a dark blue, almost black, one-shoulder floor-length gown. It clings to every single inch of my body except for the legs, which feature a slit that stops just above my left knee.

"You look like a goddess," he murmurs, circling me. "Are you wearing shape wear or does your body just look like that?

"Shape wear. I'm not having underwear lines in this thing."

"Regardless, you are curves upon curves upon a tight little waist. Are you sure you want Ben? Because you're delicious."

"Stop hitting on me, Xav, you'll get fired."

He scoffs. "Worth it."

"It looks that good?" I fiddle with the one-shoulder detail.

"Trust me," he says. "You will be the only thing anyone will be able to look at."

"I'm still me under here. Dorky, finance-y, baking-show obsessed me."

"Of course you are, dear. But don't take it offensively if the only person at the gala who cares is Ben."

"Can I take this off now?" I shift my bare feet.

Xavier clicks his tongue. "No. You have to put on the shoes and then let Daniella take a look. If any alterations need to be made, they'll need to be made quickly."

I release a long sigh before accepting the heels. They look like tiny little death bringers, but wearing sneakers with this dress would look beyond stupid.

"Hey, I have a big presentation next week. Do you think you'd have some time to help me buy a powerhouse outfit for it?" I ask as I fiddle with the shoes. "If I nail it, the company may be willing to help pay for my MBA."

"Is that even a question? More shopping and spending time with my favorite little snack? Sign me up."

*T*oday is the day. Today is the *day*. I am going to nail this presentation, get myself a little recognition and respect, and then ask Mindy about the company supporting me through my MBA. It doesn't hurt that Xavier helped me pick out the most gorgeous black business suit I've ever seen. From the squared-off shoulders to the perfect placement of the pants hem at my ankle—it's as if I could take on the world. I can do this.

"Good morning, Mindy!" I bounce into her office. "Are you looking forward to the presentation today?"

Her eyes trail from the top of my head to the tips of my brand-new shoes. "Sure, Clarke."

"I am too. I'm ready to knock their socks off."

Her brows knit together as she rises from her desk chair. "What do you mean?"

"The presentation . . ." I trail off. What am I not getting here?

She sighs, sitting on the edge of her desk. "Listen, Clarke. I appreciate all the hard work you've put into this project. You took it seriously, and I think the higher ups are going to be proud of the work. But can I be honest with you?"

I nod, despite the pit growing in my belly.

"If I let you walk in there looking like Business Woman Barbie and tell them you put this project together, they won't take it seriously. It won't matter how good the work is. They'll just see you."

Holy. Shit.

The pit is now a giant fucking black hole threatening to swallow me up. *Business Woman Barbie?*

"You're intelligent, Clarke. I know it, you know it. But you can't do this presentation."

"You were never going to let me do it, were you?" I ask. My mother's voice pounds in my ears. *Your looks. All anyone cares about are your looks. No one cares about you. You're not good enough.*

"I'm going to put you on more projects," she barrels on as if I haven't said a word. "Get you doing actual work."

"Will I ever get credit for that work?" I snap. It's as if the hinges on my sanity have been blown off. "Will I ever be promoted? Will I ever have any sort of future at this company?

Or am I going to be known as Corporate Barbie for the rest of my professional career?"

"You have to be rational about this, Clarke." Her volume increases as she stands.

Rational? I'm supposed to be rational? My boyfriend can't bear to spend more than one day in my presence, my boss thinks I'm the equivalent of a child's toy, and my own mother thinks I'm a worthless piece of shit! I'm lucky I'm still standing. Rational flew out the damn window a long time ago.

"I quit." Turning on my heel, I march back to my desk.

"No one is going to take you seriously. Especially not if you just quit," she hisses, following behind me.

"No one takes me seriously anyway. I'm done."

"'Sup Clarke—lookin' good!" Jason from HR says as I bend to grab my bag. Oh no. Nope. No.

"*Jason*," I snap, turning to face him. "As someone in HR, you should know better than to openly stare at a coworker like you do. You contribute to the uncomfortable work environment, and you should feel lucky I don't give a shit enough about you to call a lawyer. Now get the fuck out of my face."

His eyes bug out of his skull as I breeze past him.

"Oh!" I turn once more. "Consider this my notice. I quit."

With one last push of the double doors, I step into the sunshine.

"I blew up my life," I announce as I enter my apartment.

"We already did this scene, Darby." Casey sighs from the kitchen.

"I quit my job, Case." I slam my purse down on the ground. The walk home did nothing to calm me down. My hands are still shaking.

Pots clang together in a jarring mess. "Wait, what?"

"I. Quit. My. Job."

"Honey, what happened?" she asks, rubbing remnants of food off her hands with a dishtowel.

"Mindy called me Corporate Barbie. She said I'm a joke and that no one would ever take me seriously. So I quit. And now I would like to just go in my room, eat all the food we have, and wallow in self-pity. Cool? Cool." I slam my bedroom door behind me.

I'm sure I'll feel bad for snapping at Casey in a minute or two, but I just can't. I can't pretend I'm okay with this.

"I bring chocolate chip cookies and love." Casey cracks open the door. "Is it safe?"

I shrug. "I guess."

"Tell me what happened." She crosses the room, setting down the plate of cookies beside me.

"I told you what happened. Mindy had me busting my ass over this project for weeks and then told me that I couldn't present it. She said—" My voice cracks. Anger is morphing into an ache in my chest that is all consuming. "That no one would take my work seriously. That Business Woman Barbie couldn't possibly present to the partners."

"She called you that?" Casey slides her hand across the blue duvet to hold mine.

"Verbatim."

"Fucking bitch."

"So I quit. Because even though I don't believe I deserve any better, I want to deserve better."

Casey's fingers tighten around my hand. "I can't imagine what's running through your head right now. It doesn't help that you refuse to talk about whatever is bothering you. But I need you to listen and try to hear me."

She stares me down until I nod, wiping tears on a tissue I pulled from my bedside table.

"You do deserve better. You deserve a lot better than that bitch. You deserve more than the women you've had in your life, and I'm sorry they consistently disappoint you. You are an amazing woman. I see that. Dad sees that. Hannah sees that. Ben sees that."

I flinch at Ben's name.

"What? Did something happen with Ben?"

"No. Nothing has happened with him. Thank you, Casey. I think I'd just like to lie down."

She presses a quick kiss to my forehead and leaves, the plate of cookies remaining by my side.

Ben.

Part of me wants to call him, beg him to come and get me. To hold me and tell me that everything will be alright. But I don't trust that he would. I don't trust that he'd drop everything because I need him. And I can't take the rejection right now. I pull my little beluga stuffed animal to my side along with the plate of cookies.

I guess I'm on my own.

## 17

## Double Fudge Brownies

ive weeks. How did I know I wouldn't see Ben for five weeks? Love that journey for me. It doesn't help that I've been wallowing after I quit my job. And instead of being able to spend time with my boyfriend to distract myself, I've been stuck watching Paul Hollywood eat things. Not that I mind watching Paul Hollywood eat things, like yes please, but I'd much rather see Ben. Alas, we don't always get what we want.

"Casey!" I call from my bedroom. "Can you help me?"

Casey bounces in a few moments later to find me struggling with the necklace Ben bought me. "What's up, princess?"

"I can't . . ." My fingers slip again. "I can't get the clasp."

"What, is Vivica not good at necklaces?" she snarks, coming over to help me.

"She left twenty minutes ago once my hair and makeup were done. You know, I don't think I've ever had a professional glow up before."

"You look horrifying, honestly." She hooks the necklace on

the first try. Bitch. "You should sue. I may sue for emotional damages."

"I was going for horrifying, so I'm glad she performed."

She rolls her eyes before sitting on the edge of my bed. "You know you look beautiful, right?"

"Just wait until I struggle into my shape wear. All this becomes smooth as a baby's butt."

"Should I get popcorn? Watching you struggle sounds pretty entertaining."

I chuckle as I pull out the pieces from my drawer. "You joke, but by the time you're done making it, I will probably only have one foot in there."

"Who was joking? I plan on using any excess butter to help lube you up so you slip on in."

As much as I may have laughed—I swear, tears were threatening—the butter would've been a solid plan. It takes far too long to get into the shape wear and by the time I do, I'm annoyed. Why do we have to force ourselves into these contraptions?

"Come out already! Ben should be here any minute, and Hannah and I need time to objectify you privately!" Casey yells from the living room.

There's nothing I want more in this moment than to strip all this off and snuggle up with her, Hannah, and Ben on the couch. But that is not happening, so I plaster on a smile and stride out of my bedroom.

"Oh, Darby!" Hannah gasps, hands flying to her face. "You look beautiful."

"Huh, you clean up okay, don't you?" Casey smirks, standing. She approaches and circles me. "If I didn't know any better, I'd say someone poured you into that dress. But I watched the debacle, so . . ."

"Shut up," I groan. Despite her teasing, the banter does help relax me a bit. I needed the normalcy.

"Casey, stop! Darby, you look so stunning," Hannah says. Not for the first time I thank whoever sent her to us. We are not worthy of her purity.

"Thank you." I smile.

"Ben is going to be tripping over himself all night because of you." Hannah grins back.

"I hope," I whisper. I'm all but convinced he has forgotten about me. I've never felt so unstable in my life. He doesn't even know about my job.

"Spill. Now," Casey demands. I hate how she knows me.

"It's just . . ." I take a deep breath. "When we're together, everything is fine. Until he won't stop looking at his email or taking calls. And he always apologizes, but it sucks because I never see him, so I wish our time together wasn't compromised like that. It's been five weeks and I've gotten maybe one text every few days. I'm starting to think he's just not interested."

"Fuck," Casey breathes, sliding back down onto the couch with Hannah. "I mean, you've mentioned little feelings but nothing like this."

"I know. I just didn't want to complain. Especially with the wedding coming up, I mean, you have enough to think about."

"Darby fucking Clarke, when in the history of ever have I given you the impression that I'm too busy for you?" Casey demands with a ferocity that has me trying to disappear into the wall.

"I—"

"I will never, *ever*, be too busy for you. Whenever you need me, I will drop everything and be there. Hannah knows this and is prepared for it."

Hannah pats Casey's arm. "We have discussed it, yes."

"Now." Casey's storm-cloud eyes clear. "Do you need to talk?"

"I do," I admit. "But Ben should be here any minute. Can we talk either tonight or tomorrow morning? I don't know if he'll ask me to stay over."

"Hannah and I will stay here tonight so that we're available."

*Knock, knock, knock.*

"Try to have fun," Casey whispers, pulling me into a hug.

"Darby." Ben's voice leaves him in an audible gasp as I open the door. "You are . . . breathtaking."

"Thank you." My cheeks heat. No matter how unsteady I am, actually being in Ben's presence always helps. Tonight he's perfectly wrapped into a black tuxedo and crisp white shirt. He looks like a model.

"Here, sweetheart," he says, handing me a bouquet of big, sexy red roses. "I've missed you."

Have you? I bite my tongue to force the automatic response back into my throat. If you missed me, why haven't you tried to even call me? Why haven't I seen you?

"Thank you. I missed you too," I reply.

"I'll put these in some water," Hannah murmurs from where she has appeared by my side. She takes the bouquet, covertly squeezing my hand as she does it.

"Come here." Ben brings me into his arms, burying his nose in my neck. The deep inhale he takes is pushed against my chest. I take advantage of the moment we have and snuggle into his chest as much as I can. He smells of home. All moments must end, however, and he pulls back, keeping my hand in his.

"Ready?" He smiles. The dimpled one. My favorite one.

I nod. Ready as I'll ever be.

"You look beautiful, stunning," Ben says once we're seated

in the limo. Because you take limos to charity galas. Who knew?

"Thank you. Xav picked it out." I smooth my dress. "I can't take the credit."

"You can take all the credit." He chuckles, wrapping an arm around my shoulders. "Tell me, how are you? Catch me up."

Ah yes, I've quit the only job I've ever had in a most dramatic fashion. Now isn't the best time.

"I'm fine."

"Just fine? You had that project and the wedding—how's wedding planning going?"

"Well! I think it's going to be just beautiful, despite Casey being involved." I smirk.

"God, I've missed you," he murmurs before pressing a kiss to my sticky lip-gloss-covered mouth.

Liar.

"I missed you too."

There's a red carpet. Why in the history of why is there a red carpet? Are there going to be famous people here or something? I turn to Ben. Oh. Wait. I'm dating a famous person. Well, for now, at least.

"Ready?" he asks, sliding toward the limo door.

"Ready," I reply. He exits and the entire world turns into flashing lights and screaming. I can barely hear my own thoughts as I take his outstretched hand to help me out of the car. Okay, Darby, careful of the leg slit. No flashing your business to a bunch of cameras. Once I'm standing on the death stick heels Ben's arm is around my waist and he's guiding me through the madness.

"Benjamin James! Any comments on the rumors about an acquisition?" one reporter yells as we pass.

We continue without stopping as my senses are overloaded.

Flash.

Scream.

Benjamin James.

Flash.

Hey! Who is that?

Flash.

Flash.

It takes a full five seconds for me to recover once we step inside. If I was experiencing sensory overload before, I'm experiencing sensory deprivation now. I blink my eyes a few times and meet Ben's kind gaze.

"The first time is always the worst." He smiles. "Eventually you get used to it."

"Ugh," I mutter to his startled laugh.

"Yeah, it still sucks no matter how used to it you get." His hand never leaves the small of my back as we walk through the entrance and enter the ballroom.

The entire room is gold and pale pink, down to the gold silverware on the pale pink draped tables. The centerpieces on each table are extravagant white lilies in pink frosted glass vases underneath diamond-dipped chandeliers. There's a five-piece orchestral group in the corner playing something inherently too classy for my inexperienced ear to recognize. I've never felt more out of place.

"All of this for the whales?" I ask.

"Right?" Ben shakes his head. "My ex used to be on the board. The whales are just a cover to throw extravagant parties. Unfortunately, it's full of some of the most influential people in the city. It's a can't miss."

"Your ex? Will she be here tonight?" Please say no. I can't handle a gorgeous ex-wife you still post pictures of on top of everything else.

"She shouldn't be. Pretty sure she and Mr. Here Have

Some Crystals and Essential Oils moved to California or something. I haven't seen her here for the last two years." He shrugs. "Let's find our table."

Our table is off to the side by the band, thank goodness. I don't need the added pressure of being at a center table.

"Ben! Good to see you!" The first person of the night approaches him. Tonight is going to be full of small talk and mingling, or ass kissing, as Xavier described it.

"Ah, Jonathan." Ben shakes the man's hand. "Good to see you. May I introduce my girlfriend, Darby?"

"Nice to meet you." I smile, shaking Jonathan's hand. Despite everything, it warms my heart to be introduced as Ben's partner.

"Nice to meet you as well, honey," Jonathan replies, eyes spending a bit too long on my legs for my comfort. He snaps back to Ben with a creepy grin. "How about you and I grab a drink, catch up? We'll bring your lady something back." His *lady?* Why do I feel more like a car than a person?

"I'll be right back." Ben kisses my cheek, giving my hand a squeeze. *Ugh.* That man—*Jonathan*—looks old enough to be my father. At least the scent of cigarettes retreats with him.

I sit at my seat and try to relax my shoulders. Xavier told me to expect creeps and shady people, but to just stay calm and soldier through it. I thought he was exaggerating—now I can see he was being kind in his description. My eyes dance over the sea of people. Does desperation have a smell? It'll always smell like white lilies to me now. This is the kind of room my mom would kill to be in.

"I grabbed you a red and ditched Jonathan at the bar," Ben says, sitting down next to me.

"Thank you." I grin, taking a sip from the glass. The man knows how to pick a wine . . . Is that a chocolate undertone? Mmm.

"He's awful." Ben sighs. "But he's also friends with important people, so I have to play nice."

"We can't just sit in the corner and be anti-social?"

"Nope. Come on." He stands and offers his arm. "The night is still young and I have to show you off."

***

". . . And I told Maggie I couldn't possibly chair *another* event, but somehow she convinced me," the woman continues. Abigail? Annabelle? Anastasia? I think she has an A name, but I honestly don't remember at this point.

"You're lucky. I'm stuck in a boardroom all day." The man next to her groans. At first glance I thought he was her father, but his hand is quite clearly on her ass now. Yuck. "If only we could be like these girls, eh Ben?"

"I have a career in finance," I pipe up, ready and willing to defend myself. Well, maybe the alcohol is ready and willing. I'm just along for the ride.

The man turns to me and raises one gray eyebrow. "Hmmm. Yes, good for you."

Ben's arm tightens around my waist for a quick moment before the two of them dive into a conversation about the DOW.

Thanks for the support, Ben. I restrain myself from rolling my eyes.

Am I expected to just stand here as Ben mingles? Annabeth over here looks perfectly fine with it as she gazes off into la-la land. She's here as arm candy, and . . . am I here for that purpose as well? I thought I was here for support as Ben's partner, not as a trophy to brag about. Although now that my eyes trail along the room, there's a common thread. Older guy, younger girl. Granted our age difference isn't as extreme as most of them, thank God, but it still exists.

We've barely spoken in weeks. Maybe he hasn't broken up with me because he needed someone hanging off his arm at this stupid gala.

"Be right back," I whisper and unglue myself from Ben's hold. I need a moment alone. I need another glass of wine. I need a moment alone *and* a glass of wine.

Do people typically hide in bathroom stalls with an overfilled glass of wine to escape their self-destructive thoughts? Well, that's what I'm doing. Luckily the bathroom stall is big enough for me to pace a few steps back and forth. Fucking rich people.

Ben cares about me. I think he cares about me. He might care about me.

Ugh. I can't make heads or tails of what's going on with him, me, us, anything. Something about this evening is fucking with me, and I can't get this big stone out of my belly. It's like I swallowed a giant rock of insecurity before I got in the limo tonight. His voice rings in my head: *I have to show you off.*

"She's wearing the ugliest green dress, Allison, I swear," a voice chatters. The bathroom door opens and shuts. Heels click against the tiled floor.

"Jenn!" The other voice giggles. "She's at least trying. Not like that Daniella."

"I step away for two years and already the standards have fallen so low. I am almost embarrassed to be seen here." A snap of a purse hinge rings across the room.

"So dramatic. How is it seeing Ben after all this time?"

Wait. Jenn? Jenn as in *Jennifer*? As in Ben's Jennifer? Oh dear God, please let this be a coincidence of the most disgusting proportions. They're common names after all.

"I haven't spoken to him yet. I don't know if I will or not, to be honest. Not with that co-ed dangling off his arm like a cheap knockoff," Jenn scoffs.

"How young is she? Do you know? I haven't heard anything about her yet," Allison asks.

Jenn makes another derisive noise. "No. Although I did hear she was trying to brag about her career or something. What a joke. We all know she's here because Benjamin James couldn't show up without some pretty young thing on his arm. I just wonder how much she costs. Can't be much. Have you seen her in that gown? By the look of her legs, it's shapewear and God keeping her in that dress."

Tears prickle and sting my eyes as the two women laugh. There goes my hopes of this being a different Jennifer talking about a different Ben.

"You can come out." Jenn's voice is right against the stall door. "First rule of eavesdropping is don't let them see your shoes."

Fuck.

I steel my nerves, wiping at my eyes, and unlatch the door.

"What a coincidence. We were just talking about you. I'm Jennifer Morris." She sticks out her perfectly manicured fingers to shake my hand.

She's just as perfect as the pictures. If anything, she's even better in person.

"Darby Clarke," I reply.

"Can I give you a bit of advice about my ex, sweetie?" Her voice is sugary sweet in a way that reminds me far too much of my mother. Goosebumps prickle along my arms. "Ben will never care about anything more than his company. You will never be anything to him. That's not how he works."

My voice, and any arguments, are stuck like a wad of peanut butter in my throat.

"Although, let's be honest, a young girl with a pretty little face like yours? I think you already know that. After all, that outfit isn't cheap."

"Let's get going." Allison shuffles. "We're going to miss the end of the silent auction."

Jenn nods, blonde curls bouncing. "You're right, dear, thank you. See you around, Darby. It was lovely to meet you."

Their heels click against the tile floor until I'm left in silence once more.

My feet remain glued to the floor until I finish my glass of wine. I need to get out of here. All I need to do is get to the table, use my phone to get a car, and I'm home free. There's no way I'm spending a second longer at this stupid gala than necessary. I just need to put one foot in front of the other and not call attention to myself. Easy.

With a withering glance at my appearance in the mirror, and a few wipes of a tissue, I push open the bathroom door. The music is still playing over the sound of general networking and gossiping. I tiptoe all the way to the corner where our table sits and pull my purse off my chair. Step one, check. Now I just need to go outside and get a car. If Ben even notices I'm gone, which I'm honestly unsure of at this point, he can call.

One deep breath. Two deep breaths. And I'm on the move again.

"Darby, sweetheart, where have you been?"

My entire body tenses up like I've been slapped.

"Around," I reply. "I'm, um, not feeling too well. I'm just going to call a car and go home." I still haven't turned around to face him. I don't know if I can face him at this point. Not with how mixed up my head is.

"You're not feeling well? Did you eat something strange?" His hand lands on my shoulder and my entire body shivers. I feel so dirty. Bought and paid for.

"Maybe. I just need to go home," I reply, firmer this time.

"Sweetheart, talk to me," he says, walking around so I'm forced to turn my head to not meet his gaze. "Look at me."

I shake my head. "No." I'm a petulant child, but I don't understand why he won't just let me go.

"Come and talk to me for a moment. Just . . ." He tries to meet my eyes. "Talk to me?"

Fine. He wants to talk? Let's fucking talk. I notice a set of double doors across the room leading out to a terrace. I nod toward them and let my feet lead us out of the crowded ballroom and into the comfortable early summer evening.

The night is silent except for the faint sound of music and talking filtering in through the closed doors behind us. The city itself is muted by the garden and pine trees.

"Did something happen?" Ben breaks the silence.

The dam shatters.

"Honestly? I had a delightful moment of clarity thanks to your ex-wife," I snap. Oh, there's that fourth glass of wine I had. I was wondering when it would hit.

"Jenn is here? Shit. Shit, sweetheart, what did she say? I'm so sorry." he says.

"Don't be sorry, she saved you a lot of grief. She explained a few things that I didn't understand, and now you and I are on the same page."

"I don't know how that could be true considering she's borderline insane. Darby, whatever she said to you I promise that there's no truth to it."

I turn to face him and I've never seen him seem so small.

"Ben, it doesn't matter what she said to me! What matters is that I couldn't fight her. I couldn't sit there and lie saying that you care about me. And now, now I understand how you see me. I understand that to you, I'm no different than any of the other plastic trophy girls waltzing around tonight."

"Wait, what?"

"You've been buying me. With each gift you were buying my presence at your side like a glorified sugar baby. You bought my affection, my attention. Hell, you even bought my virginity! I just didn't realize how cheap it was."

His eyes are practically bugging out of his face. "Darby, I didn't—"

"I'm a prostitute, Ben. I'm your personal prostitute who mistakenly thought she was your girlfriend." Tears flow down my face. "You haven't introduced your friends to me. You didn't introduce your sister to me until you were forced. You don't talk to me on the one date we go on each month. Your ex-wife, the ex-wife you still post pictures with, thinks I'm only with you for your money. So tell me, do I look like a prostitute to you?"

"Of fucking course not, I—"

"I can't believe the man I—" I forcibly choke down the word love. This man doesn't deserve to know that I love him. "I can't believe you think so little of me."

"Please, sweetheart, let me explain." His hand grasps mine in a touch I would've welcomed readily. I know every callous, every wrinkle, every imperfection on that hand.

"I don't want to hear it," I snap, snatching my hand away. "I'm nobody's Barbie doll to be pulled off the shelf and admired as they please, Benjamin James. I'm nobody's trophy, and I'm no longer your business."

With that, I fly off the terrace and toward the limo. Let Benjamin James, CEO, find his own way home.

***

My ears ring. Even as I tell the driver where to go and we cruise further and further away from downtown, I can't hear a thing. Just ringing. I can almost taste the bitter sting of adrenaline on my tongue that's making my entire body shake. But I can't hear a damn thing but the ringing.

I slam the limo door shut once we arrive at my apartment. Still only ringing.

I punch the button for the third floor in the elevator. Still only ringing.

I fumble for my keys in the overpriced bag Ben bought me instead of seeing me two weeks ago. Still only ringing.

The door falls open and the ringing stops. The apartment smells of Casey and brownies and home, and before I know it I'm on my knees. My eyes swim with tears as I sob on the wooden floor.

What have I done?

"Come on, Darby, come on," Casey's voice calls to me. She must be miles away; it can't be her hands that soothe over my arms. Phantom touches pull my head onto a phantom lap to stroke my hair. Her voice is too far away.

"I'll get a brownie," Hannah whispers from somewhere above.

"Bring the entire goddamn tray. Darby, honey, come on," Casey repeats, voice clearer now.

I don't want comfort. No.

"Mm fine." I struggle uselessly against Casey's hold.

"Of course you are. Do you want to get out of that dress?" she asks, brushing a few tears off my face.

I nod, allowing her to take most of my weight and get us both standing. When did my shoes come off?

"That's it. We'll get this ridiculous outfit off, eat some brownies. I'll take care of it." She leads me into my bedroom. "I'll take care of you."

The dress comes off easier than it went on.

"I can take my makeup off by myself," I say as Casey follows me into the bathroom.

"Less than five minutes ago you couldn't walk by yourself, so excuse me if I'm your chaperone for the rest of the night," she replies, leaning in the doorway.

"Fine," I concede. It's not like she's wrong after all. The world seems more manageable now that I'm in baggy sweat-pants and a T-shirt three sizes too big.

"So. Seems like we need to talk," she continues as I wash my face.

I conceal a sigh underneath the sound of running water. "Yeah. I think I broke tonight. And I'm not sure I can put myself back together."

"You survived your mom. You can survive this. It's just a matter of dealing with it."

"Yeah. Yeah, I don't think I can keep going on like this."

"Let's sit down, work this out. There's never been a problem that you and I can't solve when we put our minds to it. We're far too stubborn." She grins, standing up straight again. We walk hand in hand out to the living room.

"Here's the brownies, and I made you both some hot cocoa with marshmallows. I'm going to head out, let you two talk," Hannah says, placing everything on the coffee table. "I'll come by and check on you in the morning."

"Thanks, love," Casey murmurs, pressing a kiss to Hannah's cheek. "Let me know when you get home."

The gentle *snick* of the front door closing is the end of all noise in the apartment. So much silence tonight.

"You've eaten two brownies." Casey pushes the tray out of my easy reach, bringing me out of my thoughts. "Can you walk me through tonight?"

"I think . . ." Fuck. "I have to start earlier than tonight."

"Then start from the beginning, whenever that is."

"What if I don't know where to start?" I wring my brownie-crumb-covered hands.

"Just talk and we'll figure it out." She smiles, relaxing into her side of the couch.

My head falls into my hands. "I think it starts with me."

Deep breath, Darby.

"I broke up with Ben."

"Okay. Why?"

"Because I'm in love with him and . . ." Fucking tears. "I don't think he feels the same."

"Did you ask him how he feels?"

"No. But I didn't want to. I didn't want him to tell me that I'm pretty and beautiful and whatever else. I didn't want him to tell me the truth because I'm scared he'll prove me right."

"I'm missing a big chunk of this, babe. Start from the beginning," she says, rubbing my knee.

"I've been feeling insecure." My voice trembles. "I think it started when he wouldn't pay attention during our dates. He was always on the phone. He made such an effort in the beginning to be present and pay attention, and then slowly he stopped seeing me as often and talking to me. Then the presents started coming and I've never felt so . . ."

"Bought off?" she supplies, a sympathetic smile on her face.

I exhale. "Yeah. It was as if he had bought the right to treat me however he wanted. And he'd open up a little when we saw each other, but then close right back up. So going into tonight I was in a bad place. Especially with everything that happened with my job. My mother's voice was in my head telling me that all I'd ever be good for is my looks. Then, Case, he just walked me around like some human Barbie doll. I was treated like a moron! And then while I was in the bathroom I met his ex-wife."

Casey's eyes bug. "His ex was there? Shit."

"She wondered how much I cost. She said he would never love anything but his job and that they'd never see me again."

My hands sting with how hard I'm wringing them. "She said some other mean things, but it doesn't matter. So I tried to leave and he stopped me and I basically accused him of treating me like a prostitute and stormed out."

"Fuck. You used the word prostitute?"

"Yeah. And I didn't let him say anything, and I may have had four really big glasses of wine."

"I mean, it sounds like you had every reason to be upset. I can't imagine what he'd have to say for himself regardless. I mean, I like the guy, but goddamn. What are you going to do now?" She pushes the brownie tray closer to me again.

"Case, I have no fucking idea. I feel so in over my head, and I can't see a way out on my own."

"Can I give you some advice? A little tough love?"

"Please," I sob.

"I think you should go see a therapist. I love you, but you have had to deal with some serious trauma in your life and you have never addressed it. Dating Ben seems to have exacerbated the situation. I wonder if you would've been more confident and more willing to create open communication if you weren't so closed off. You've been upset with Ben for a while, apparently, so why are you just now telling him? Why is it your mother's voice in your head at that event? I think you need some help, honey."

I exhale a trembling breath and make my way into her arms. She wraps around me like a mother koala and squeezes me just short of too tight.

"I think you're right."

## 18

# Lemon Cake with Chocolate Frosting

"I quit my job," I say into the silence that has fallen. My eyes are glued to the mug of hot tea in front of me and haven't moved since we sat down.

"Casey called and told me, kiddo," Dad replies. "And I do want to talk about that and why you didn't want to tell me. But I'm just worried. You've been quiet for a while, and I don't think it's because of that."

We're sitting outside on Dad's back porch. His house lies among tall pine trees as far as the eye can see. Hawke runs and plays among them, sniffing out new scents to chase.

"You're right. I want to talk about Mom."

His own mug clatters against the wooden outdoor end table between our Adirondack chairs. "You're ready?"

I chuckle out a half-hearted laugh. "No. Is anyone ever ready? But I need to. It's time."

"What do you need? How?"

"I remember." Deep breath in, exhale. "I remember how angry she was all the time. How disappointed she was with her life and how things had played out for her. As a kid, I couldn't . . . I couldn't understand why she was so unhappy. The only thing that made sense was that it was me."

"You were a fantastic kid, Darby, you still are," he murmurs.

"As an adult, I'm starting to piece together that I wasn't the source of her unhappiness. That the responsibility didn't fall on my shoulders. But growing up, all I knew was that I had a mom who didn't like me. I had a mom who didn't want to play with me, who didn't think I was smart or funny. I had a mom who was angry and it had to be my fault. I had to be doing something wrong."

"That's a lot of responsibility, kiddo. I had no idea you felt that way."

"Neither did I until I started thinking about it. Casey and I had a talk, and she convinced me to see a therapist. My first appointment is this week." My eyes lift from the steaming cup.

"I am so proud of you. This is going to be good for you." His eyes swim with tears.

"I need to know something, but I'm afraid to ask you. I'm scared you'll think I'm attacking you or blaming you."

He runs a hand through his hair, shaking his head. "You shouldn't ever be afraid to ask me anything."

"Why didn't you leave her? When I was young, I mean. You left once I was in high school, but what about the years before that? You guys were constantly fighting, so I know she was just as awful to you."

Hawke barks, drawing our focus to where he plays in the backyard. He's found a branch almost as big as he is and he's parading it around like a trophy.

"I was terrified of losing you to her," Dad replies, so quiet I can barely hear him. "I was terrified that it would be just my word against hers and we'd get shared custody, or worse. She's vindictive and would've tried to steal you away. I was scared the court would favor her and you'd be stuck alone with her forever. At least if we were married, I could be with you as much as possible and shield you from her."

A lump presses against the back of my throat. "Daddy . . ."

"I have no idea if it was the right thing to do. I wonder all the time if I could've done better, but at the moment it was all I could think to do."

"I'm sorry, Daddy. I'm sorry that you suffered too." I reach for his hand across the table. Our fingers link as Hawke continues barking, trying to chase a squirrel with the branch still in his mouth. My heart aches with each beat in my chest as we sit together in silence. As we grieve together in silence.

The sun has dipped lower in the sky by the time Dad and I meander back inside, Hawke hot on our heels. We haven't said everything, but we've said enough for today. We've opened up the conversation and I'm proud of us for that bit of progress.

"So." Dad clears his throat. "You're unemployed, huh?" We make our way into the kitchen to prepare lunch. Although, at this point, it's more of an early dinner.

"Yep," I reply, opening the stainless-steel refrigerator. "Dad, you have no groceries."

"Right. I was planning on shopping this weekend, but I got caught up with Lisa. You aren't making any money now, how about I take you out to dinner?" he asks.

I roll my eyes with a laugh. "I don't think we have a choice."

"Want to invite Casey and Hannah? We could even call Ben, make it an impromptu fancy dinner." Dad scoops up some food into Hawke's bowl to his delighted barks.

"We already celebrated my birthday two months ago. All this attention will spoil me," I deflect, chewing my bottom lip.

How do I tell Dad that I ruined my relationship? That I'm so damaged I couldn't voice my needs and instead exploded like a bomb?

Dad's eyes raise from the silver dish Hawke is annihilating. "You're not spoiled."

"Can it just be you and me? I promise to order a decadent dessert to make up for it." There's no use fighting him, definitely not when he's using his dad face on me.

"So long as you promise." He chuckles, appeased. For now, at least.

I stagger back into my apartment hours later with an entire two-tier lemon cake with chocolate frosting. Apparently because the restaurant was "right near a bakery, Darby" and "you just lost your job, Darby" and "I'm your dad, Darby, I'll buy you a cake if I feel like it." What a dork. A loveable, irreplaceable, damn amazing dork.

"Dad?" Casey asks from where she's snuggled up with Hannah on the couch. She's already eyeing my cake. Little bloodhound can smell everything.

"Dad," I confirm, making my way into the kitchen.

"Want us to pause so you can join? We just started the movie," Hannah pipes up from where she's buried in Casey's arms.

"No, that's not necessary. It's been a tough couple days. I think I'm just going to get a big slice of this cake, a bath bomb, a romance novel, and lounge in the tub for a while. You two pretend I'm not even here." I smile. Truly smile. Despite how fucking awful I feel and how much I wish the past few days played out differently, I'm hopeful. Hopeful that I'm making real steps toward better mental health and better health in general. Okay, maybe not better health in general—I have too much of a sweet tooth for that nonsense.

## 19

## Cookie Dough Ice Cream

My phone shakes with every breath. All I want to do is scroll Instagram, actively avoiding Ben's, and yet my hands won't stop trembling. I've never liked doctors' offices, and apparently psychiatrists' offices are no different—no matter how sunny this one tries to be. I'm alone, other than the receptionist, in the Japanese garden-style waiting area. From the bamboo chairs to the oriental lamps to the babbling jade fountain underneath the floor-to-ceiling windows, the obvious theme is relaxation. So how come I'm buzzing like a bumblebee? It's even a gorgeous, sunny day. The sunlight bounces off the water in the fountain to create small rainbows across the white walls. It's perfect in here. And I just want to go home.

"Darby Clarke?" The door to the private room swings open.

Well, so much for running away. I rise from my chair and follow the small brunette woman who emerged.

"I'm Dr. Yang, it's nice to meet you. Sit wherever you feel comfortable," she invites. The inside of her office matches the waiting room. She even has one of those sand pits with a little rake on the low table in front of the couch. I choose one of the fluffy armchairs instead. I've seen too many movies with someone dramatically splayed out on their therapist's couch. I can't take it seriously.

"Nice to meet you," I reply.

She chooses the rolling chair opposite me and picks up a notepad and pen. "You look a bit nervous, Darby."

"What was it that gave it away? The fake smile or the uncontrollable shaking?" I joke, clenching my hands together in my lap.

"I understand. You're not the first person to come in with reservations or nerves. How about I tell you a bit about myself first?" She smiles. She's a tiny thing. She can't be much taller than five feet, with dark brown hair tied up in a bun at the nape of her neck.

"Okay." I resist the urge to pull my knees to my chest like a child.

"My name is Dr. Penny Yang, and you can call me whatever you like. Most of my patients call me Dr. Penny, but you do what makes you comfortable. I'm from Seattle, born and raised. I have four sisters, and yes, I'm the middle child. So I've always been a mediator." She chuckles. "My entire philosophy is simple. We need to find out what you need and execute it. We will get to a place where you understand that putting yourself and your needs first is not always a selfish act. Self-love and self-care helps us love and care for others."

"That all sounds good. I guess." I take a sip of water from the unopened bottle in front of me. Maybe I can do this.

"So the dreaded question: what brings you in to see me, Darby?" Dr. Penny asks, crossing her ankles.

I take a deep breath. I can do this. "I'm having trouble

dealing with some issues and some things from my past. It's obvious that I'm not dealing with any of it. I need help."

"Okay, that's good. Being able to voice your needs is a big step. What is it that you're having trouble dealing with?"

"My mother. I wasn't treated well." Each word is drawn out. I'm still struggling to vocalize what's in my head.

"I see. What is your relationship with her like right now?" Dr. Penny writes a few notes.

"I don't speak to her. I haven't since I was eighteen. She still texts and calls me, but I don't answer."

"Has that been good for you? Not communicating with her?"

"Yes," I reply. "It's just not enough."

"Why don't you tell me a moment from your relationship with her that you would like to share? From there I can ask some questions. Does that sound good?"

I nod my head, flipping through memories like pages of a book. The clock on the wall ticks away the seconds.

"I think I have one."

***

"When I was sixteen, my dad and mom announced they were divorcing and putting the house I grew up in up for sale. It was a long time coming. I had been asking if they were going to get divorced for as long as I can remember. My dad was the one who moved out, although I'm still not sure why or how. All that matters is that I was left alone with her for the first time in my life." I dig my nails into my palms, trying not to cry. "I lasted about a month before I begged him to take me with him. He immediately came and got me. About two weeks later, I was in the neighborhood visiting my best friend Casey and I wanted to grab some clothes from the house. She came with me for moral support. When I tried my key in the front door, it didn't fit. I walked around the entire house trying every door, and each one failed. I finally called my mom, who was out for drinks with some girlfriends, and asked her why my keys wouldn't work. She explained that she had all the locks changed. She said it wasn't my home anymore. If I wanted a key, I could move back in. Otherwise, if I wanted to visit my own house and have access to my own things, I could call her to set up a time."

There's silence in the room for a few moments, the only noise coming from the ticking of the clock and the sniffles I'm trying to contain.

"I'm sorry, Darby." She pushes a box of tissues into my easy range. "I'm sorry she did that to you."

I shrug. "I shouldn't have been surprised."

"It sounds to me like your mother is very selfish. Did she give you ultimatums regularly?"

"Yeah." I nod. "It was either her way or no way."

"How did you feel when she did that to you?"

"Stuck."

"Stuck?" she repeats.

"I felt like there was no way out. That she had boxed me in yet another corner. My life has felt like a series of games, and she won yet again. She always cared about winning more than she cared about me."

"That's an awful way to have a relationship with someone, let alone your own mother. I'm interested to know why you chose that memory. Is it your worst of her?"

I snort a laugh. "God, no. Not at all. I'm not sure why I chose it. It just was the one I was ready to tell."

"That makes sense. Darby, I'm getting the impression you don't talk about your mother or the impact your relationship with her has had on your life very often. Is that part of why you've come to see me?"

The clock ticks another second. Two.

"Yes. I . . . I've never been able to vocalize what happened, and I've come to the conclusion that I have to face it. I've spent so much of my life forcing down these memories, just telling myself that the past is in the past. But I don't think that's true. I think I have to accept all parts of my life, not just the good parts."

She smiles. "It takes people a long time to figure that out. I'm proud of you. I think discussing your past will be helpful, but I think what will be most helpful will be addressing how your past impacts your life today. We can dissect each moment of your life, but if we don't address how those moments influence your quality of life, then we won't get far. So, I'll ask you: what do you need?"

My hands smooth out invisible lines in my jeans. "I need to improve my mental health. I need to learn how to accept and love myself. I need to accept the failures of my upbringing and stop bringing them into my future. I need to learn how to live my life in a way that brings me joy."

"Then that is what we'll do," she replies, a triumphant grin on her face.

I can't help but mirror her expression. Fuck yeah.

"Usually people have a moment that causes them to want to reach out to a therapist. Rock bottom, if you will. Not everyone, but I have a feeling you may have. Would you feel comfortable sharing?" Dr. Penny asks, pen lifted and ready.

Well, okay. Jumping right the fuck in, then. "My boyfriend and I broke up."

She lifts a single, perfectly manicured brow.

"Well, I exploded at him and stormed off, telling him I was no longer his business after quitting my job," I add.

"I see. Before we get into that, where is your relationship at now?"

"Nowhere. We haven't spoken since."

"Has he reached out? Have you?"

I shake my head, a few tears escaping.

"Okay. What prompted the explosion, the breakup?"

"It was a long time coming. I had been feeling uncertain and uncomfortable, but I never brought it up. He's an incredibly busy man and I guess . . . I don't know, I didn't know how to handle it. So, all my feelings just . . ." I mimic an explosion with my hands.

"Lack of communication is a common issue in relationships, romantic or otherwise. What were your concerns?"

"Like I said earlier, Ben is a very important man. He's the CEO of S—" I stop myself. He deserves his privacy just as much as I do. "He's the CEO of a major company. Because of this he works a lot. More than a lot. He works every single day."

"That's a lot of stress on him, I imagine. And on you."

"At first he made an effort to see me and I appreciated it. I also understood it may not always be that way. But I guess I didn't really. He started working more and seeing me less, and then when we would get together he'd be sending emails or taking calls."

"That must've been frustrating," she supplies, writing faster than I've ever seen.

"It was, but I tried to understand. I tried to think about how much pressure he must be under, and I felt so selfish for wanting more of his time. My mother always said I was selfish."

"It isn't selfish to want to see someone, and it's not selfish to be open and honest about what you need in a relationship. A partnership is between two people, and it can't be successful unless both parties get what they need."

"I never had the discussion." I reach for a tissue from the flower-printed box. "I was too scared."

"What were you afraid of?"

"I was afraid he'd leave. I was afraid I'd rock the boat and lose him. I just . . . I just wanted to be loved."

"And you believed that if you told him you needed more communication during your one-on-one time that he'd leave?"

"I believe that I'm not worth the effort," I snap. My hand covers my trembling mouth. Where did that even come from?

Her grin falls just a tad. "And why is that? What makes him worth the effort, but not you? What makes it okay for you to jump through hoops to make the relationship work but not offer him the same opportunity?"

"Because that's what I've heard my entire life. I've heard that all I'm good for are my looks. All I'll ever be good for is my looks, and that I'm not worth the effort."

"Darby." She leans forward. "In sitting with you for the last twenty minutes, I can already tell that you're worth it. You are an intelligent, insightful, caring woman. And it's okay to know that. Knowing that doesn't make you selfish, knowing your worth doesn't make you selfish."

"Are you sure?" I hiccup on a sob that's been threatening to burst.

"Positive. I'll be the first to tell you if you're heading into selfish territory." She winks, leaning back.

"Okay," I whisper.

***

"Tell me about the explosion, I think is what you called it. What happened?" Dr. Penny stands, fetching me a fresh water bottle from the pink mini fridge under her glass desk. Who doesn't love a woman with a pink mini fridge?

"Thank you." I accept the bottle. "We were at a charity event. It was the first time we'd seen each other in over a month, and I was stressed. I had just quit my job, which is a whole other can of worms."

"Mm." She nods.

"And we barely spoke the entire night. It was all about walking me around like a prize horse at a convention. Me and all the other dates. We weren't expected to contribute to the conversation, just gossip and look pretty. And his ex-wife was there and she was saying the nastiest things and I drank four glasses of wine . . ."

"Sounds like a terrible situation."

"It was. So I tried to leave, and he tried to stop me." My eyes sting. "And I couldn't take it anymore."

"It sounds like you regret how things happened."

I nod. "I do. I really do. I said some horrible things to him. But when I look back at it with a clear head I realize that I meant them. I accused him of treating me like a prostitute, but I felt like a prostitute. Every time he cancelled a date, he would send gifts or offer his credit card. As if money and presents could buy my silence. It wasn't okay."

"You regret how you addressed the situation, how your feelings came out. But you were honest about how you felt?" She's still writing. I'd pay a lot to see what's on that paper, but I don't think it's included in my bill.

"I was."

"And what did he say?"

"He didn't. I didn't allow him to. I ran away. I didn't want him to confirm that I was right. I didn't want to take the chance that I was right."

"I wonder how he would've responded if you'd allowed him the opportunity. But what matters here is the future. We want a future where you feel comfortable sharing your feelings with your partner before they reach a boiling point. Where you feel worthy of reciprocation, where you feel worthy of someone's best efforts. What do you think?"

"I think that would be amazing."

Dr. Penny glances at the clock on the wall. "Our time for today is almost up. I want you to share one more memory of your mother with me. Something that we can both think about and discuss next time. Something you think encapsulates your daily relationship with her growing up. Then, I'll give you an assignment and let you go."

"I almost feel like I'm back in school." I chuckle.

"Sometimes therapy is a bit like school," she agrees, the corners of her mouth twitching.

"Okay. I think I have one," I say, surprised at how quick it came to mind.

"Whenever you're ready."

"I was maybe fourteen or so." I toss off my sneakers and tuck my feet underneath me in the plushy chair. "I had already given up on ever pleasing my mother. My hopes of being enough for her were dashed a few years prior. My mom had a friend—more like a frenemy—named Cynthia, who had a daughter one year older than me named Selena. Selena was, and I'm sure still is, an incredibly intelligent girl. She was in all the gifted programs and the accelerated classes. She had straight A's and never acted out. Well, she hadn't acted out *yet*. She hit her rebellious stage later. But anyway. My mom hated coming back to me after talking to Cynthia, because Cynthia would talk about Selena's accomplishments, and my mom didn't have anything to say about me. Being embarrassed like that always put her in a foul mood. So I'm minding my own business and watching TV and my mom storms in. She asks what I got on my last science quiz, and I told her I failed it. We started yelling at each other, which was the norm. Around this age I was attempting to fight back, to stick up for myself. Maybe I wanted any form of attention, even negative attention."

"That makes sense." She nods. "Go on."

"So we're screaming at each other at this point. Lord knows why. Our fights never made sense. She would just be in a bad mood and pick little useless things to berate me over, and I'd do it back to her until we'd be shouting across the house. I remember I told her that she was pathetic and that I never would be as smart as Selena with a mother like her. The house went so quiet in that moment. Right up until she walked up to me and smacked me across the face. I remember her pulling her hand back and the look of utter disgust on her face. She told me I was a horrible daughter and then sent me to my room."

"Wait." Dr. Penny puts a hand up. "She hit you?"

"I mean, yeah." I shrug. "It didn't hurt, she was as skinny as a twig. Plus, parents used to be more physical in their discipline. Spanking, slapping, whatever."

"What you described to me wasn't discipline. What you described to me was a fight that escalated to physical violence."

I search Dr. Penny's face. And I'm not loving the pitying look in her eyes. "I never thought of it that way. I just thought it was her version of spanking."

"Darby, I won't get into why I don't agree with any physical discipline because that's a different topic altogether. But I can assure you that wasn't discipline. How often did she hurt you?"

Why does it suddenly seem like I'm in one of those movies where the abused wife is unaware that she's being abused?

"Um . . ." I twist my fingers together in my lap. "A few times."

"So more than once?" She's writing furiously again. I crane my neck, but she's just far enough away that I can't make any of it out.

"Yeah. More than once."

"Slapping children, no matter how hard, is not the norm." She pauses until I meet her eyes. "I would *never* touch my kids in anger. And I imagine you would never do that to any of your future children, should you choose to become a parent."

I shudder. "No. Never."

"I don't want to put you on the spot or make you uncomfortable. But someone needed to say that to you, because I don't think anyone ever has. Your relationship with her wasn't normal, it was abusive."

I nod, all power of speech gone. It's like a lightbulb has turned on in my head and I can see. There's a name for what I went through.

"How are you feeling?" She reaches for me, holding her hand out palm up.

I place my hand in hers. "I don't know, to be honest."

"That's okay. I think it'll be good for you to take a step back until our next session and think. We made a lot of progress today. I have two assignments for you, if you're up for them."

I nod again.

"First, I want you to start journaling. The point isn't necessarily to write about your mom, or Ben, or anything important. I want you to practice recognizing how you feel and expressing it. Each journal entry should start with one thing you like about yourself. From there you can write whatever you want. I'll even give you a journal so you don't have to go out and buy one." She stands, walking toward her desk.

"That's not too bad." I chuckle. The sound is hollow as it reverberates against the walls. "What's the second part?"

"I want you to talk with your friends and family, your support system. You don't have to force yourself to open up or say things you're not ready to say. But I think you'd be surprised to hear about their own experiences with your mother. I think you'd learn a lot." She pulls a light brown notebook out of the center desk drawer. "That's more of a long-term goal, though."

"I can do that."

"What are your plans for the rest of the evening?" she asks, crossing the room to hand me the notebook.

"I plan to eat an entire carton of cookie dough ice cream, watch *The Great British Baking Show*, and cry," I reply.

She breaks into a huge grin. "Sounds perfect."

## 20

## Red Velvet Cupcakes

The hotel room is lit by one hundred fake votive candles and the television screen in front of us. The entire living area has been cleared out to make way for a giant blanket and pillow fort the likes of which hasn't been seen since Casey and I were in high school.

"Dude, you're getting married tomorrow." I roll onto my side.

"And here I was thinking you used the last of your money on a humongous hotel room because you were going to try and seduce me." She rolls over to face me. "I dressed in my sexiest sweatpants for nothing!"

"I knew you did that on purpose, you temptress!" I throw a handful of popcorn at her. "And I have a second interview in a few days, so hopefully it's not the last of my money. More wine?"

She sticks out her novelty bachelorette glass I bought for the occasion. "Absolutely! This stuff is amazing. How did you find it?"

"Ben and I drank it together once," I reply, pouring the

bottle. I suppress the full body shiver I get whenever I mention him. It's been a few months, but I still can't get him out of my head.

"Did he ever call? Even once?" She reclines back on the pillow bed we've created for us to share.

I shake my head. "No, not that I blame him. But tonight isn't about him, or me, it's about you. We're celebrating your last night as an unmarried woman!"

"By drinking wine, eating copious amounts of food, and watching movies. My favorite!"

"You wouldn't let me get you strippers, so I figured sugar is the next best thing."

"You know." She cracks open a box of expensive French chocolates. "I know tonight is supposed to be about me or whatever. But I'm proud of you. These last few months you've taken hold of your life in a way I've never seen you do before. You're interviewing at a company that would value you, applying to an MBA program, taking care of yourself, not waking up in the middle of the night because of nightmares."

"Wait, you knew about those?"

"Sometimes you'd scream. Or cry. But I knew if I came in and checked on you, you'd just ignore it and pretend nothing happened."

My eyes lower. "Probably. I wasn't in the best place."

"That's my point, though! You've made so much progress."

"And there's one thing left to do. I wanted to save it for us." I lift my phone from the blanket mess below us.

Casey's head cocks in confusion just like Hawke.

I smile, opening the text message exchange with my mom. "It's time to block her."

And with one press of a button, the weight of her falls fully off my shoulders. The past will still hurt, the way she treated me won't change. What's changed is me.

"Pick up a chocolate!" She demands.

I do as she says, lifting an eyebrow at her. She smacks our pieces together with a huge grin.

"A chocolate toast! To you, my best friend."

"I hate you." I smile, popping my chocolate in my mouth.

"Do you think you'll date again?" Casey asks, another glass of wine and a bag of popcorn later.

"I don't plan on being a spinster." I snort. "But I'm not in any hurry."

"You haven't talked much about him since the breakup." She's gazing at the twinkly lights taped to the top of our fort.

"No."

"Do you miss him?"

I sit up. "Isn't this supposed to be your bachelorette party? Why are we talking about Ben of all things?"

"Because it's my party and I can choose the topics of conversation," she says. "Why are you avoiding talking about him?"

"Because I'm still in love with him," I reply. Apparently the wine has loosened my tongue, which she must've accounted for.

Bitch.

"Why haven't you tried calling him?"

"Despite the way I attacked him, he made himself unavailable to me. Yes, I should've voiced my concerns. I should've done a lot of things differently. But he wasn't perfect. There are a lot of things I'm still not clear on. And I'm not ready to be the one to put myself out there."

She makes a face. "Therapy has made you so mature."

I throw a pillow at her face. "Shut up."

"You'll just have to date Paul Hollywood instead. Bit bigger around the middle and older than Ben, but he's got the same blue eyes. Don't tell me you don't have a hard on for him." She waggles her eyebrows. "You watch too much of that stupid show to be there just for the baking."

"I admittedly have a half chub for the guy. What can I say? I want to be up close and personal with his buns."

Casey cackles, sending leftover popcorn kernels flying. "You said half chub!"

"And I regret it. Just like I regret being friends with you. Can I send you back for a newer model? Maybe someone who doesn't talk back as much?"

"Oh shush. You love me and wouldn't change me for the world."

I grab her in a surprise hug, squeezing as tight as I can. "You're right about that, my little weirdo. I love you."

$\mathcal{M}$y alarm sings at a volume too high for the early morning light filtering through the windows, forcing me to crack open my eyes.

"The fuck did we set the alarm to that song?" Casey mumbles from underneath a mountain of pillows.

"Probably in the middle of our impromptu Disney marathon," I reply. Why am I so cold? "You stole all the blankets, you bitch."

"I'm used to having Hannah snuggling with me!" she whines, burying her face further into her cocoon. "I'm so cold without her."

I roll my eyes, digging my fingers through the literal mountain of blankets she's under. "You can see her in a few hours."

"I miss her," is the dreamy response.

"The sooner you wake up, the sooner we can get you married," I tease.

She pops up out of the mountain like a daisy. "Let's go!"

I recoil in mock horror at her appearance. "Oh. Oh, you need a shower. Now."

"Was that an invitation?"

"Shut up. And remember to keep your hair dry! The stylist said dirty hair styles better."

"What if there's chocolate in my hair . . ." she trails off with a guilty smile.

I push her up toward the opening of the fort. "Only you. Only fucking you. Go!"

She scrambles out, running off with a cackle. Weirdo. I survey the area for damage, and yeah, I may owe the hotel extra cleaning services because this is damage. Thankfully, I don't see any red wine stains. Just a few chocolate stains and popcorn kernels.

I untangle myself from the blankets and pull myself to stand outside of the fort. No matter what this may cost me, the night was worth it. Despite living together Casey and I haven't done something like this in a long time. I wipe away the first stray tear of the day. The first of many, I'm sure.

Two showers and a quick breakfast later and we're off to the venue. Casey and Hannah's little Woodinville winery is perfect for their intimate ceremony. My insides are fluttering as I drive along the quiet Saturday morning streets. Well, they would be quiet if Casey wasn't blasting Smashing Pumpkins through my car stereo.

"I'm tempted to yell apologies to the poor people trying to sleep," I say over the noise.

"What?" she yells.

I shake my head with a smile. "Nothing."

My dress and hers hang against the windows of the back seat, vibrating along with the music.

"Despite all my sage, my house is still haunted and lame," she belts. I wish she could carry a tune, but the poor girl is as tone deaf as I am. Doesn't stop her from trying, no matter how much I wish it would. She could at least attempt to get the lyrics right. With a dramatic flourish, she kicks off her "Bride" sandals and sticks her feet on my dashboard.

"Nope!" I turn the volume down and swat at her. "Absolutely not. Off!"

"I'm getting *married*! Stop being such a poop."

"You can blast music as much as you want, you can even fuck up all the lyrics, but get your stinky feet off my car."

"Fine, Mom." She rolls her eyes, turning the volume back up.

For the first time in years, that word doesn't make me cringe. Doesn't make me want to fold in on myself and hide. It's just a word.

It's just a word.

"According to Hannah's schedule, we are on time," I announce as we walk up to the winery. Hannah produced a color-coded schedule that she laminated. Laminated.

"You should've seen her making these babies. My woman is so hot," Casey chirps, opening the front door for me.

The winery is a mid-century modern dream, the floor a shiny, polished concrete and the ceiling covered in beautiful wooden beams. In the middle of the main room sits a large bar, and fridges full of wine line the wall. The best part, and where they'll be married, is the outdoor area. The smallest rocks follow a tree-lined path, framed by a stunning bright red wall. It's the perfect place for a summer wedding.

"Casey? Nice to see you again." Raina, the day-of wedding coordinator, spots us from across the room. "Hannah is already set up in her bridal suite. You'll be downstairs as discussed."

"Perfect. Let's go get moderately attractive!" Casey smiles, leading me downstairs.

The room is small and private, with a long table in the center. We throw all our stuff down before hanging our dresses on the hangers provided for us.

"Hannah and I decided to invite Xav last minute. Is that okay?" Casey asks, pretending to busy herself with her dress.

It's no secret the three of them hit it off and have been hanging out. I just haven't mentioned it because I didn't want them to feel like they had to choose between him or me.

"Of course it is," I reply. "I like Xav, it'll be good to see him."

"And you're not lying?" She faces me, hand on her hip.

"I don't lie to you, you cow." I roll my eyes. "I like Xav."

She nods. "Good. So lunch should be here soon, according to the schedule. Then hair and makeup arrive, pre-wedding photographs, and away we go."

"How you feeling? My car has a full tank of gas just in case."

"I feel amazing." Her eyes light up. "I've been wanting to marry that girl since the moment I met her. I don't know what the fuck she sees in me, but damnit if I'm not the luckiest person on this planet."

"You are. Hannah is one in a million, and I am so happy you two found each other."

"No mush!" she insists, waving her hands. "No! I will be crying enough today, and I will not start this early!"

I chuckle, nodding in agreement. "As you wish."

***

I swish my dress back and forth in front of the floor-length mirror. The light green, high-neck dress comes to my mid-thigh. The skirt itself has a layer of tulle over the solid fabric, making it a flirty, summery choice. All Hannah. The shoes are a classic, strappy flat sandal for which I am grateful. Walking on those little stones lining the aisle in heels? No thank you. My hair is down in beachy waves, a headband of cream-colored flowers nestled amongst the black strands. Maybe someday I'll stop dyeing it, let it be naturally blonde again.

"You look beautiful, girls," Dad says after knocking twice on the big double doors.

I turn and smile at the embrace Casey and Dad share. Her satin dress is just as perfect as the day she tried it on in the shop. Only now her hair is curled in gentle, strawberry blonde waves that frame her face. I've been fighting tears all day and I'm losing the fight. Thank God for waterproof mascara.

"Stop!" she whines once she notices me. "No tears until the ceremony!"

"I never promised that." I sniffle.

Dad gives his own watery chuckle, making his way over to give me a big bear hug.

"You look dashing, Dad," I whisper into his suit.

"I better. One of my girls is getting married." He wipes a tear from his eye.

"I will kick both of you out!" Casey stamps her foot. "No crying!"

Dad and I share a look before rushing over and locking her in a group hug just as the photographer arrives.

Raina bursts through the double doors after we are finished with our first round of pictures. We aren't allowed to leave the room for fear of seeing Hannah before the ceremony.

"It's showtime!" she announces.

"Is my father still pouting in his seat or has he decided to man up and walk me?" Casey rolls her eyes.

"Pouting, last I checked." Raina smiles.

"Shocker." She chuckles. "Darby, would you mind if I asked Dad?" She won't meet my gaze.

"I'd be offended if you didn't ask him," I reply, laughing at the shocked face I get in return. "What? He practically raised you. I'm not going to horde him."

Raina nods. "I'll grab him. Remember, Darby you're down the aisle first, then Hannah's maid of honor, then Casey, then Hannah."

"What happens if I fall?" I ask to Raina's retreating form.

"We all get a good laugh," Casey replies.

Bitch.

***

The cello player readies her instrument, looking to Raina for the cue to begin. From where I stand in the winery, I can see the setup perfectly. Light green flower petals lay along the aisle, framed by gold-dusted glass vases with white flowers and candles inside. There are maybe fifty chairs lined up in front of the red wall, and a cream frame marks the spot where Casey and Hannah will say their vows. If I ever get married, I'm having Hannah help.

"Go." Raina nods with a smile.

With a deep breath, I step outside and the cello player

begins. It's a perfect summer Seattle day, not a cloud in the sky. I focus on keeping my head up and not going too fast with each step. One step. Two steps. Three steps. Ben.

Wait, what?

I resist the double take that threatens to snap my neck in two. It's just someone who looks like him. Yeah. How many brunette men with exceptional style exist in this city? A million, at least. No way it's him. I reach my place and turn to the crowd. And there he is. Benjamin fucking James, sitting there with his perfect face and his sweet smile and his adorable dimples. In a gorgeous navy blue suit that brings out the blue in his eyes. Casey has a lot of explaining to do. I may kill her. I don't care if it is her wedding day. She can warn me about Xavier, but not Ben?

I school my features, plastering on a happy smile. Here I was in my little bubble thinking that I'd never see him again. Or if I did, it would be on my terms, with a plan in place. Not all willy nilly. How am I supposed to function when I can barely breathe? How am I supposed to get through this wedding, standing in front of all these people, when all I want to do is collapse? I love this man with my entire being and I . . .

I think my heart may fall out of my butt. Yep. It's a goner just like me.

My eyes plant themselves on Casey and Hannah at my side, refusing to budge. But he's looking at me. The quickening of my heartbeat, the shiver that tingles down my spine, tells me he's watching me. How dare he watch me. I'm supposed to be paying attention! *He's* supposed to be paying attention. Am I sweating? Did it get thirty degrees hotter?

Casey's clear voice cuts through my own thoughts. Vows. Wedding. Paying attention. This is going to be a hell of a night.

"I'm married, bitch!" Casey screams as Hannah finishes signing the marriage license.

"You won't be for much longer if you keep screaming like a banshee," I snark. My sob fest during their vows made me a little less murder-y, but I'm still a little mad at Casey.

"Saw Ben, huh?" Casey replies, puffing her chest out a bit. "He looks good in his suit, doesn't he?"

"You're a manipulative little—"

"No!" Hannah interrupts. "Most of the time your banter is cute. But not today. This is my wedding day. We are going to go take pictures, eat delicious food, dance, and bask in our love for one another. Capisce?"

It takes me a moment to close my gaping mouth.

"Mmm, baby," Casey murmurs, wrapping Hannah up in her arms. "You know I like it when you get bossy. Usually only happens in the bedroom, but I like."

"I need to scrub my ears with a brillo pad." I wince.

"Photos!" Hannah claps. "You can kill Casey when we see you tomorrow at brunch. Although, if you could put it off until after the honeymoon, I'd prefer it."

"Consider it my wedding gift." I smile, allowing Hannah and an amused Raina to herd us outside.

"Wait, you didn't get me a wedding present?" Casey demands.

I cackle all the way outside and to my chair.

Usually at weddings I always choose chicken. It's hard to fuck up a chicken dish. But Casey insisted I go with the beef and dear God I may forgive her for Ben purely for the heads-up on dinner. The entree is a wagyu beef tenderloin drizzled in a red wine sauce, accompanied by green beans and mashed potatoes. My ass is in heaven. It helps that Ben and Xavier are seated on the other side of the dining room. I'm able to hide behind an elaborate candle centerpiece instead of making eye contact.

"This is delicious," Dad comments, having picked the beef as well. I almost feel bad for Lisa as she gazes longingly at his plate. Don't get me wrong, the chicken looks excellent but . . . wagyu beef.

"*Delicious*," I agree.

"Have you talked to the Fairbanks at all yet? I can't believe they'd come all this way and not participate in their child's wedding," he grumbles.

I throw a glare their way. They both are cutting their meat as if everyone is watching. "I'm not all that surprised. They didn't even show up to the engagement party. Assholes."

"Language," Dad replies. "But agreed."

"I'm sure they'll corner me at some point. They always do." I roll my eyes. "How are you, Darby? Still working at the firm, Darby? How's your mother, Darby? You know the Bible says respect your elders, Darby?"

"It's insufferable when people use the Bible to justify their own stupid opinions." Dad shakes his head. "But enough about that."

I nudge his arm with my elbow. "I'm glad she had you to walk her. You've always been there for both of us."

"Always will be. One kid walked down the aisle, one to go."

Ouch. Right in the gut, Dad. My eyes flicker over to Ben of their own accord, the traitors. He's gazing at me in that way he used to. That way that makes me feel like the only woman in the world. He catches my eye and gives a small wave. I twist my hands together in my lap to resist the urge to wave back. I can't let myself hope that he's here for anything more than a friendly gesture. I can't let myself dream that all he wants is to have me back. That things would be different even if I went back.

Where the fuck is dessert? I eye the table I helped curate. Fuck it, I'm grabbing one of those red velvet cupcakes and screw anyone who tries to stop me.

****

I don't see them until it's too late. The Fairbanks. Eye contact has been made, there is no escape. Only death could save me now. From here it seems as though Mrs. Fairbanks has lost about twenty pounds, and Mr. Fairbanks's waistline found each one.

"Hello, Darby," Mrs. Fairbanks drawls in a put-upon fake Southern accent. You raised Casey in Seattle and have lived in Texas for eight years. Stop pretending.

"Mrs. Fairbanks," I reply, engaging in a two-cheek kiss with her. Can you get a contact high from perfume? Because the sheer amount this woman is wearing is just . . . there must be a hole in the ozone above her head.

"How are you, Darby? Still at the firm?" Mr. Fairbanks asks, shaking my hand. I knew it. I knew he'd ask that.

"No, Mr. Fairbanks. I'm in between opportunities right now. But I'm applying to a program to get my MBA."

"Ah." He sneers just the slightest bit before smoothing it over with a fake smile. "Good for you!"

"Thank you. How are you both? Enjoying Texas?"

Dear God, someone save me.

"Excuse me, may I interrupt?"

Anyone but *him*.

I turn to face Ben, a dimply, sweet, sexy Ben who is so much more attractive up close than I remembered. Damn those wispy silver hairs at his temples. There are a few more than there used to be.

"I'm sorry, I'll catch up with you two later." I smile, giving Mrs. Fairbanks her two kisses. They walk off together, seemingly just as pleased not to be in my presence any longer.

"I, well, you looked pretty uncomfortable so I figured you could use a save," he says, scratching his stubble.

"I appreciate it. They're Casey's parents," I explain, rubbing my shoe into the floor.

My eyes dart around the room of their own accord as we stand in perfect silence for one second.

Two seconds.

Three.

"Would you want to talk outside?" He nods his head toward the door. "Only if you want."

I sigh. He deserves an explanation and so do I. "Okay."

I follow him through the door and into the cooler night air. The twinkly lights in the trees are aglow, making the red wall seem on fire. The question now is who's going to talk first?

"How've you been?" he asks as we walk toward the small waterfall.

"I've been alright. Applied to an MBA program," I reply, picking at my fingernails.

His face lights up. "Darby, that's fantastic!"

I can't help but mirror his expression. His joy is as contagious as always. "Thank you. How about you?"

"Good. The contracts for the acquisition are all signed. We should have a press release going out next week."

I nod, both of us stopping in front of the running water. For a few moments all we do is breathe and listen to the sounds of the evening.

"I'm seeing someone," I blurt out into the lingering silence.

The fake grin that's plastered on his face falls. "Oh. I, well, I'm . . . I hope you're happy."

"Oh! Oh, no that's not what I—I'm not *seeing* someone. I'm seeing a therapist. You know, to talk about me and my issues," I explain, hugging my arms around myself. How could he think I'd already be seeing someone new? Not unless . . . Could he?

"That's good. I'm"—he coughs—"I'm proud of you."

"Would that be so awful?"

"Would what be so awful?"

"Would it be so awful if I were seeing someone else?"

His eyes bug at the question. I guess therapy has made me bold, or at least used to asking invasive questions.

"Honestly? Yeah. Yeah, it'd be fucking awful."

It's my turn for my eyes to bug. This may be one of the most open conversations we've ever had.

"Then why haven't you called?" I ask in a small voice.

He lets out an audible breath, hands twitching at his sides. "Because I fucked up, Darby. And you deserve a hell of a lot better than what I put you through."

"I'm pretty sure I'm the one that verbally assaulted you at a charity function," I half-heartedly joke.

"You had every right to. There's. . . shit, there's a lot I want to say to you and a lot I'd like to explain. But I'd understand if you don't want to hear it. I wouldn't like it, but I'd understand it." He kicks a little pebble into the water, making a plop.

"You're not the only one who needs to explain themselves." Okay, Darby, let's fucking do this. "Do you remember the date we had that you planned? The one to celebrate me for no reason?"

He winces before scrubbing a hand over his face. "Yeah, yeah I do."

"I was unhappy, but I didn't tell you. I didn't tell you during the date what I was feeling and what I wanted. Do you know why? I was so scared that if I even pushed you a little, you would leave me. I was willing to compromise myself and my happiness. I didn't believe I deserved you. While yes, you work too fucking much, that lack of communication and self-confidence is my problem. I need to be able to stand up for myself and to tell you what I want without being scared of you leaving. I wasn't in that place. I wasn't ready."

He stares at me in silence, eyes watching my face. Listening to me.

"Our relationship never would've worked because I wasn't ready to be my own advocate. To tell you what I need. I don't . . . I don't like the way I was treated. I didn't like feeling bought off, and I didn't like feeling secondary to everything else. And I need an explanation for that. But I also need to take ownership of my own problems and my own issues." It's like a weight has lifted. Everything I've needed to say to this man, to the man I love, has been said.

"You're magnificent," he breathes.

My cheeks burn hot. "Ben . . ."

"I'm serious. That fire, that bite you have. It used to come out every once in a while, and goddamn if it's not my favorite thing about you. I'm sorry you didn't feel safe enough, that I didn't make you feel secure enough, to voice your needs."

"No, Ben, you can't take that on. That's me and my issues from being abused by my mother. I never would have felt safe," I explain. "But I do need to know what you were thinking."

"I was being a balls-less coward, or at least, that's how Xav put it. I buried myself in my work on purpose. Work has always been my sanctuary. My safe place. Work is what healed me after my divorce, what healed me after my parents died, what helped me come back swinging. And work is what allowed me to hide from the fact that I love you. I love you more than anyone I've ever loved before and that scared the living shit out of me."

My heart jumps right up into my throat. He loves me?

"Yeah, that acquisition had me busier than I've ever been. I wasn't going to be available all the time, but I could've delegated. I could've put my fucking phone down. But, shit, you got under my goddamn skin like no one ever has. I didn't introduce you to my friends because I knew they'd love you. I didn't introduce you to my sister because I knew she'd love you. I knew if they met you, I wouldn't be able to pretend like you're not the fucking love of my life."

"Ben," I croak. My face is covered in tears, overwhelmed by this man in front of me.

He reaches for me, calloused fingers wiping away tears like he's been by my side for months. "I'm sorry I never told you. I'm sorry I never explained myself. I'm sorry I hid behind my money and my job instead of trusting my gut. And I'm sorry for not calling. But I needed to get some things settled first."

"Things?"

"I pulled back at work."

My mouth hangs open.

"I'm stepping down as CEO effective at the end of this month. I'm going to be on the board now, exclusively. Being with you made me realize that I hide in that big office. I hide from my divorce, from how much I miss my parents, and I don't want to hide anymore. Even if you decide not to give me another chance, I can't keep hiding. I have to live my life again. And I want to thank you for that, sweetheart."

"I love you. I always did and I never stopped," I hiccup, grasping onto his suit jacket.

He growls, pulling me into a kiss so passionate my legs go weak beneath me. His arms squeeze that much tighter around my waist, holding me up as I cling to him. To whatever piece of him I can reach. I don't care that we're in public, I don't care that the entire wedding can probably see us, and I don't care that I just heard Casey whooping from somewhere.

"You must allow me to tell you how ardently I admire and love you," he says.

I snort a watery laugh. "You're quoting *Pride and Prejudice* to me? I wasn't paying attention either time we watched it!"

"Maybe not. But when we first watched it, that moment was the first time I realized I was falling in love with you. As I watched that movie, and watched you sleep on my shoulder, I could see myself making a grand speech to you instead. I could see us making our own love story, far greater than anything in fiction."

I'm speechless.

"You." A kiss to my nose.

"Are." A kiss to each cheek.

"The." A kiss to my forehead.

"Love." A kiss to my chin.

"Of." A kiss to my ear.

"My." A kiss to my neck.

"Life." A peck on the lips.

"And I'm never letting you go again," he promises, sliding his nose against mine.

"I wouldn't let you if you tried." I smile.

# EPILOGUE
## DOUBLE CHOCOLATE CHUNK CROISSANT

### BEN

"May I please have a grande strawberries and cream Frappuccino, a double chocolate chunk croissant, and a small piece of carrot cake?" Darby asks the barista with a smile, cheeks rosy from the cool spring morning.

It's been two years and I still can't figure out how the fuck she puts away all these sweets. I never thought I'd meet someone who could keep up with me and my sweet tooth, but she puts me to shame. Her blood sugar should be through the roof, and yet she always comes back from the doctor with a clean bill of health. But that's my Darby, she makes no goddamn sense. And I love every second of it.

"Want anything?" she asks, turning to me with a smile that makes me want to give her anything and everything I can get my hands on.

"Croissant and a coffee." I turn to the barista. "Medium roast, please."

Does she realize that it's been two years to the day that I met her in this exact Starbucks? Does she know that's why I dragged her out of our bed—our pillow-covered bed—this morning to bring her here? I wouldn't be surprised if she suspected something. She's smarter than her own good, and I'm fucking awful at keeping secrets from her.

"Sit with me." Her brown eyes twinkle as she takes my hand and leads me to the same couch we sat on. Yep, she's onto me.

"Whatever you want." I shrug, trying to be calm. The engagement ring weighs heavily in my pocket. I have the whole day planned. I hope she doesn't guess and ruin it now.

"Love you," she says instead, cuddling into my side.

I kiss the top of her head, inhaling the smell of coconut and gardenias. Darby. The scent of home. "I love you."

Just wait until she finds out that Paul Hollywood and Prue Leith are presenting her engagement ring on a handmade cake.

HE END

---

## SUGAR Spotify Playlist

---

Playlist can be found on Zoe Shae's socials
(not in any specific order)

- Sugar by Maroon 5
- Issues by Julia Michaels
- This is Me from The Greatest Showman
- Hey Look Ma, I Made It by Panic! At The Disco
- Burn by The Pretty Reckless
- I Won't Give Up by Jason Mraz
- Fix You by Coldplay
- Mama Who Bore Me from Spring Awakening
- Mama Who Bore Me (Reprise) from Spring Awakening
- I Don't Want Your Money by Ed Sheeran and H.E.R.
- Human by Christina Perri
- Warrior by Demi Lovato
- I Was Made For Loving You by Tori Kelly and Ed Sheeran

- Why Don't You Love Me by Hot Chelle Rae and Demi Lovato
- It Ends Tonight by The All-American Rejects
- Stolen by Dashboard Confessional
- Not About Angels by Birdy
- It'll Be Okay by Shawn Mendes
- Nothing Breaks Like A Heart by Mark Ronson and Miley Cyrus
- Falling by Harry Styles
- Don't Look At Me by Zoë
- Light Switch by Charlie Puth
- Hold You 'Til We're Old by Jamie Miller
- You Are The Reason by Calum Scott
- Anyone by Demi Lovato
- Like Everybody Else – Acoustic by Lennon Stella
- Praying by Kesha
- I GUESS I'M IN LOVE by Clinton Kane
- Love Me Like You Do by Ellie Goulding
- 2 Be Loved (Am I Ready) by Lizzo
- I'm Tired by Labrinth and Zendaya
- Worst Case Scenario by Loveless

# About the Author

Zoe Shae has always been fascinated by stories. Whether she was creating them with her father, or reading them, they have always been a constant. One of her favorite memories is of receiving a pre-ordered book at midnight in high school and hiding under the covers until the sun came up to finish it. No, it wasn't a certain sparkly vampire book.

It might've been a certain sparkly vampire book.

Zoe spends her time pretty much the same way each day. Writing, reading, singing, and chasing around her rambunctious toddler. She hopes to show her daughter how to follow her dreams.

You can find all things Zoe Shae here: https://linktr.ee/AuthorZoeShae and follow her on Instagram and TikTok @AuthorZoeShae